Shamini Flint began her career in law in Malaysia and also worked at an international law firm in Singapore. She travelled extensively around Asia for her work, before resigning to be a stay-at-home mum, writer, part-time lecturer and environmental activist.

Shamini also writes children's books with cultural and environmental themes, including *Ten* and *The Seeds of Time*, as well as the Sasha series of children's books.

Visit Shamini's website at:
www.shaminiflint.com

By Shamini Flint

Inspector Singh Investigates:
A Most Peculiar Malaysian Murder

Inspector Singh Investigates:
A Bali Conspiracy Most Foul

Inspector Singh Investigates:
The Singapore School of Villainy

Inspector Singh Investigates:
A Deadly Cambodian Crime Spree

Inspector Singh Investigates: A Deadly Cambodian Crime Spree

Shamini Flint

piatkus

PIATKUS

First published in Great Britain as a paperback original in 2011 by Piatkus
Reprinted 2011, 2013 (four times)

A CIP catalogue record for this book
is available from the British Library.

ISBN 978-0-7499-5347-8

Typeset in Caslon by M Rules
Printed and bound in Great Britain by
Clays Ltd, St Ives plc

Papers used by Piatkus are from well-managed forests
and other responsible sources.

MIX
Paper from
responsible sources
FSC® C104740

Piatkus
An imprint of
Little, Brown Book Group
100 Victoria Embankment
London EC4Y 0DY

An Hachette UK Company
www.hachette.co.uk

www.piatkus.co.uk

For Christine 'Aunty Mum' Siva-Jothy

'I did not join the resistance movement to kill people, to kill the nation. Look at me now. Am I a savage person? My conscience is clear.' – Pol Pot

Prologue

My feet sink into the mud as if it is quicksand. Black stuff oozes between my toes and makes a squelching noise as I walk. Each sound fills me with terror. Perhaps the men ahead of me will hear. And then, instead of following them at a safe distance, I will be one of their captives, head bowed and arms tied behind my back in flesh-cutting twine – just like my father. I can see the small group ahead, walking in single file – a cadre followed by three prisoners and then two more cadres. *Khun Pa* is the one in the middle, I can tell because he is the shortest. I am so terrified I have to bite my inner cheek to stop from whimpering. They will surely hear that. We have only been in the countryside for a few short months but already I know that sound travels quickly and clearly across the flat square grids of the paddy fields, ducking around small bushes and between the trunks of tall sugar palms until they reach the sharp ears of the soldiers.

The little procession up front pauses and I think back over

the events of that evening. Shivers run through my body like ripples on a pond when the fish are jumping: Khmer Rouge cadres, dark men with badly cut hair and rotting teeth, arrive at our regulation-sized hut in the late evening. They smile and say not to worry. They just need *Khun Pa* to attend a re-education camp for a few weeks because he was one of the 'new' people, recently arrived from Phnom Penh. My mother falls to her knees and begs them not to take him. Her coppery skin is streaked with tears. It offends the leader that she does not believe his protests that Pa will only be gone for a short while. He shouts at her to be quiet. I steal a quick glance at my father to see how he reacts. He says nothing. Perhaps, like me, he knows that coming to Ma's defence will only make things worse.

Pa gets to his feet slowly, a slight man with sticking out ears and a kindly blank gaze. His pale yellow skin marks him out as part-Chinese. He blinks at the guards in their black pyjamas, red and white checked *kramas* hanging loosely around their shoulders. I can see from his slight squint that he is trying to focus. Pa hid his glasses on the long walk from the city – rumours were swirling that 'intellectuals' were being targeted. Glasses were proof of mysterious and dangerous city influences that the new regime had sworn to eradicate. Now, the precious delicate circles of smudged glass, held together with thin wire, are wrapped in a piece of cloth and hidden in the hollow of a bamboo pole.

'We need to be sure that you support our glorious peasant revolution,' explains cadre number one. He is much shorter than the rest and his black outfit, baggy shirt and drawstring trousers are shiny with newness. He turns to look at *Khun Ma*

2

and I notice that he has a birthmark, a rose-coloured oval shape the size of a palm, on the side of his neck. He looks healthy – and well fed. This means he is senior within the Khmer Rouge. As the final evidence of his stature, he is wearing a gold watch, obviously confiscated from some new arrival. He wears it loosely around his wrist as if it is a gold bangle rather than a timepiece. I note that it is upside down. *Khun Ma* – before she fell silent with hunger – was quietly scathing about the 'savages' stealing things they did not understand. Perhaps she was not quiet enough. The Khmer Rouge have eyes and ears everywhere as neighbours trade neighbours for an extra portion of gruel. I shake my head and feel the rough edges of my hair brush my cheeks. I must not blame Ma or the others – I know instinctively that this is what they want.

Pa nods in response to the cadre's expressed doubt about his loyalty to the new regime. He is not agreeing with them, only acknowledging their desire to re-educate him. This is not the first we have heard of the 're-education' camps. Uncle Lay was taken away last week and one of our neighbours as well. Someone told them that the men used to be in Lon Nol's army. But my Pa was not in the military. He has never fired a gun. He was a pharmacist, running a small ill-stocked apothecary on the edge of Phnom Penh.

Pa licks his dry, cracked lips quickly with a furtive tongue. Is *Khun Pa* afraid? My own father who urged us to be brave, carried my two younger brothers, one on his back and one in his arms, and walked courageously at the head of our little family column when we were evacuated from Phnom Penh? My own fear is like a stone in my chest, making it difficult to breathe.

3

The cadres drag Pa out of the small hut on stilts that has been our home for six months. Ma's sobs become loud, uncontrollable. One of the men aims a kick at her with big dirty feet. I notice his sandals, made from the black rubber of car tyres, and wonder at myself that I can absorb this irrelevant detail while Pa is being taken from us. *Khun Ma* cowers but cannot or will not stop crying. My brothers crowd around her, seeking comfort or giving it – I don't know. I have made up my mind. I wait a few moments and then slip out after the men. I need to know where they are taking him.

Now as I drag my tired legs through the paddy fields, I regret my hasty decision. But always the sight of my father ahead of me, stumbling as he walks without his glasses, keeps me going.

At last, the procession in front of me stops. In the light of the full moon, I see their silhouettes against the night, like characters in a shadow puppet play. Snatches of conversation are carried to me on a gentle breeze that runs curious fingers through my short hair. I cannot make out individual words even though I am straining as if I were lifting heavy sacks of rice. I crouch behind a bush. I do not know the name of the plant but it has a fragrant smell that perfumes the night. There is so much I still don't know about the countryside. I slowly make my way, bent over almost double, to a clump of sugar palms. I need to get closer to see what is happening. Something slithers across my foot and my blood runs cold. There is no medicine under the Khmer Rouge to treat snakebite. I do not want to die, not now, not here.

The prisoners are doing something – bent over, working with slow repetitive strokes. I am puzzled. It is dark. The digging and planting of rice seedlings is daytime work, even under the Khmer Rouge. As I get closer, I crawl on my hands and knees along a dyke. Even if they see me they will assume that such a small black figure is a stray dog or a wild pig. I just hope that none of them has a gun and decides that he would like meat in his stew.

The leader leans forward and snatches something from Pa's hands. I see from its shape that it is a shovel. Why are they making the men dig trenches in the middle of the night? He barks a command in the harsh tone that the Khmer Rouge soldiers use to communicate. I pray to the Buddha, seeking his intervention to help Pa, knowing it is futile. In my mind, the Buddha is the impassive stone statue, cool to the touch, in the *wat* near our Phnom Penh home, not the compassionate being of my mother's simple faith. I know that the Buddha will not help because I have seen the others – so many of them – beg for his aid: pregnant women giving birth by the side of the road, young mothers with sick babies, old people, the wounded and the disabled, abandoned on the long march by families that cannot care for them any more. They all called for help from the Buddha and he did nothing – why should I be different? We must help ourselves and each other. That is the only truth. But how can I help *Khun Pa*? I lean my forehead against the trunk of a palm and its cool rough surface reminds me of that statue of the Buddha. For a brief moment, I am comforted by the misleading sensation of familiarity.

The prisoners fall to their knees on the soft earth. One of them utters a soft moan. I cannot tell if it is my father. I hope not. I peer into the night. My eyes are accustomed to the darkness now. The light of the moon seems as bright as the paper lanterns in our old living room. The prisoners are on their knees in a row, facing away from me. A cadre barks an instruction and all three men bow their heads as if in prayer. I am still trying to understand what is going on when the short cadre with the gold watch raises the shovel and brings it crashing down on the back of *Khun Pa*'s head. In that instant the only thing I can think of is that Pa will not need his glasses any more.

One

Cambodia. What did he know about Cambodia of all places?

Inspector Singh held out his passport and carefully printed e-ticket to the woman at the counter. At least, in a previous era, the sheer complexity of the ticketing documentation suggested that an adventure was in the offing. Now catching a flight was like boarding a bus. Except that buses didn't travel thirty-eight thousand feet in the air or at nine hundred kilometres per hour. Singh reminded himself that flying was, statistically speaking, safer than driving a car. It didn't help his pre-flight nerves.

'Frequent flyer?' The smartly dressed woman had enough paint on her face to have sufficed for Picasso.

'No,' he snapped. 'As little as possible, actually.'

She giggled, baring two front teeth that were edged in crimson. He supposed it was lipstick – it looked as if she had been nibbling on livestock.

She tried again. 'No, sir. I mean are you a member of any frequent flyer programmes?'

He shook his head resolutely, his turban making an emphatic hundred and eighty arc. He was not a frequent flyer although at the rate his bosses were sending him on bizarre assignments as far away from Singapore as possible, he soon would be.

The woman was typing furiously. He craned his short neck, wishing he could see what she was doing. How could it possibly require so much input to assign him a seat? Maybe, she was writing a novel between passengers. Maybe she was writing a novel *about* passengers.

'Aisle or window seat?'

'Aisle,' growled the inspector. 'Definitely aisle.' It was closer to the emergency exits and had less view of the distant ground. He watched his small suitcase roll away on the conveyor belt, wheels wobbling uncertainly. He hadn't locked the bag. Any Cambodian airport staff with light fingers would be very disappointed to discover a stack of carefully ironed identical white shirts, two pairs of dark trousers and white socks. He didn't even have a spare pair of shoes. The comfortable shiny white sneakers encasing his big feet were quite sufficient. He wasn't planning on visiting any fancy restaurants with dress codes, assuming there were such things in Phnom Penh.

'Visiting Angkor Wat?'

'What?'

'No, *wat* – you know Angkor Wat!'

He looked at her suspiciously. Was she trying to be funny? Or worse, friendly? He'd rather she just gave him his boarding pass. Singh was highly sceptical of the polished pleasantness of airline staff, convinced that the glib good nature was based on carefully rehearsed lines from an expensive training manual.

'I'm attending the trial of the ex-Khmer Rouge leader, Samrin, for crimes against humanity at the Extraordinary Chambers of the Courts of Cambodia in Phnom Penh.' Singh resorted to the sort of pomposity he despised in his superiors to create a barrier between himself and this highly-powdered woman.

He was handed his boarding pass without further attempts at conversation. The policeman felt a moment of guilt that he had thwarted her attempt at friendliness. Still, she was probably relieved to get back to her novel or resignation letter or whatever it was she was typing with such firm strokes.

An hour later he was on a plane. Only Silk Air flew this route and they didn't have the wide-bodied jets of the Singapore Airlines fleet, which was a shame, as he preferred planes with more engines and more space. The passenger next to him, a large man with a Roman nose, had laid claim to their shared seat divider by placing a hairy arm on it immediately upon boarding. Singh scowled but did not contest this pre-emptive possession. The policeman's feet were as far under the seat in front as he could get them, which was not far at all. He gulped his orange juice from the plastic container provided, stuck it into the seat pocket, checked again where the nearest exits were and stared at the in-flight magazine, hoping to while away the time. Photos of Angkor Wat dominated an article on Cambodia. It was an enormous complex of temples built around the twelfth century by a Hindu king. There were majestic towers, careful decorations and detailed bas reliefs – including an enormous array of well-endowed, scantily-clad women. He pictured his wife, her mouth puckered in a censorious grimace. She didn't approve of images of voluptuous naked women and it made no difference whether it was in a magazine, on the internet or on an ancient Cambodian temple monument to the god-king Vishnu. She had a point, he supposed. Would eight hundred years of history render *Playboy* magazines objects of genuine artistic and historical interest, carefully preserved in glass cases?

He closed his heavy-lidded eyes, folded his arms across his belly and contemplated his mission. His bosses had really outdone themselves this time. He had known he was in their black books after his cavalier treatment of due process in the last murder he had investigated in Singapore. But he had expected to ride it out, as he had done throughout the course of his career. He had planned to work diligently on a few low-key murders – those that did not have his superiors breathing down his neck – the killing of someone 'unimportant'. A maid perhaps or a foreign labourer. Singh didn't mind those cases where he was not the front-page news every morning. Indeed, he preferred them. His satisfaction was from lining up his turban and his broad nose in the direction of a killer, in ensuring that the victim did not go unavenged. In a murder case, reparation was impossible, of course. The killer had taken something that he could not return – the life of another human being. It was Singh's life mission to tramp after the murderers in his snowy white sneakers, following the evidence and his instincts, ignoring the advice and warnings of his superiors, stopping only for regular meals, cold beer and the odd afternoon nap, until he had ensured some justice for the dead.

Superintendent Chen had other ideas.

'We're sending you to Cambodia,' he said importantly from behind his big empty desk.

'Have I won the police sweepstake?'

Superintendent Chen responded through clenched teeth, the mere sight of his chubby subordinate probably too much for his fragile nerves. 'It's an assignment. You've been volunteered by the Singapore government to hold a watching brief on behalf of ASEAN at the war crimes tribunal in Phnom Penh.'

He was met with silence.

'Some of the other ASEAN countries were worried that we might not be able to spare our top murder cop,' continued Chen, referring to the Association of South East Asian Nations and rubbing his hands together. He added, grinning slyly at his unhappy subordinate, 'I assured them it was no trouble – no trouble at all.'

Singh scowled. Superintendent Chen always gave him indigestion, which was a shame as he had enjoyed his long curried lunch.

'Why in the world would you send me?'

'You like murder investigations, right? After all, aren't you *the* Inspector Singh, leading criminal investigator in Singapore? Well, I'm giving you a whole genocide. Think of it as a late Christmas bonus.'

Singh rubbed his eyes and smelt the faint whiff of curry from lunch on his fingers. The traces of chilli, impossible to wash out first time, made his eyes water.

'But what am I supposed to do there?' he demanded.

'Nothing at all,' admitted Chen. 'You're just window

11

dressing so that the Cambodians – they're very sensitive about their place in ASEAN – think we give a damn about their war crimes tribunal.'

It seemed he was to twiddle his thumbs at the trial of a man accused of killing thousands of his compatriots. Singh screwed up his face and stuck out his pink bottom lip. He guessed the boss was hoping for a refusal so that he would finally have an excuse to get rid of his recalcitrant subordinate. The inspector held his tongue. He wasn't going to give the other man the satisfaction. Instead, he nodded curtly, indicating his willingness to go. After all, it might be interesting and Cambodian food, whatever it was, might be good. Singh's brow creased in concentration as he contemplated his new and unexpected mission attending the trial of a man accused of mass murder. What was it that Stalin had said? Kill one person and it's murder, kill a million and it's a statistic?

François Gaudin stood outside the gates of the French embassy. The usual traffic of motorbikes, tuk tuks and cyclos hurtled by, their drivers shouting out offers of transport. The gate, in this era of truck bombs and suicide bombers, was a sturdy iron retractable construct embedded in a thick high wall with spikes along the top. Security personnel glared at him from within a fortified glass cubicle. They were armed and alert, watching him with cold eyes. These days, everyone was an enemy, a potential threat, a suicide bomber, until proven otherwise. That hadn't been the case in the old days. Despite the Cold War, despite Ho Chi Minh, despite Kissinger, it had seemed like a safer world then to a naïve young French teacher at a school in Phnom Penh.

François was an old man now, slightly stooped with thick white hair in tight curls around a thin long face. Sunken grey eyes suggested a man who had suffered some emotional torment in the past which was never quite forgotten, always on the edge of memory. After all these years, what had it been – thirty? – Gaudin had finally plucked up the courage to return to Cambodia, to try and find out what had happened to his wife and children.

Yes, it was almost exactly thirty years since he had left Cambodia to visit an ailing mother in a comfortable Paris suburb. He had plucked up the nerve, it had taken weeks, and told his parents that he had a Cambodian wife and two young children. He had been afraid, rightly so as it turned out, that his foreign bride would be too much for their conservative middle-class prejudices. There had been tears and recrimination, shock at the double life he had been living for the last three years.

At last he had found the guts to put his foot down. They would gain a daughter and two beautiful grandchildren or lose a son. It was their choice. His parents had succumbed to the pressure and promised reluctantly to welcome his new family. He agreed to bring them back to France after his tenure teaching at the French lycée was over or if the situation in Phnom Penh – torn between the communists, Sihanouk and the American puppet government – became too dangerous. His heart overflowing with joy, he booked his flight home – he called it home – distant Cambodia, a country which he had learnt to love in parallel to his wife. The date stamped on his return ticket was April 17th, 1975 and he waited anxiously, excitedly, happily for the day to arrive. That day, the Khmer

Rouge overran Phnom Penh and all international flights into the city were cancelled. He had not seen his wife and children since.

Chhean glanced at her watch. She still had a couple of hours before she had to hurry to her next assignment, and as always she planned to use it sitting in on Samrin's trial. The Cambodian woman wrinkled her small nose in disgust. She'd really drawn the short straw this time. When she had signed up to be a court liaison at the war crimes trial, excited at the chance to use her language skills, she had envisaged an important role explaining the function of the tribunal to senior diplomats and academics. Instead, she'd been instructed to babysit some lowly policeman from Singapore who was attending the trial on behalf of ASEAN.

Chhean stood in line outside the court room, her tapping foot the only overt sign of her impatience, waiting to be ushered in by the various functionaries. The tribunal guards were dressed in light-blue shirts and heavy gold braid. She supposed this fondness for colourful costumes was a subconscious effort to forget the days when authority had worn black collarless pyjamas and red chequered *kramas*. If only it were so easy to dress up or disguise the past.

A sudden awareness grew that she was being watched and she turned around. A small-sized man in baggy well-pressed trousers was beckoning to her. He was a clerk at the documentation centre for the tribunal, usually buried under a mountain of paperwork. Chhean had asked for his help, and now he beckoned her over with five-fingered urgency. Was it possible that he had found something?

She hurried towards him, fine hair blown away from her face by the stiff breeze, short legs pumping energetically. As she reached him, he said in an undertone, 'New documents have been found, buried in the ministry archives.'

Chhean's face brightened.

'I have no time to go over them,' he explained apologetically.

Chhean was not surprised. Her friend was stretched for time dealing with the enormous amount of paper that the trial of Samrin had generated.

'Would you like to look at them yourself?' He explained quickly that he could arrange for her to have access to them, provide her with the necessary credentials.

Chhean, who had been about to suggest the same thing, smiled at him broadly and was rewarded by the sight of her friend blushing bright red. It was mean of her to exploit the crush this man had on her – God knows what he saw in her, a short, stocky and determined woman – but she needed as much information as possible.

Chhean knew the clerk thought she was on a wild goose chase but she didn't mind. She had been doing this for so many years now, looking for traces of her family history in yellowing documents that hinted at secrets within. So far she had not found anything – not a single thing – but every time a fresh cache came to light, she would trawl through the sepia photos and mildewed paper looking for a hint of the past, her past. So now, she accepted the clerk's offer gleefully. She would continue the hunt for her parents, her family and her identity in this new treasure trove of possibilities, her only clue the photo in her pocket. She took it out now and glanced at it although every detail of the image was burned into her memory. It was her talisman, her link to a world beyond the harsh reality of the refugee orphanage on the Thai border where she had grown up. Chhean's face lit up as she imagined the day when she would finally find the people in the photograph, her family.

Her friend, worried by her sudden radiance, raised a finger warningly. 'Remember, you might not like what you find. Sometimes, it is better to let the past keep its secrets.'

Two

François Gaudin reached into his wallet and took out a single snapshot, a black and white picture fading to grey of a young woman, her face turned away slightly as she looked down at the laughing child clutching her skirt, a baby enfolded in her arms. He felt the wetness of tears on his eyelashes and blinked them away. He needed to be in control of his emotions.

Back in Cambodia for the first time in so many long years, he had been unnerved by the grim concrete layer of modern development and the innumerable brothels. The only thing unchanged was the grinding poverty on the faces of the people. He hadn't known where to begin in his search for answers. François already knew that none of them, his wife or children, had returned to the family home: his mother-in-law had written and told him that. Neither was there a trace of them in the village from which the family had originally fled. It was as if they had been swallowed up by the earth. Later, when the truth of the Khmer Rouge era was revealed,

François realised that that was probably what had happened. The polished ivory-coloured bones of victims of the killing fields were still dug up each planting season. He had assumed that this was what had happened to his family, had a nervous breakdown and been dissuaded by his parents from making the trip back. After all, what was the point? If they were alive, they would have contacted him. His in-laws had already searched long and hard. In the end, he had fallen in with his parents' wishes. His wife and children, missing, presumed dead. A statistic to add to the other statistics.

Until now. He was old and close to death and so he had decided to return. After days of wandering the streets, a ghostly figure lost in the shadows of the throbbing dusty reality of twenty-first century Phnom Penh, he had finally remembered that many Khmer women with French husbands had sought shelter at the French embassy during the fall of Phnom Penh. It was one of the few places that his wife's family might not have investigated. And so he had made his way slowly, on foot, along the long walls on Preah Monivong Boulevard. Perhaps Kiri had sought refuge for herself and the children. It would, after all, have been the sensible thing to do. And he knew that his wife had a streak of common sense as wide as the Mekong.

He was ushered through the grounds of the embassy by a young Frenchman. The modern building with its flat roof and white façade bore no resemblance to the place he used to come to renew his passport and notify the consulate of his whereabouts. But he had not seen the embassy in the days after the fall of Phnom Penh, with the gates barricaded shut, Khmer Rouge soldiers camped opposite and terrified individuals within. A picture formed in his mind of people clumped together on a lawn. He'd seen it in a newspaper after the fall of Phnom Penh, the negatives for the photo smuggled out of the country by one of the last foreign journalists to leave Cambodia. The men and women were Khmer refugees. Their meagre possessions, salvaged from their homes before the arrival of the first Khmer Rouge soldiers, were piled up beside them in little heaps, small monuments to hope. Perhaps his wife and children had been amongst them.

After much consultation between bureaucrats while François sat patiently in a chair against the wall, he was shown in to see an elderly attaché who wore an expression that combined sympathy and irritation.

'You have left it a long time to trace your family.'

'I knew if they had escaped, survived, they would have contacted me.'

The attaché shrugged, a purely Gallic gesture that could have been acceptance, disgust or an acknowledgement of his explanation.

'I was afraid to know the truth. I didn't want to know what they had suffered.' François was garrulous in response to the man's quizzical expression, seeing judgment, fearing judgment, where perhaps there was only curiosity.

'And now?'

'And now . . . I am old. I wish,' he paused – seeking the right words, 'I wish to have some rest.'

François didn't need to say more. He could see the understanding in the pale blue eyes deep set in a wrinkled brown face. This was a career diplomat who had spent most of his time within hailing distance of the equator. François took a small folded piece of paper torn out of a notebook and slipped it across the table. The names of his wife and children were written on it with a tentative hand.

'Did they have French passports?'

François shook his head.

'Any proof of marriage?'

'No, we were married in a Cambodian ceremony. I hadn't registered the marriage with the embassy when Phnom Penh fell.'

'It happens,' said the attaché. 'We cannot predict the future. You shouldn't blame yourself.'

The Frenchman buried his face in his hands. 'I was afraid that word would get back to my parents if I informed the embassy . . . that's why I didn't register the marriage.'

'Ah . . . I see.' Unable to absolve François of blame in the light of this new information, the attaché busied himself with checking the names against a central database.

He shook his head with genuine regret. 'We have no records of them, I'm afraid.'

'Does that mean they didn't come here?'

'We didn't take down the names of all the Khmer – not once it became apparent that the communists would insist they leave the grounds to join the forced evacuation of the city.' There was a lop-sided smile on his face as he added, 'The Khmer Rouge didn't have much time for niceties like the sovereignty of embassy grounds.'

François nodded his understanding.

'I was here,' the other man said unexpectedly.

A spider web of lines formed across François Gaudin's thin face. 'What do you mean?'

'Those last days . . . I was a junior official at the embassy. The day we ordered the refugees to leave was probably the worst of my life. The Khmer Rouge liaison said they had to be turned out – or they would invade the compound. We had so many embassy staff, French nationals, foreigners – Russians, Vietnamese – we had a responsibility to them. In the end, we agreed.'

'My God . . .' whispered François.

'God?' remarked the attaché. 'God was not in Cambodia that day – or for the next four years.' He continued, 'We turned the Cambodians out. They didn't make a fuss or beg to stay. We must have sent so many of them straight to their deaths.'

François took the photograph out of his breast pocket, the one of his wife and two children, and held it out reluctantly to the other man. He had turned to gaze out of the window, his vision blurred with tears, so he did not see the other man grow pale beneath his tan.

The Mercedes-Benz pulled up by the gates of the National Museum. Despite the poverty in Cambodia, there were pockets of wealth, the government and business elite, who travelled in style behind darkly-tinted glass in bloated limousines. None of the passers-by spared the vehicle a second glance. Mostly they were not interested but there was an element of fear as well in the averted eyes. The privileged classes protected their privacy and wealth with a certain disdain for the rights of others.

The rear window wound down slowly and a balding, middle-aged man peered out. His attention was on the small coterie of men selling postcards and books to foreign tourists by the museum entrance. Two of them were in wheelchairs and one leaned on a single crutch: the one he wanted – Cheah Huon. He'd been given a cursory description but there could be no mistake. The amputated leg was not sufficient to identify the man – in Cambodia such injuries were common – but the scar tissue on the man's face and neck were horrific even by the standards of the country.

'Huon,' he called and then again, louder.

One of the wheelchair-bound men said something and gesticulated in his direction. He couldn't make out what had been said but the amputee turned to stare and the man in the car beckoned him over. Huon leaned his crutch against a wall and snapped on an artificial limb. He hobbled over to the car, his expression a combination of curiosity and wariness.

'You are Cheah Huon?' asked Judge Sopheap.

The man nodded, the scars on his neck bunching and stretching like a collection of centipedes.

'I hear you sell books.'

There was a quick affirmative nod from Huon. 'And postcards,' he added.

'Bring them over – I'd like to have a look.'

Huon did not question or hesitate – one didn't when instructed to do something by a social superior in Cambodia. He loped off in an ungainly fashion and returned with the cardboard box of books.

'You want me to show you some titles?'

The judge shook his head. 'I'll take them all. Pass them over.'

Huon's expression was puzzled but he obediently pushed the box through the car window.

Sopheap reached inside the inner pocket of his jacket, extricated a thick envelope and handed it to Huon. 'This should cover the price.'

Huon's eyes lit up as he felt the thickness of the envelope. 'Thank you,' he whispered.

'Now, remember.' Sopheap's voice had grown cold. 'I have met your demands. My client expects you to keep your mouth shut. Do you understand?'

There was no hesitation on the part of the amputee. 'Yes, sir. I understand. Please tell your client that his secret is safe with me.'

Singh awoke suddenly and clutched the seat rests like a lifeline. As the aircraft banked, he stole a glance out of the window. The city of Phnom Penh was spread out and low-rise, in contrast to the skyscrapers that clamoured for attention on the approach to Singapore's Changi. Here, muddy brown rivers snaked together like overfed pythons to meet at the city centre. He guessed that two of them were the Mekong and the Tonle Sap; he had no idea what the third river was called. He had read about the Tonle Sap and was fascinated by the idea that it flowed from the highlands to the sea for part of the year – and then reversed its flow for the rest of the time. Sungei Kallang, the longest river in Singapore, all ten kilometres of it, did not indulge in such erratic behaviour.

In a few short minutes, the plane came in to land at Pochentong Airport, now renamed the Phnom Penh International Airport. It had recently been refurbished and modernised by the looks of things. It even had an aero-bridge. There was no need to clamber down steep steps onto grey tarmac. It was still a distant cry from the imposing cathedrals built for the worship of incoming tourists in other Asian cities like Singapore and Kuala Lumpur. Phnom Penh airport was a yellow building built in practical rectangles. The locals just didn't have the tourist dollars to indulge in architectural extremism. Alternatively, surmised Singh, this might be his introduction to communist architecture.

He wandered through immigration, denied hotly that he needed a visa – it was probably an attempt to extort a few dollars – collected his bag from one of only two carousels and walked out to the waiting area. Here he changed some money to *riels* and noticed that each note was decorated with a picture of Angkor Wat.

As he lumbered out of arrivals, blinking against the bright light, Singh was immediately bombarded with offers of rides that seemed to range from taxis and tuk tuks to 'motos', whatever those might be. He ignored the enthusiastic solicitation, relieved that he didn't have to try and choose a reliable driver from amongst the hordes. He had been informed that, as befitted the ASEAN observer to the war crimes tribunal, he would be met at the airport – but he had no idea by whom. He squinted at the various young men carrying pieces of cardboard with names scrawled on them in marker pens. He spotted a placard written in a neat hand and held aloft by a stocky woman whose expression was in marked contrast to the beaming faces around her. He grinned, baring his brown-stained smoker's teeth. The sign read, 'Inspector Sing'. He wondered whether to interpret this as an instruction. That would certainly attract the attention of the dour creature waiting for him. He walked over, panting slightly in the heat, which, although not as intense as Singapore, was still in marked contrast to the air-conditioned building from which he had just emerged. He felt sticky damp patches form under his armpits.

'I'm Inspector Singh,' he said.

She looked at him and her thick straight eyebrows arched. He wondered what she had been expecting – not a short, fat, turbaned Sikh apparently. Mind you, relative to her height, he was a giant of a man. Despite her diminutive stature she grabbed his bag with a determined grip, waving away his protests with the other hand.

She said in English, 'My name is Chhean. You come with me this way please. We go to the car now. Then to hotel in Phnom Penh.' There was very little in the way of pauses between sentences and a strong accent to boot. Singh wondered whether this staccato tone was going to characterise their whole relationship. He would need to work hard to participate in any conversation with this woman. He chortled inwardly – not that different from his communications with Mrs Singh then.

Singh followed obediently in her wake as she marched towards a waiting taxi. He noted that she was as broad-hipped as she was broad-shouldered and walked with short but quick steps. Unlike many of the airport greeters, Chhean was not dressed in native Cambodian dress but instead wore a pair of black trousers and an oversized blue shirt that reached to mid-thigh and covered her posterior. Her trousers were too long and she trod regularly on the hem.

Their driver, a grinning lad in a baseball cap, was leaning against the side of the car. A cigarette dangled from his lip.

Singh reached for the packet in his breast pocket, tapped out a stick and slipped it between his thin upper lip and plump lower lip. The driver whipped out a coloured plastic lighter and held the flame to the tip. Singh inhaled slowly, watching the tip glow orange. He exhaled a stream of grey smoke and noticed that the taxi was doing something similar through its exhaust pipe. Perhaps he should have just stood downwind and taken a deep breath. Glancing around, Singh saw that most of the skinny young men with the dark skin and jet-black hair of the Khmer were puffing furiously. It was typical and rather sad. Poor third world countries were the few places where there were still no laws, or where the laws were not enforced, forbidding the advertising and selling of tobacco to the young and vulnerable. There wasn't even a health warning on the packet he had bought at duty free. Still, from what little he knew of Cambodia's history, cigarettes were probably fairly low down the list of major killers.

Singh clambered into the back of the car with some difficulty while the young man slung his bag into the boot like an Olympic hammer thrower. Chhean slipped in next to him and he noticed that she had sweet features in the broad face, small ears and hair that had an auburn tinge.

'Where do we go now?' he asked politely.

'Hotel Cambodiana. Many of the foreigners stay there.' She made it sound like a criticism. When he did not answer, she snapped, 'Prices in US dollars – only UN can afford it.' She glanced at him slyly, 'Also ASEAN.'

Why did he always get the women with attitude? wondered Singh, his lips turned down despondently. He supposed he should be grateful that she spoke English. He certainly didn't have a single word of Khmer at his disposal.

They set off at a cracking pace and Singh yelped with shock. It took him a moment to realise that he hadn't found a suicidal driver. Apparently, they drove on the wrong side of the road – or the right side if he was to be accurate – here in Cambodia. A legacy from the years of French rule, he supposed. That and the six-lane wide, straight-as-a-die boulevards they were hurtling down. The traffic was the usual third world mix of motorbikes, four-wheel drives and crowded minibuses. The signboards were in Khmer, whose script looked to Singh like so many dancing earthworms. His driver pulled into a station for fuel, narrowly avoiding the vehicles that had formed an extra lane going in reverse to the main flow. It was a Total station. Across the road, he spotted a Caltex. The foreign powers which had treated Cambodia as their personal plaything were now back, this time in the guise of commercial interests. On the other hand, thought Singh, reading the road signs with interest – Rue Sihanouk was followed by Rue Nehru and Rue Mao Tse Tung – the Cambodians had sought some of their heroes elsewhere.

The driver, perhaps disappointed with Chhean's uncommunicative silence in the back seat, turned around and said, 'You want I take you to place for tourists? Very good price. We go Royal Palace, National Museum, Tuol Sleng museum, Choeng Ek killing fields?'

Chhean snapped something in Khmer, or at least Singh assumed the breathy language was Khmer, and the driver subsided into grumpy silence.

'Only in Cambodia tourist highlights include torture chambers and mass graves,' she muttered.

Singh, unable to think of a suitable response, focused his gaze on the dilapidated shops with corrugated roofs and faded, peeling paint. Goods were stacked on the pavements outside as if the shop owners doubted that any customer would choose to enter their premises. Singh didn't blame them. Half-dressed, plump, grubby children played by the roadside, oblivious or indifferent to the traffic. He noticed the familiar mansions of the corrupt protruding grotesquely from the surrounding slums, their architectural styles derived from watching too many episodes of *Dallas*.

Like the *riel* notes in his wallet, the beer advertisements on the roadside billboards were decorated with the *stupas* of Angkor Wat. Communists or not, these people weren't above sticking their most iconic monument on the front of a beer bottle. The inspector nodded approvingly. With that kind of entrepreneurial spirit, the country would soon emerge from its communist constraints into a haven of commercial enterprise and consumer excess like his home town.

Singh glanced at the frowning profile of the young woman beside him. 'It's very pretty here,' he said ingratiatingly. Compliments, however untruthful, always softened one of Mrs Singh's moods.

Chhean glanced out of the window and snorted.

So much for polite chit-chat, thought Singh wearily. He tried again. 'You speak English very well.'

This overture earned him a sweet smile and an explanation. 'I grew up in a refugee orphanage run by Americans,' she explained.

Singh breathed a sigh of relief. It appeared that his minder was not quite as terrifying as he had first assumed.

The Cambodiana's concession to its location and name was an excess of gold-trimmed pointy roofs in a sort of modern 'wat' style. Communist architecture in royalist colours with faux historical roofs – an uncommon mix, thought Singh, quite possibly only found in Cambodia. Just as well too. He didn't think it was an architectural style that would catch on.

Chhean escorted him in, led him to the reception counter, spoke rapid Khmer to the woman in charge, almost snatched at the key she was handed and gave it to him silently. She rummaged in her capacious practical bag and produced a thick blue file tied up in pink string which she handed to him officiously. 'Update on present trial for crimes against humanity of Samrin.' He grasped the file with stubby fingers, immediately rueing its thickness. This shabby scowling figure had provided him with enough reading material to last quite a few evenings.

'I will pick you up in the morning at eight o'clock for tribunal,' she said, in lieu he supposed of the more traditional words of farewell.

He nodded his great head, uttered his thanks to a retreating and indifferent square back and gratefully accepted the escort to his room of a decidedly less taciturn female bellhop wearing a short skirt that made the most of her short legs.

A few moments later he drew the heavy layered curtains and looked out over the Mekong River, the major artery that linked the countries of Indochina. The sun was setting and the waters glowed red and orange, reflecting an angry sky. He could see the dark silhouette of numerous fishing boats on the river and the glinting yellow lights from shacks along the banks. The noise of scooter engines and minibuses on the road below was a rumbling, muffled soundtrack to the extraordinary view. For the first time, Singh felt the mystic charm of the small isolated country. Like it or not, for better but almost certainly for worse, he was in Cambodia for the foreseeable future. He would have to make the best of it. The fat policeman admired the scene for an instant longer, drew the heavy curtains, chucked the folder on the bed and reached for the room service menu.

'I knew them,' said the French embassy attaché. The words were like heavy stones dropped into a deep pond. They sank without a trace, a few ripples the only evidence that words of such enormous importance had been spoken.

'What do you mean?'

Gaudin's appearance reminded the attaché of the Edvard Munch painting, *The Scream*. Without opening his mouth, this elderly gentleman from France gave him the impression of a man in anguish. He answered quickly. 'They were here – they asked to be allowed to remain, to be evacuated with the French nationals as the wife and children of a French citizen.'

'And . . . ?' There was hope in the voice, like brittle glass.

The attaché shattered it with his next words. 'We couldn't let them stay. They had no proof, you see. No proof of marriage.' His voice tailed away for a moment and then gathered strength. 'I believed them. I begged the authorities to issue them a passport, some papers, anything to give them what little protection the embassy still had.'

'Why did you believe?'

'They were . . . they were clearly part Caucasian, the children that is. Dark hair but not black, hazel eyes and rosy cheeks.'

'Then why wouldn't the authorities let them stay?'

Blue eyes met grey. The official shrugged, a knowing gesture, one man of the world to another. 'They could have been illegitimate. We had no way of being sure.'

'What happened to them?'

'They were here right until the end. It was my fault. I gave them hope, you see.' He winced. 'In the end, it was just a handful of Khmer left on the grounds including your family. The trucks were due to arrive the following morning to take us to Thailand. The airport was off limits so our escape was overland.'

'What *happened* to them?' François's voice was a decibel short of a scream.

'We let them out at night to give them a chance to sneak past the Khmer Rouge guards at the entrances. But the baby . . . the baby started to cry. She couldn't make it stop. I watched from the gate as they were picked up.' He took a deep breath and found the courage to be honest. 'Your wife tried . . . she wanted to toss the baby back over the gate. The Khmer soldiers grabbed her arms and stopped her. I swear to God I don't know what happened to them after that.'

There was no response from the other man. He was staring at the table top as if it was a flat screen television playing out the events that were being described.

'With their mixed blood, the Khmer Rouge would have targeted them. There is no possibility they could have survived,' whispered the attaché.

It was dusk. Only a car aficionado would have been able to identify the make of the car he was driving. The dents, dirt and add-ons from other vehicles rendered it anonymous. The driver smiled, exposing teeth worn to the gum. He was amused by the idea that someone might recognise his vehicle. There weren't many car experts lurking in the paddy fields of Cambodia and he wasn't driving one of those bloated Mercedes belonging to the corrupt nouveau riche of Phnom Penh. The man pulled off the road – if the typically pot-holed, randomly-tarred track deserved such a title – next to a cluster of bushes and extricated his square frame with difficulty. He was already wearing dark clothes but he poured some water from a bottle into the dirt, rubbed it in with his booted foot and scooped up a handful of mud. He carefully applied the mud to his face and hands, not forgetting the ears as he had been taught almost too long ago to remember. He leaned into the car, opened the glove compartment, slipped out a revolver and tucked it into his trousers. He could feel the cold metal against the pale skin of his back and it was reassuring. Guns, any weapons, were terrifying – unless you were the one behind the trigger. He wondered a bit at this – even with his background he wasn't sure it was entirely normal to find such physical comfort in a weapon. He didn't want to think that his balance was slipping. It was of utmost importance that he had complete faith in his mental equilibrium. Otherwise, he wouldn't trust his judgment in matters that were of significance to him – matters of life and death.

He took a deep breath, enjoying the scent of the yellowish-white flower of the *rumdul* tree. He paused to contemplate the glow of a pink and orange sky. The colours were so intense that they belonged on a canvas, an exaggerated depiction of the traditional glorious sunset. Such beauty had no place in the real world. It mocked the suffering of individuals that their gods were too busy mixing colours to notice their pain. The man forced his mind to the job at hand in the way farmers channelled waters to their fields, suppressing his burgeoning sense of injustice with an effort of will that was almost physical. It left him sweating and the breeze felt like a cold compress against his high, lined forehead. There was no time for any hiatus before action. He needed to focus on what was important, what he had come to do. His muscles became taut like a boxer anticipating a punch. He felt his senses sharpen and he slowed his breathing intentionally.

He walked quickly towards the fields. The haphazard geometrical shapes of individual paddy fields were obscured by tall brown stalks that swayed rhythmically to the music in the soft breeze. It was almost harvest time so if he kept to the dykes and kept low, he was as invisible as the wind but just as potent. In the distance, he spotted a man walking with a leisurely step, leading a docile water buffalo towards a clump of houses that formed the small village, identical in size and configuration to thousands of others scattered throughout Cambodia. The old man whistled as he walked. It was not surprising – the rice plants were golden and heavy. The crop this year would be bountiful. After the planter threshed the stalks and milled the grain, there would be rice to sell in the markets and to exchange with the fishermen and farmers for their produce, not forgetting, of course, to set some aside for the saffron-robed monks with their alms bowls. The farmer looked up. The final rays of the sun had turned the sky a deep purple, the colour of shrouds, and mild gusts brought the coolness of evening after a scorching day.

At last, the man leading the buffalo drew level. The assassin stepped out in front of him, more shadow than substance.

The farmer gave a start, but it was an instinctive response to the unexpected. There was no trace of fear in it.

'*Chom-reab-suor*,' he said politely, a formal greeting for a stranger. His elderly face creased into a gap-toothed smile.

The man pulled the revolver from his waistband in one smooth unhurried action and, arm outstretched, pressed it against the farmer's forehead. He noted the thin grey hair cut close to the head. It was so sparse that in better light he would have seen the pale scalp gleaming through.

'Why?' whispered the old man.

It was an interesting response. He was not begging for his life although there was fear now, visible in the rheumy whites of the man's eyes even in the half-darkness. Some of the others had grasped him around his knees and wept for the right to live. This man's voice was leaden and dull – as if he had emotionally forfeited his life the moment he saw the gun.

'I think you know.'

From the suddenly downcast eyes, he knew he was right. This victim, confronted with sudden death, was resigned. Only a slight sad wobble around the mouth suggested he regretted the appearance of the grim reaper. The killer became

34

aware that he despised his victim. It annoyed him. It contradicted his self-portrait, that he was an agent of justice, not revenge.

He pulled the trigger quickly, such a small shift in weight with his index finger and in front of him a man died. The loud report caused a flock of swifts to launch themselves into the air, screams of indignation issuing forth from open beaks.

There was no need to check for a pulse. The peasant lying on his back in the dirt with a gaping dark hole in the middle of his forehead was most definitely dead. As he walked back to the car, the killer noted with satisfaction that the evening's work brought his tally to eleven.

Three

Justice always seemed to wear robes, decided Singh. He wasn't sure why it was necessary for such an excess of heavy cloth. Perhaps it was to convince ordinary folk that serious matters were at hand. How could one gainsay a judge in a costume that swept the floor with regal disdain as he walked? The Extraordinary Chambers in the Courts of Cambodia (ECCC), funded in part by the United Nations, had really gone to town on the outfits. The judges, and he counted at least five of them – three Cambodian and two foreign – wore red shiny robes, gathered in pleats around the shoulders. The prosecutors and other lawyers had opted for rich purple. White bibs were draped across their chests as if they might nip out for a hurried meal between proceedings. Singh folded his arms across his belly and wondered whether consultants had been hired to design the ECCC and its accoutrements. It looked like they'd obtained the services of a theatrical company by mistake.

The Sikh policeman felt out of place in his usual uniform of dark trousers, white shirt and white sneakers. The last part of his ensemble already looked grubby. He thrust out his bottom lip in an irritated pout. Every time he was sent overseas on a work trip, his shoes were the first to acknowledge the distance he had travelled from Singapore – physically, economically and hygienically.

Singh looked around. Here at the ECCC, every effort had been made to turn a large air-conditioned room in a complex of military buildings into an international war crimes tribunal. All the parties sat behind waist-high polished wooden ramparts. The policeman noted the large flags, that of the Kingdom of Cambodia (no surprise that, like the currency and the beer, it depicted Angkor Wat) as well as the more familiar sky blue of the United Nations, draped behind the judges' dais. The entire trial chamber was encased in bulletproof glass. The glass walls gave the proceedings a slightly unreal air, as if he was watching the trial on a massive television screen rather than in real life and real time.

Singh turned his attention to the accused. Samrin sat quietly in the dock, a carved wooden affair in the centre of the room. He had neat grey hair, small regular features except for a long thin nose and fair skin. His eyes were rheumy and tired and he had neat bags arranged in semi-circles under each one.

In the first trial before the ECCC, Comrade Duch had been tried for the death of an estimated twenty-one thousand people at Tuol Sleng prison, or S21 as it was sometimes called, and sentenced to life imprisonment.

Now, Samrin, accused of being the commandant at the Choeng Ek killing fields, faced the same fate, life imprisonment for crimes against humanity. Indeed, the only reason that he had not been charged with genocide was that his victims had been chosen generally without reference to ethnicity, race or some such feature. Singh closed his eyes, the dark lids like heavy curtains. It really was quite extraordinary to think that the Khmer Rouge killings had been so indiscriminate that a charge of genocide as defined in the UN Convention on Genocide wouldn't stick. He would bet his next curry that the framers of the definition hadn't expected such an irony.

Singh had read in the handwritten notes provided to him by Chhean that Samrin professed to be a born-again Christian. Very convenient, thought Singh, his lips pursed together grimly, and not an option that his victims were allowed. Most Cambodians were Buddhists and had a simple faith in the cycle of rebirth until a state of Nirvana was attained. Singh, an atheist, particularly disliked the idea of being reborn, one's status in the new life determined by one's conduct in the old. It was asking for trouble. Especially as Singapore was quite happy to hang all the murderers he apprehended. An eye for an eye. A life for a life. He was pretty sure that everyone he had sent to the gallows had been guilty. But that might not be enough of an excuse under the pacifist Buddhist doctrine. He, Singh, might be reborn as a cockroach, or worse, a vegetarian.

Singh took off the large earphones. The added layer on top of his turban was making his ears itch. Still, he needed the headphones for the simultaneous translation of a multitude of languages: Khmer, English, French and Vietnamese, carried out by court officials. To his relief, he noted that while his headphones had been resting on his ample lap rather than wound around his ample head, proceedings had been adjourned for lunch. Samrin was led away to a small building adjacent to the compound. It looked like a small home on the edge of suburbia but was actually a prison for those appearing before the ECCC.

A tight voice at his elbow muttered, 'Under the Khmer Rouge, millions died from starvation – but he still gets three meals a day.'

Singh looked down at his minder, the Cambodian woman with the short glossy hair, square, almost masculine face and perfect rose-petal skin. 'It doesn't help reconciliation if we behave like our enemies.'

It was trite and Chhean wrinkled her nose in disgust. Singh was not sure he believed his own platitudes.

'That's why we have a judicial process,' he argued, determined to play devil's advocate. 'So that we don't behave like those in the dock – Samrin executed the poor bastards who were sent to him, no questions asked.' He wondered for a moment if he was trying to convince Chhean or himself of the value of due process.

'They made everyone work as farmers but no one had enough to eat.'

The policeman nodded. The Khmer Rouge era had been riddled with ironies.

Chhean grinned suddenly at the fat man, her gaze resting for a moment on his belly. 'I suppose right now you also do not have enough to eat?'

Singh guffawed. This small creature with the unexpected sense of humour that punctuated her usually stern demeanour was growing on him.

'How come you got the job of looking after me anyway?' he asked.

'My official title is court liaison but that just means we have to do all the odd jobs.'

Singh contemplated the reality that he, the leading murder cop of Singapore, was nothing more than an 'odd job' to his Cambodian companion as they walked slowly towards the canteen reserved for staff. The other canteen was heaving with Cambodians from all walks of life, queuing for food and waiting to get into the trial chamber. He noted the subdued air – justice could be hard to stomach sometimes. Singh's own tummy growled audibly and Chhean raised an eyebrow that was so fine it looked as if it had been plucked by a professional. Singh doubted this. Chhean did not strike him as the sort of woman who spared a thought for her personal appearance. Her entire concentration was devoted to the war crimes tribunal.

'Why are you so angry?' he asked suddenly.

She did not pretend to misunderstand him. 'You have heard what they did to my people . . .'

Singh suppressed a smile – her command of English was excellent but her accent was pure Cambodian, every other hard consonant abandoned so that what she had said sounded more like, '*Yu haf hear wha they di to mhy peepo.*' Still, if he concentrated he had no difficulty, well, almost no difficulty, understanding her.

'Yes, but your countrymen – many of them are not

interested in this tribunal. They want to forget, to put things behind them.'

'Probably all Khmer Rouge,' she muttered darkly.

He raised an eyebrow, tufty and grey and in complete contrast to hers.

'Even Hun Sen is ex-Khmer Rouge.' Singh knew she was referring to the Prime Minister.

'Well, he did flee to Vietnam and return with the troops that liberated Cambodia from the Khmer Rouge.'

Chhean waved a hand dismissively.

Singh abandoned his defence of Hun Sen. For this woman, everything was in black or white, there was only cadre or victim, she had no faith in the grey area of ex-Khmer Rouge turned good guy. She had a point as well, conceded Singh. Who knew what atrocities had been committed by any of these men before their defection? And could one ever atone for the past? It was a difficult question. The inspector felt strongly that there should always be room for forgiveness, even redemption. But his position was held in the abstract, as a principle. It had never been properly tested and he hoped to God that it never would be.

He reverted to his original theme. 'But many of the victims want to forget as well. Why are you so different?'

'They used engineers as farmers and tried to build irrigation channels to make water run uphill. They murdered people for wearing glasses or having a book.'

He continued to look at her quizzically. These were all good reasons but not the real ones. Singh was surprised and discomfited to see tears well up in her eyes. 'I was brought up in a refugee camp after the war. The Vietnamese soldiers found me wandering alone not far from Tuol Sleng prison. No one knows what happened to my family. The Khmer Rouge, I hold them responsible.'

Jeremy Armstrong smiled and held out his hand. His wife slipped a thin hand into his and he gave it a comforting squeeze, noting – as if it was for the first time – the way his big hand engulfed her slim pale one.

He stated, 'I saw you in the public gallery this morning.' His tone was edgy, but it was the sound of worry rather than anger. 'You know I don't think you should attend the trial. Not all day, every day. It's not good for you.'

'You're doing it,' replied Sovann, smiling at her husband, a demure curving of the lips that did not reveal any teeth.

He had always loved her smile, so different from that of the American women he knew with their wide grins and enormous, shiny, orthodontically-perfect teeth.

'That's different, you know that.' Jeremy was impatient and it showed in his tone. 'It's my job to be there. I don't have a choice.'

He worked for a Cambodian-American society representing a group of victims. He had worked for years with these survivors. It was how he had met Sovann in the first place, the quiet girl with the stricken face who had been unable to articulate her grief, to talk about her past. Now, he was attending the trial, tasked with presenting the written testimony of those victims who were too old or too afraid to appear before the court.

His wife said, 'It's your job, I understand that, but it is my duty. I have to be present for those . . . for those of my family who cannot be here.' Her voice was almost inaudible, not a whisper with its feathery sibilant sound, but just words spoken at a volume so low that he could barely hear. 'I need to understand.'

Jeremy closed his eyes briefly and his short white-blond eyelashes, the same colour as his hair, rested on his cheeks. He had listened to so many tales of hardship that he was almost inured to the pain. And then he would remember what Sovann had been through and he would feel the suffering of the victims amplified through his love of his wife – he was not so hardened after all. He spoke, his voice loud and determined. 'There is *nothing* to understand. A bunch of mad men took over the country for a few years . . . it's in the past now. There's just no point in putting yourself through the trial.'

'You know it's not as simple as that. Besides, I signed and filed a witness statement. I don't know if they will use it – there are so many after all – but it means I am part of this too.'

He loved her accent, Cambodian with a soft American lilt from the West. She was a frightened refugee but also an independent-minded cowgirl. This wife of his was a creature of immense contradictions.

Jeremy stood up and wrapped his arms around Sovann. He could feel the slender bones under her simple white cotton blouse. She felt like a sparrow in the hand – fragile and yet pulsing with life. She put her hands on his chest, and pushed gently, seeking an escape from his embrace until she had his agreement on her attendance at the trial. He let go and they stood apart, the few feet between them representing a gulf of experience. He smiled a little to see the *sampot*, the wrap-around slim skirt made from fine silk that she was wearing.

Back in the United States, she rarely wore traditional Khmer clothing. When he had first met her she had adopted a Western style of dress – another attempt to distance herself from the memories. And now, thirty years after she had fled a Thai refugee camp for the United States, she was attending the war crimes tribunal and reverting to Cambodian attire.

'You said that you just wanted to get re-acquainted with your home, your country. To bury the past.' His tone was accusing now. She had lied to him. She had not come to forget, to finally say goodbye. On the contrary, she had come to remember, to rake up every memory.

And what about him – could he give her the courage to live with her experiences – as he had tried to do when they had first met so many years before? Jeremy acknowledged in a small quiet place in his heart that, truth be told, he was part of the problem. The secret that he carried within him could well be the cudgel that finally broke his wife's determined resistance to the memories. The knowledge made him brusque and angry. He squeezed his eyes shut. His whole life since those early days had been an act of atonement. And yet it was not enough. Nothing could undo the damage, but there was nothing more he could do. He shoved two fists into the already distended pockets of his suit jacket and reverted to his original theme. 'I don't want you at the trial.'

Her enormous, light-brown eyes gazed at him as if she was a small child seeking absolution for breaking an ornament. He noticed that her pupils reflected the light and were flecked with gold.

'Sovann . . .' he whispered, savouring the word, knowing that it meant 'golden', just like her eyes that were the windows into her past, 'I just want to save you from the memories – from the pain.'

She smiled but the expression did not touch her eyes. 'It's a bit too late for that.'

Chhean left the inspector at the tribunal canteen looking miserably at a bowl of fish stew. He was definitely going to lose some weight if he did not quickly develop a fondness for Cambodian cuisine. That would at least appease his doctor, a large Tamilian at the Singapore general hospital who was given to prodding Singh in the belly with a long finger and sighing.

The last time Singh had turned up reluctantly and late for his appointment, the doctor had looked him over carefully, poked a thermometer into his ear, tied a blood pressure gauge around his arm and a held stethoscope to his chest. He had then energetically stuck a needle into a fat vein to extract some blood. They had both watched as the rich liquid slowly filled the vial. Singh was struck by the fact that he usually came across this particular substance in less salubrious surroundings, pooling around a dead man's head or staining the front of a shirt around a knife entry point. He didn't like the stuff. Blood was so rich and red, so heavy with life – even after death.

The doctor distracted him from his melancholy contemplation of his own life blood with his next remark.

'You hunt murderers, right?'

'Yup,' agreed Singh suspiciously.

'Well, I think *you're* a cold-blooded killer.'

'Eh?'

'You're killing yourself,' said the doctor, turning red with amusement, his loud chuckles no doubt audible to the taciturn nurse and impatient patients in the waiting room. 'Look at you: food, fags and beer – death by a thousand cuts.'

'But not so painful,' pointed out Singh.

'We can discuss that again after you've had your heart attack.'

Singh scowled at the memory. Why did the medical profession take such an interest in trying to ruin his simple pleasures?

Food, fags and beer. In Cambodia that translated into fish soup, Angkor beer and Ara cigarettes – this latter product asserting firmly on the box that it was of 'international quality'. Did that mean it killed you just as fast?

The policeman scooped up some soup, blew on it gently to cool it down and sipped it reluctantly. He grimaced, plump bottom lip curved downwards. It was disgusting, fishy without being tasty. He imagined that cat food tasted like this.

The woman across from him had been watching his facial contortions with amusement. She said now in a soft voice which he had to concentrate to hear, 'I think you do not like our Cambodian cuisine?'

'I'm not a huge fan,' he admitted. He hadn't meant to offend the Cambodian beauty sitting across from him. She had delicate features and kind eyes, her hair tied back from her face in a neat bun.

She smiled and it emphasised her cheekbones, high and sharp. 'This canteen food is not an example of our finest.'

He nodded and spooned more of the stew into his mouth heroically.

She nodded approvingly at his willingness to give the dish a second chance even if only to appease her. The flush of blood under her pale skin gave her face a rosy hue. She wasn't young, at least forty he would have guessed from the fine tracing of lines fanning out from her eyes, but she had aged gracefully.

'Any better?' she asked. He noticed that she did not show her teeth when she smiled.

He grimaced and pushed the bowl away with an air of finality. Some of it slopped onto the plastic table top. 'I'm afraid not.' He glanced around and wondered at the other diners who were slurping away without hesitation or complaint.

'We in Cambodia have some experience of going without food,' she explained. 'So we are less fussy about taste.'

He managed to keep an expression of chagrin off his face. This country was impossible – he couldn't even abandon a truly awful meal without having the past flung at him like a wet blanket.

She must have noticed his discomfiture because she sought to put him at ease by changing the subject. 'What are you doing here?' she asked. Her tone was friendly.

Apparently this creature was thoughtful as well as beautiful. Singh found himself almost tongue-tied. 'Watching brief – ASEAN,' he said, more abruptly than he had intended.

The woman held out her hand. 'My name is Sovann Armstrong.'

Singh wiped his hand on his trousers and shook the thin fingers gingerly. The delicate appendages looked as if they might snap like dry twigs if he exerted any pressure. 'Inspector Singh, Singapore police.' He sounded – staccato and verbless – as if he was reading from a telegram, not speaking. The policeman took a deep breath, coughed as his tobacco-damaged lungs protested at the influx of oxygen and added, 'That's a beautiful name.'

'My husband thinks so too.'

Had he behaved so ridiculously that she felt obliged to bring up a spouse in order to thwart any further foolishness? He felt his cheeks grow hot and was glad that his dark complexion would disguise it even from the most discerning of observers. He was behaving as awkwardly as a pimply schoolboy in the presence of this exotic woman. He was curious about the husband as well. From the name, he was a foreigner. From Sovann's softened tone when she referred to him, there was love and dependency in the relationship.

'ASEAN has not been a good friend to Cambodia,' she remarked, following on from his earlier explanation.

'What do you mean?'

'They demanded a Vietnamese withdrawal from Cambodia after 1979. Didn't they realise that would have meant the return of the Khmer Rouge?'

Singh could only shrug his burly shoulders. 'Cold War politics,' he murmured.

'Is that an explanation or an excuse?' she asked and Singh realised that this fragile creature had a core of steel.

He scratched his nose with a blunt fingernail. There was nothing he could say, no defence to be made for a foreign policy that, if it had succeeded, would have resulted in innumerably more deaths.

'Well, perhaps *you* are here to make amends.'

Singh didn't even bother to explain that he had neither the ability nor the means to make amends. There had been a sardonic hint to her suggestion that indicated she understood the realities of politics all too well. This woman would have been a kid in those days of the Khmer Rouge but she had learnt her history lessons. He focused on her accent. 'You went to the US?'

'Yes. After a couple of years in a Thai refugee camp I managed to get an exit visa.' She added thoughtfully, 'I was one of the lucky ones.'

The policeman from Singapore had seen a lot of death. Sometimes being the one who survived could be very difficult indeed. Every moment was filled with guilt at the things left unsaid because death had intervened to form a permanent barrier between loved ones. It explained her married name as well. She must have met her husband – lucky man – after she had escaped to the United States.

Sovann rose to her feet and her hands met, palms together, in a gesture of farewell. He noticed that she had not touched much of her food as she turned to walk away. 'You haven't eaten,' he exclaimed.

'I don't have much of an appetite,' she said apologetically. 'You're right, of course. It is shocking of me when so many died in my country from lack of food.'

'That's not what I meant,' explained Singh hurriedly. 'I was just . . . concerned, that's all.' He was embarrassed at his instinctive honesty. She would think he was mad giving a damn whether a complete stranger had finished her lunch. Perhaps he *was* mad. But this woman, with her natural elegance, a complete contrast to his own gross fleshiness, and gentle manner, had provoked an unusually chivalrous response from him. An image of Mrs Singh flashed into his mind – scrawny elbows protruding from colourful caftan and voice raised in admonishment. No wonder he was drawn to Sovann.

She smiled at him and walked away in the direction of the courtroom. He realised that he had no idea what she was doing here. Was she a witness, an observer, a victim? He felt a strong curiosity to know more about this woman with the kind eyes that were more inward-looking than outward-looking.

He turned his attention back to his lunch. Sovann was quite right. It would be shocking to waste the food. On the other hand, he really, really didn't think he could eat this cold fish soup. One thing was for sure, Mrs Singh might not have the grace or the delicately modulated voice of his erstwhile luncheon companion but she would never have expected him to swallow this stomach-churning lunch.

Four

Singh wandered towards the police headquarters at the tribunal site. It was in one of the – no surprise, pale-yellow – buildings on the outer perimeter of the compound. The buildings, which housed courtrooms, offices, media rooms and hostels, formed three sides of a rectangle around an empty grassy area. It must have once been used as a parade ground before the military turned the premises over to the ECCC. The grass was so dry that the inspector kicked up little puffs of dust as he walked.

Looking around, Singh noted that policing on the premises was discreet, limited to a few friendly unarmed guards except for a machine-gun-toting fellow at the main entrance next to the metal detectors. It seemed inadequate considering the identity of the detainees. Just that morning he had read about some vigilante who was hunting down ex-Khmer Rouge. The death toll had reached ten and a hysterical editorial wanted to know why the police weren't doing more. The restrained policing indicated a general distrust of the local coppers that exceeded the need for an overt police presence despite the threat.

Singh pushed open the swing doors. He had been instructed to present his credentials and inform the Cambodian police that he was in town. It was the courteous thing to do. And ASEAN, with its policy of non-interference in the domestic affairs of fellow ASEAN nations, was always keen to be polite. The inspector had very strict instructions to keep his big sneaker-clad feet off any toes. For once the fat policeman was happy to comply.

He wandered into the small air-conditioned anteroom, waved his letters of introduction at them and was immediately shown in to see Colonel Menhay. Such was the power of colourful letterheads. The colonel was smartly dressed in the green uniform of the Cambodian military police. He was a squat, powerful, harsh-featured man who wore large gold-rimmed Rayban dark glasses. The inspector hitched up his trousers. The Cambodian's shoulder to stomach ratio was the exact opposite of his own. Indeed, Menhay looked more like an extra from a war movie about Vietnam than a policeman. However, when he spoke, the colonel sounded competent, his English almost accentless.

'Welcome to Cambodia, Mr Singh.'

Singh nodded his thanks.

'You are attending the war crimes tribunal?'

'Yes, but purely as an observer. I'm holding a watching brief to indicate ASEAN solidarity with Cambodia during these difficult times. I have no desire to get in your way in the execution of your duties.'

Colonel Menhay nodded, apparently pleased rather than sceptical at this orotund politeness from his rotund counterpart. He walked around his desk, opened the door to his office and shouted something in Khmer. 'We will have coffee together,' he explained.

Singh nodded enthusiastically. He was especially pleased when the coffee arrived. It was hot, sweet and milky and more importantly, accompanied by two dry biscuits. For a man who had eschewed his fish soup at lunch, it was a welcome nibble. The colonel eyed him with curiosity and then pushed his own plate of biscuits over.

'How are things going?' asked Singh. He had no real interest in Cambodian police work but he had to buy time to finish the biscuits.

The colonel shrugged. 'It is difficult to be a policeman in Cambodia. Our police and military force was formed through the merger of the militias of the different political entities. Sometimes, they forget that their first loyalty is to the country, not political parties. And then there is the corruption.' His eyes brightened and his short neck lengthened with interest. 'I hear that in Singapore the police are not corrupt?'

'For one thing, they are paid enough so there is less temptation,' explained Singh.

'Our policemen, they get maybe just a few *riel* a month. Sometimes they work at night as bouncers or guards. Other times . . .well, you can guess.'

Singh's eyes widened. That was even less remuneration than he would have expected. No wonder graft was rife if the cops weren't paid enough to make ends meet. Even he, a man of simple tastes, might have found the straight and narrow difficult if he was regularly deprived of his beer and curry, not to mention cigarettes, for lack of funds.

His host's expression had become steadily more gloomy, drooping jowls softening the edges of his square head. It had not been Singh's intention or inclination to draw the man's attention to the shortcomings of the Cambodian police force. He asked, changing the subject quickly, 'How about here at the ECCC? What is your main security concern?'

'Samrin!' snapped Menhay. 'Someone might try to kill him.'

'The accused has been a free man for thirty years. Why should they come for him now?'

'It is the Cambodian way to wait for as long as necessary to exact revenge. Thirty days or thirty years, the desire for retribution stays fresh.'

Singh remembered that many of the Khmer Rouge leaders had been in hiding or in safe areas, not in the open as they were now.

The colonel was still speaking. 'Sometimes months, sometimes years . . . if you have harmed someone in Cambodia, you can never feel safe. Your family will never be safe. These trials – they have opened many old wounds, brought back so many memories . . . I don't know where it will *end*.'

There was something in his voice that caused Singh to seek an answer in the other man's carefully expressionless face. 'Are you worried about the serial killings?'

'I see that your reputation is well-deserved,' remarked the

colonel, revealing for the first time that he had heard about the policeman from Singapore before this meeting.

'I read about it in the newspapers,' confessed Singh.

'An organised campaign – ex-Khmer Rouge are being targeted.'

'How do you know? It could just be individual acts of revenge.'

'The MO,' said the colonel.

Singh smothered a smile. Even in Cambodia, cops talked like they watched too much *CSI*.

'Single shots to the head – execution style,' continued Menhay. 'That's not the Cambodian way. Usually, revenge here is much messier. It is quite common for victims to be disembowelled, their livers cut out and cooked. Acid attacks are quite common here too. These murders have been clinical.'

'Are you in charge of the investigation then?' Singh could not keep the note of surprise out of his voice. The small office did not look like the epicentre of a major criminal investigation.

Menhay grimaced. 'No – not since I was sent here to the tribunal. But I keep an eye on what's going on at HQ.'

Their eyes met and there was no need for further explanation. This policeman was champing at the bit because the policing action was going on elsewhere. Singh knew the feeling all too well.

As if to emphasise his conclusion, the colonel said snidely, 'There are murders to investigate but I'm playing security guard to a mass murderer.' His face brightened. 'Still, maybe someone will try and kill Samrin.'

'He must be an obvious target for your serial killer,' suggested the Sikh inspector.

The colonel became serious again and parallel lines of worry filled the space between receding hairline and sparse eyebrows. Singh noticed for the first time that the other policeman had the round small ears perpendicular to the head that he had noticed on a number of Khmer already. It was a peculiar and distinctive genetic trait.

'The killer seems to be picking easy targets – avoiding big names like the men we have locked up here.'

'I read that there have been ten murders so far?'

The colonel nodded in agreement.

'But you're sure the victims are all ex-Khmer Rouge?'

'Yes.'

'Any other clues?'

'The murders have taken place on the weekend, usually within about fifty kilometres of Phnom Penh.'

'So a killer with a day job in this town?'

'That's what I figured.'

Singh smiled at the choice of words – this policeman had probably been sent on some policing course to the US and adopted the speech patterns. The inspector leaned back in the white plastic chair which strained to hold his weight without buckling. He asked, his interest piqued, 'Have you spotted any other links between the victims?'

The other man shook his head emphatically. 'They have a few guys looking into the background of the victims – but nothing yet.'

A policeman knocked on the door smartly and, upon a nod from the colonel, walked in and handed him a folded piece of paper. From the colonel's expression, Singh had no difficulty in deducing that the news was not good.

'What's the matter?' he asked.

'The death toll has just reached eleven.' Menhay's words and a deep sigh were intermingled. 'A farmer – shot in the head.'

Singh adopted what he hoped was an expression of sympathy, checked the saucer to make sure the biscuits were finished, rose to his feet hurriedly and shook the other man's hand. 'Good luck with everything,' he said firmly and marched out of the police HQ. Biscuits or no biscuits, frisson of curiosity or not, the last thing he wanted to do was get involved in some dodgy Cambodian murder investigation.

He stopped on the veranda and squinted at the sky. There was not a cloud to be seen and the sun was at its zenith. Beads of sweat popped out along his forehead and he mopped them up with a large handkerchief. He thought about what the policeman had told him – someone was bumping off Khmer Rouge cadres one by one. He cast his mind back to the newspapers that morning. All being said and done, he didn't envy Menhay his job.

A voice at his elbow demanded, 'What were you doing? I was waiting for you outside the courtroom.'

It was Chhean, addressing him in her usual brusque style. He remembered his lunch companion, Sovann. She was closer to the stereotype he had expected of Cambodian women, the demure beauty with downcast eyes, refined manners and gentle voice. The refugee orphanage that had raised this stocky young woman had certainly not sought to produce cookie-cutter Cambodians for public consumption. Mind you, there had been depths to Sovann that he could only guess at after such a brief acquaintance. It would be a mistake to treat any of these Cambodian women lightly – that much was certain.

He reached for his cigarettes and answered her question cheerfully. 'Just saying hello to your local cops.' He brushed the biscuit crumbs off the front of his shirt.

'The police are *all* criminals,' she said dismissively.

Singh raised an inquiring eyebrow and added a puff of grey smoke to the otherwise clear sky. They watched it ascend and then dissipate slowly into nothingness.

Chhean added as an afterthought, 'In Cambodia, I mean.'

'Colonel Menhay seemed all right.' Singh had no real evidence of this one way or the other. But there was something about the squat man, his honesty about the vendetta killings or the problems within the Cambodian police force, that had given Singh a good opinion of him.

'You're just saying that because he gave you biscuits.'

Singh looked at his companion admiringly. 'You should be a policewoman,' he said. 'That was a very good deduction based on, literally, a few crumbs of evidence.' Was there an irony in discussing corruption within the Cambodian police force when his goodwill could be purchased for a couple of stale biscuits? It was like they said – every man had his price. Singh had hoped that his would be a little higher, that's all.

'Actually,' Chhean admitted, ignoring Singh's earlier compliment, 'I have heard that the colonel is a good man. The UN asked for him – they are very concerned about the rumours of corruption around this tribunal. But with most policemen in

Phnom Penh, it would be like asking the civet cat to guard the chicken coop.'

Singh had read as much in her notes. Dozens of Cambodians associated with the trial – judges, lawyers, clerks – had come under suspicion of everything from outright graft to influence peddling. It was causing enormous ineffectual hand-wringing within the international community, especially amongst those nations who had donated funds for the setting up of the tribunal. As far as he was aware, ASEAN's only contribution to date was his own presence – and he was not exactly worth his weight in gold.

'Good man or not, he has a lot on his plate.'

'What do you mean?' she demanded.

Singh inhaled deeply, feeling the tobacco-laden breath fill his lungs. It felt good to smoke a cigarette hundreds of miles away from his wife, his doctor and Superintendent Chen. In fact, it felt good to be away from all of them, full stop. Chhean was looking at him expectantly, still waiting for his response. He said firmly, 'That's police business, young lady.'

They were back in the courtroom. Singh was not looking forward to the session but he was grateful for the air conditioning. He scratched his belly thoughtfully like a classical guitarist plucking at strings and leaned over to his companion. 'What now?' he whispered audibly.

Chhean scowled at him, eyebrows meeting in a 'v' above her short nose. 'Shhh!'

Singh was aggravated. Her shushing him was more disruptive than his question. He was prevented from making a fuss by the ponderous announcement that the judges were making an entrance.

They all stood as the judges walked into the room in single file and took their places on the dais. Singh tried morosely to put a number on the times he had dragged himself to his feet for the arrival of these so-called embodiments of justice. Still, this group had a lot on their plate. He didn't for a second envy them their colourful robes and high-backed chairs. From what little he had seen, Cambodian society had as many layers as an onion and every time a layer was peeled back an odour attached to the fingers and the eyes began to smart. He smirked – perhaps that was taking the metaphor too far.

There was much rustling and shuffling of papers, fiddling with microphones and important whispers behind palms as if the audience consisted of seasoned lip-readers. The next witness for the prosecution was announced. 'Ta Ieng.' There was a hum of anticipation from the crowd.

The tall man was so thin that he looked emaciated, half-starved. He reminded Singh of the hollow-cheeked pictures of Moslem men at Srebenica and the black-and-white grainy photos of survivors of the concentration camps of World War Two. It worried him that, although the Cambodian genocide had occurred on Singapore's doorstep, he was more familiar with the images of massacres from far away.

Despite his appearance, however, this man was not one of the good guys. He had been an executioner at Choeng Ek, one of those charged with killing prisoners trucked over from Tuol Sleng prison.

'I had no choice,' Ta Ieng explained in a low voice. 'I had to do what I was told.'

Singh noted that his gaze remained focused on the ground beneath his feet – he did not look up at the presiding judge or the lawyer who was putting the questions to him in a clear voice that carried to the galleries.

'Otherwise, he would have killed me.'

'Who would have killed you?'

Ta Ieng nodded quickly in the direction of Samrin, sitting rigid in the dock, and then let his chin sink back to his chest.

'Let the record show that the witness has identified the accused,' intoned the lawyer.

Was following orders to protect one's own skin ever an excuse? It had been used as a defence by foot soldiers and lower ranks since the Nuremberg trials – *I was only following orders*, they would say, as if it was an excuse, absolution, a defence to unthinkable behaviour. What would he have done when presented with such a stark choice? Singh preferred to believe that he would not save his own life at the expense of another. He stared at the skinny man in the witness stand. He very much feared that this man would have said much the same thing if he had been asked the question any time before he was put in that invidious position.

'How do you know he would have killed you?' The lawyer was professional, his tone even, without any implication of judgment. Singh admired him for it. He was, even as an observer, struggling to maintain a sense of autonomy. He had no idea how the hordes that packed the public gallery felt. He had been told by Chhean that they were mostly survivors of that period, coming to find answers, closure, retribution. But this man was a witness, not a defendant. The multi-million-dollar war crimes court had no remit to try the lower ranks of the Khmer Rouge.

The answer to the lawyer's question came in a whisper from Ta Ieng. 'It happened to others. If Samrin suspected that they were not committed to the revolution, he would arrest them and send them to Tuol Sleng prison. Soon they too would confess after the torture . . . that they were CIA agents, KGB, or worked for the Vietnamese, anything really.'

'Did you believe their confessions?'

He shrugged, one thin shoulder raised above the other, as if there was a misshapen coat hanger inside his shirt.

Singh was not sure what the gesture indicated. That he hadn't believed? More likely it meant that his own beliefs were irrelevant to the process or the outcome and it was naïve to suggest otherwise.

'Surely it would have been better to refuse to assist in the killings and take what punishment came to you?'

'If I had refused, I would have been killed.' He bowed his head. 'Maybe that was an acceptable price to pay.' He looked up and faced the lawyer squarely. 'But you must understand that someone else would have done it. I would have saved no one – not one single person.'

The inspector felt as if his earphones were clamped to his head like a vice. It was the strain of listening to Ta Ieng's jus-tifications. Was his decision to comply with the macabre instructions of his superiors that hard to understand when his refusal would have made no difference?

'Did you play a role in the torture?' The lawyer was persevering.

There was a brief but definite nod.

'Who told you to do it?'

'Samrin.' His whisper was accompanied by another sidelong glance at the accused sitting within a semi-circular wooden dock with unexpectedly Romanesque balustrades. After thirty long years, this skinny man drumming his foot up and down on the floor was still terrified of the Choeng Ek commandant.

'What sort of thing did you do?'

'The usual . . .'

'Perhaps you could elaborate?' asked the prosecutor, two hands clasped behind his back.

The thin man's right hand went to his throat as if the words he wished to speak were stuck in there. He had a quick sip from a glass of water. His voice, when he finally spoke, was loud and high-pitched, as if he had resolved to tell the truth. 'We were instructed to remove toenails and fingernails if the prisoner did not confess. Also, sometimes we placed poisonous creatures, snakes and centipedes, on their bodies.'

The lawyer nodded encouragingly.

'If the confession was not in enough detail, we would reduce the daily food ration from two condensed milk tins of rice gruel to just one.'

Singh winced.

'What was the worst thing you ever did?'

There was a silence and then the hurried pre-emptive defence. 'I didn't want to do it. Samrin made me. I was just following orders.'

'What was it?'

'We had to kill the children.'

'What do you mean?'

'If there was a confession, if the prisoner was a traitor, his whole family was purged. You see, the leaders did not want to risk any relatives seeking revenge. They were tainted – after all, the fruit does not fall far from the tree. Pol Pot used to say, "To kill you is no loss, to keep you is no gain".'

Every eye in the courtroom was fixed on this man who was resorting to expressions from the Khmer Rouge leader's personal cupboard of revolutionary maxims.

'Even the children?' asked the lawyer.

'Yes.'

'How?'

'You see, the regime didn't have enough bullets.'

'How?' snapped the lawyer. His hands were gripping the balustrade separating him from the witness. Even from where Singh was sitting, he could see that the man's knuckles had turned white. He was asking the questions, but like almost everyone in the room, Singh included, he barely had courage to face the answers.

'I smashed their heads against trees – there was a special killing tree at Choeng Ek.' He swung his long thin arms in a wide semi-circle like a man wielding a baseball bat. 'You know, like this . . .'

Singh glanced around the court. Amongst the worn, shocked faces of the spectators, one stood out – a tall, elderly Caucasian was leaning forward, his hands clasped together tightly. Tears, unchecked, perhaps even unnoticed, were coursing down his cheeks. They dripped from his chin like rain off the eaves of the policeman's Singapore home.

The inspector remembered the serial killer who was hunting down ex-Khmer Rouge one by one. All his long years of pursuing murderers, of siding with the victims whatever the motivations of the killer, did not prevent Singh from wishing that the vigilante would track down Ta Ieng.

Singh had not known what to expect from the next witness but it had not been this wrinkled man wearing an oversized shirt and a pair of baggy tan shorts that revealed he had a prosthetic limb attached to the stump of his left knee. His artificial leg was an aluminium rod with an old running shoe on the end. On his good leg he wore a flip-flop. As the gnome-like figure sat down, Singh saw that one side of the man's face was eclipsed with thick dark mounds of scar tissue. The man's left eye was shut and deeply indented, as if the eyeball within had been removed.

'You are Cheah Huon?'

The other man answered in Khmer, 'Yes,' revealing teeth that had yellowed like old ivory.

Singh reached hurriedly for his earphones.

'You are originally from Kompong Som province?'

Cheah Huon nodded and was requested to speak his answers for the court by one of the crimson-clad judges. He gave them an informal grin and answered loudly, 'Yes.'

'You were sent for re-education by the Khmer Rouge?'

'Yes, I was.' The left side of his mouth was misshapen and from the tentative translation in his ears, Singh guessed that his speech was distorted and difficult to understand.

'Why?'

Huon cupped a hand behind one ear and leaned forward

towards the lawyer who recognised his cue and repeated himself, much louder this time. To Singh's amusement, the voice in the earpiece grew more distinct too. This was not so much a translator at work as a method actor.

The witness focused his good eye with disconcerting intensity on the questioner who took an inadvertent step backwards. No surprise there. Singh was reminded of the proverbial stare of the basilisk. 'One of the *schlops* heard me talking to my wife,' he said.

A judge from Europe leaned forward and spoke into her microphone. From her accent Singh guessed she was French. 'What is a *schlop*?'

The inspector realised that the word had not been translated with the rest of the sentence. Was it such common parlance in Cambodia that an interpretation was unnecessary?

'It means a spy,' explained the Cambodian lawyer.

'Many of the "old" people would hang around outside our huts or near us when we were eating or working in the fields. They were listening for information that they could pass on to the bosses,' continued the witness.

Singh knew – again he had Chhean and her notes in the blue folder to thank – that 'old' people referred to the peasants, especially those who had been living within Khmer Rouge-liberated areas before the fall of Phnom Penh. 'New' people were city folk who had been purposefully scattered throughout the country after the cities were emptied.

'What did you say to your wife that the *schlop* reported?'

'I spoke in French.'

'What did you say?'

'I can't remember,' he said sadly, shaking his head from side to side. 'Anyway, the *schlop* who turned me in did not speak French.'

Singh scratched his bearded chin.

'They said I was an intellectual – because I spoke French, not Khmer – and needed to be retrained to understand the new socialist order,' he explained further.

'And they sent you to Tuol Sleng prison?'

'S21, yes.'

'When did you first come across the accused, Samrin?'

Samrin was sitting on Huon's blind side so he had to turn his head a full half circle to see him. Singh noted that he did not seem afraid, despite Samrin's reputation for cold-blooded cruelty in the service of the revolution. Probably, after what he had been through as evidenced by the blasted heath that was his face let alone the missing limb, he was beyond fear.

'After I had confessed to being a CIA agent.' To Singh's amazement, Huon chuckled. 'We all confessed eventually, of course. I confessed everything that I could imagine they wanted to hear even *before* they tortured me.' He spat on the ground suddenly, amusement turning to anger that was visible in a reddening of the scar tissue so that the wounds looked almost fresh. 'They tortured me anyway. They were sadists, all of them.'

'What about Samrin?' prompted the lawyer.

'When they were tired of me, they sent me to Choeng Ek, you know, the killing fields outside Phnom Penh. Samrin was there. I saw him often because I was put on duty to cover the graves.' He responded to the expression of puzzlement on the lawyer's face, 'You see, the prisoners dug their own graves and were then executed, usually by being

67

bludgeoned to death with ox-handles – but when they were dead there was no one to,' he made a sweeping motion with his hand, 'spray chemicals – to disguise the smell – and cover the bodies with earth. They asked me to do it because I was not in as bad shape as the others from Tuol Sleng.' If the lawyer found any irony in the crippled man asserting that he had been in relatively good shape, he kept any hint of it out of his voice.

'What was Samrin's role?'

'He would supervise each mass execution: give instructions of how deep the earth was to be dug, tell the prisoners to line up on their knees, check names against the master list he had been sent from the prison. Sometimes, he would take part in the killing as well if they were short-handed although usually he left it to junior rank cadres.'

'How did you survive?'

'I was still on duty when the Vietnamese came. Samrin ordered that all the prisoners be killed so that no one could speak of that place, tell what had happened there. It was a messy business, there were so many to be killed at once. I pretended to tumble into the grave. No one bothered to help me – I'm not sure they saw me – or maybe they thought I would suffocate. That happened quite often, whenever a blow was mistimed or the aim was not good and the prisoner didn't die immediately.'

He stopped speaking and silence reigned in the court as if it too was a mass grave.

'What happened next?' asked the lawyer, hitching his gown higher onto his shoulders as if he could feel the chill of the tomb.

Singh adjusted his headphones so that they sat tight on his ears. He didn't want to miss anything.

'I lay in there with the bodies. When night fell, I managed to scramble out. The guards, Samrin, everyone had fled. The next morning the Vietnamese arrived.'

Huon did not embellish his tale any further. There was no need. Everyone in the room was imagining what it must have been like to be in a deep, stinking, bloody pit, hemmed in on all sides by the dead and the dying.

'Is that how you received your injuries?' asked the lawyer sympathetically, clearing his throat and finding his voice again.

Huon gestured at his artificial limb and ran the other hand across his scarred cheek gently. He turned his head from side to side so that the audience could see the full horror of his injuries. 'Yes, I believe it was the chemicals they sprayed on the bodies – it ate through my skin like acid.'

In the silence that greeted this last piece of information, Singh heard a quiet sound, like the slow exhalation of air from a balloon. He turned his head and was just in time to see Sovann, the beautiful creature who had not finished her lunch, half rise from her seat, close her eyes and slip to the ground in a dead faint. In a few moments, she was surrounded by concerned people and lost from view. Singh remained seated. There was nothing he could do. She was too far away, there were others to help and he had no real *locus* to interfere.

The lawyer for Samrin's defence rose to his feet. He was a middle-aged Englishman with a paunch that overhung his belt like a waiting avalanche.

'You claim that you saw my client, Samrin, supervising affairs at Choeng Ek?'

'Yes . . . him!' Huon pointed at the defendant with an angry finger.

'But we have only your word for that – and you are not a very credible witness. I am sure you mean well but the suffering you have undergone means that your recollections cannot be trusted.'

Singh suddenly understood the thrust of the defence. With so many witnesses dead or disappeared after thirty years, linking Samrin to the atrocities was not a straightforward job for the prosecution. Everyone knew full well that Samrin had ordered the executions at Choeng Ek but the evidentiary trail was intermittent.

And Samrin believed he had a chance. He had pleaded 'not guilty' to all the charges against him, spurning an invitation to admit guilt and seek clemency from the court on the grounds of age and infirmity.

'Why should I lie?' demanded Cheah Huon.

'I am not suggesting you lied,' explained the barrister smoothly, 'just that you might be mistaken.'

'That is not true!'

'I guess we differ in our opinion then.'

The Cambodian lawyer rose to his feet. 'Is there anything else you would like to share with the court?' he asked.

Cheah Huon was leaning forward, still angry at being disbelieved. He gripped the balustrade with both hands and bit out his next words. 'I know many things that this court would be interested to hear. Not just about Samrin but about others too. Remember, a small axe can fell a big tree if it is sharp enough. My body is injured' – he scowled at the English lawyer – 'but my mind is still sharp and I can prove it!'

There was a whispering in the courtroom that sounded like a stiff breeze through long grass.

One of the judges, a sleek, well-fed looking Cambodian man with receding dark hair said, 'That is very interesting, Mr Cheah Huon. We look forward to hearing your testimony – but it will have to wait until tomorrow.' He looked around at his fellow judges and intoned, 'Court is adjourned until nine a.m. in the morning.'

Five

François Gaudin sat on a low bench against a recently painted cream wall and pillowed his head on arms folded across his knees. At last he straightened his spine with a conscious effort. He took a few deep slow breaths, as if air was precious and to be savoured. The smell of fresh paint had an oddly medicinal property – almost like the old-fashioned smelling salts he remembered his grandmother clutching in a loose-skinned, plump-veined hand. It cleared his head and he was able to stand.

Ta Ieng's testimony had made him physically ill earlier that day as he had heard, first hand and for the first time, what the Khmer Rouge had been prepared to do to children. But he knew that, if it was possible to grade the horrors of the past, then what lay ahead of him was probably going to be worse. He was outside the notorious Tuol Sleng prison, known as S21 by Brother No.1, Pol Pot, and his henchmen. He flinched at the anonymity of numbers so beloved by the Khmer Rouge.

It worked to distance the perpetrators from the crimes and removed any vestige of humanity from the victims. They were not people, just ciphers – involuntary participants in a grand revolution for which sacrifice was necessary. The prison had been the subject of numerous books, films and documentaries; a museum of horrors that was open to the public so that tourists could gape and stare and wonder what madness had led to such things and whether those seeds of insanity still lay within the smiling, friendly Cambodian people.

The multi-storeyed building looked like a school, and indeed it had been before it was taken over by the regime, the classrooms divided into cells with hastily constructed rough-edged brick walls, crude checked barbed wire fixed between roof and balcony to prevent untimely suicides. The short grass in the compound was dry and had a brownish tinge. A couple of tall palms stood like sentries at the front.

The attaché at the French embassy had pointed out that his wife would have been considered an enemy of the state because of her relationship with a Frenchman, the evidence there for all to see in their mixed-blood children. She might have been arrested right away, sent to a convenient prison nearby – just like this one, perhaps even this one. After all, S21 was the biggest and was known to have housed foreigners: Vietnamese and Thais but also Americans, Frenchmen and Britons.

François screwed up the courage to go inside. He knew what to expect, of course. They even sold postcards of Tuol Sleng on the streets. Small children offered up souvenirs of death to the *barangs*, the foreigners. He knew what to expect and yet he didn't. He had not realised that, like the Mona Lisa, the rows and rows of victims, each holding a card with a number on it, followed a visitor with their eyes. He had not known that the subjects had their hands tied behind their backs so that each one looked like their arms had been lopped off at the shoulders. The photos were in black and white, the eyes dark haunted hollows. The victims silently begged him to come to their aid or accused him with dead eyes for having survived, for having escaped, for having left his wife and children behind.

He stumbled upon an exhibition of paintings by Vann Nath, one of only seven people known to have survived the prison. He read on the notice board that Vann had been a prisoner, but kept alive – there was a note on an execution list in Duch's hand, 'Keep the painter' – because the prison boss liked his depictions of Pol Pot. The artist had spent the years after the regime's collapse painting his memories, trying to exorcise the ghosts he carried around in his head.

François turned a corner and was confronted with the next canvas.

The Frenchman sank to his knees and his sobs came from the depths of his soul, first loud and anguished and then a continuous soft sound, like bubbles bursting against a wall. He lay on the ground, curled up as tight as he could, hands around his knees, eyes open and yet unseeing, all his focus concentrated within. The guards came to fetch him with the quiet professionalism of those who had seen others collapse under the weight of memories at Tuol Sleng.

'A *barang*,' observed one of them. 'Unusual.'

The other was looking at the painting which had broken the man before them, seeking a reason for his collapse.

It depicted a young woman with dishevelled dark hair, her

face creased with desperation but also a single-minded concentration. A guard in black pyjamas and a blue *krama* was yanking her small baby from her hands as she fought to hold on. Another cadre was beating her back and legs with a rod, trying to persuade her to let go of the child.

'Why does this canvas affect the *barang* so much?' asked the second guard as they led the hunched sobbing figure away.

The other one shrugged. 'I have no idea.'

'I don't trust Cheah Huon.' The voice was firm.

The judge held the receiver hard against his ear as if he feared that the words might be overheard although he was alone in the room. He sat behind a desk, staring blankly at the opposite wall. His glasses, thick black plastic frames, were perched on the end of his nose. He scratched his hairline, which had receded so far back that he looked like a Chinese eunuch with a shaved scalp.

'I don't understand – I paid him off, just as you asked. He promised to keep his mouth shut. What's the problem?'

'I thought the situation was under control as well – he keeps quiet about what he knows, he stays alive and gets a pension. But now I am not so sure.'

Judge Sopheap reached for a tissue from a lacy receptacle on his desk and dabbed his high forehead. 'I think you are making too much of this – I am sure we can trust him. I explained the situation when I met him.'

'They are all talking too much. Not just Huon. Why would Ta Ieng speak of killing the children? Is he trying to make himself important? They are showing off to the court and the press and the public . . .'

'Even if you are right, what can I do?' Sopheap took off his glasses and pressed an index finger and thumb against his closed eyelids. Trying to reverse the pressure he could feel from the inside. It dismayed him that the caller knew so much of the day's events. He had observers present, determined to shroud the past in secrecy to the extent it affected his interests. So much for truth and reconciliation, he thought bitterly. Like Cambodia itself, this tribunal was becoming a battleground of competing interests.

'You must stop him from revealing any further secrets – don't give him any opportunity to speak.'

'I cannot stop him from testifying. It's not my decision. There is no way the other judges will agree, not even the Cambodians.' He could hear the pleading note in his own voice, begging tones that held so many echoes of the past. The muscles in his shoulders and neck were tense with memories. He added, 'Already there was surprise from the other judges when I halted the testimony of Cheah Huon. I had to say I was feeling ill.'

The caller wilfully misunderstood his point. 'You did well – but we must have a more permanent solution.'

'Give me time to think of something . . .'

'There is no time,' snapped the man at the other end. 'Perhaps I could arrange for the other judges to fall ill – Cambodian food can be very suspect sometimes.'

Sopheap shook his head, trying to dislodge the fear that preyed on his mind like maggots on a corpse. He picked up his glasses and put them on carefully. He looked out of the window. A row of saffron-robed monks with shaved heads was accepting alms from strangers. Some of the monks were mere youths, novitiates learning the way of the Buddha. He too had spent a part of his boyhood in a rural *wat* being trained by the monks. It was a rite of passage for boys of his generation. But then the Khmer Rouge had exterminated the monks – they were 'useless mouths' without value in the godless, lawless Cambodia of Pol Pot. Unfortunately, despite the peaceful image of monks re-integrated within Khmer society outside his window, parts of Cambodia remained lawless and godless.

Sopheap tried to sound reasonable, thoughtful – fearless. 'It doesn't matter if you replace *all* the judges with your henchmen, such a decision – to prevent further testimony – will cause consternation. It will be in the newspapers – the foreign press too. It won't solve anything. Instead, questions will be asked. Your secret will surely be found out.'

'Very well – I understand your difficulty.'

Sopheap sighed – an audible sound of relief that must have carried to his caller.

'That is good. I am sure you have nothing to worry about and he won't say anything. You are quite safe.' He was using too many words, prolonging the conversation when he needed to terminate it, his fear making him garrulous and incoherent.

'Oh! I'm not worried,' explained the man.

Something in his tone filled the judge with foreboding. He asked the question, pulling nervously at a loose strand of red thread on his gown. 'What do you mean?'

'One way or another – and I really don't care how you do it – *you* have to stop Cheah Huon from talking . . .'

'But how am I to do that?' spluttered Sopheap, flecks of

saliva landing on the papers on his desk. The pattern reminded him of the configuration of bullet wounds from an automatic weapon.

'You're a smart man – I'm sure you'll think of something. Otherwise . . . otherwise, you know what will happen.'

Singh was slumped in an armchair in his hotel room contemplating the day's testimony. He cast his mind back to when he had investigated a murder in the aftermath of the terrorist bombings in Bali. At the time, it had seemed that the callous snatching of life in a terrorist attack, without any nexus between murderer and victim, was the most grievous expression of cold-blooded murder possible. He would have to revise that thought. The murder of innocents without malice aforethought but with a cynical, clinical cruelty over a period of months and years, that was worse. Kill or be killed, torture or be tortured, follow orders or have the same fate befall one as the would-be victims.

He cast his mind back over the murders he had investigated over the years. So many killers, so many victims, so many motives – but none as powerful as the desire for revenge. And yet, as far as he was aware, there had been no attempt on the life of Samrin or Ta Ieng. Was this society that forgiving? He remembered the eleven ex-Khmer Rouge who had been killed recently. Perhaps not.

He wondered idly – the policeman in him was like a dog with a bone when there was even a hint of murder in the offing – whether the wave of killings had been sparked by the commencement of the trials. It could be that repressed memories had surfaced with the tribunal or that the testimony of a witness had acted as a trigger. Otherwise, why were the murders happening now, after all these years?

There was a sharp knock on the door which he had already learnt to identify as belonging to Chhean. Her aggressive rat-a-tat was quite different to the gentle scratching of room service. He opened the door with trepidation. He was not sure if he could cope with Chhean's view of the world – black and white with no shades of grey.

Chhean was as crisp and efficient as ever. 'It is time for dinner. We will go to a street market for food. It will give you a chance to understand Cambodian culture.'

Singh, unusually for him, was feeling a complete lack of inclination for dinner. The testimony that afternoon had destroyed his appetite, he who had always gone home after a grisly day at the office and tucked into a good meal cooked by his skinny wife.

'What is the matter? Why do you not answer?' demanded Chhean, excluded from this sudden wistfulness.

'Nothing – it's fine. Let's go.' He should venture out into Phnom Penh. He needed to see a more normal aspect of Cambodian life – to believe that the horrors he listened to daily were not the sum of the place or the people.

Chhean led him directly to a small motorbike. She whipped a cloth out from under the seat and wiped it down.

'You can't be serious!' exclaimed Singh.

Chhean, who was always serious, looked at him, smooth brow creased into puzzled lines. 'What is the matter?'

'I'm not getting on that thing!'

'But I have no car. The driver has gone home – also there is traffic. Moto is the best way. Very fast.'

Chhean, her short legs straddling the machine, sat as far forward as possible to make room for him. Singh adjusted himself to make sure his centre of gravity was firmly in the middle of the seat and felt the scooter sink under his weight. He wondered about the Cambodian etiquette on pillion riding – was it acceptable to clutch at this small, square human being who was young enough to be his daughter?

'You must hold on!' said Chhean, revving the small engine. It sounded like a lawn mower.

It was soon apparent that their moto, despite the presence on it of a Sikh gentleman of ample proportions, was lightly laden compared to the others. Another one sped by, driven at speed by a teenage boy with at least four other children hanging off it. All were laughing, tongues hanging out in delight like dogs next to an open car window.

The dust in the air was making his eyes and nose smart. Chhean had tied her *krama*, the ubiquitous Cambodian multi-purpose scarf, around her face and he noticed a number of other drivers and riders had done the same. He wished his turban had the same flexibility of use.

He shouted over the wind whistling in his ears as if he was in a wind tunnel. His voice was hoarse. 'What did you think about today?'

There was silence up front although he felt her back stiffen. He had dispensed with considerations of etiquette and was now hanging on to Chhean like a lover.

He was about to repeat his question when she said, 'Someone should murder them!'

'Who?'

'Samrin, Duch, Ta Ieng – the whole lot.'

They came to a standstill at a crossroads. One road led directly towards a large yellow Art Deco building that was teeming with people.

'This is where we buy dinner. New Market.'

'Is it new?' asked Singh doubtfully, looking at the architecture and the peeling paint.

'No, no – more than seventy years old,' she said impatiently. 'Sometimes people call it Central Market.'

'Oh! It's centrally located,' said Singh, trying to get his bearings.

'No – actually we are not near the centre of Phnom Penh.'

She looked at his bemused face and cracked a smile. 'You try Cambodian food.'

Singh looked at the nearest vendor. Various insects had been fried and stuck on a spit. Singh shook his head while Chhean purchased a stick with a handful of *riel* and dragged a toasted grasshopper off with her neat, even teeth.

A stray dog with a mangy coat and teats hanging so low that they brushed the ground looked longingly at Chhean.

She tossed a fried insect on the ground and the dog pounced on it. 'This is a brave dog,' she muttered.

'Why do you say that?' asked Singh, taking a step backwards to get away from the creature and almost knocking over a trolley of pirated CDs.

'A few years ago, the mayor said we should all eat more stray dogs to keep down the population in Phnom Penh.'

'Dog or human population?' demanded Singh. Surely – taste for dogs or not – no one would eat a creature in the condition of this unhappy animal?

The inspector turned away hurriedly and walked down the

road. He immediately developed a following of small, grubby children with wide eyes and brown skin. A particularly dirty child, naked except for a large pair of shorts tied on firmly with a piece of twine, tugged at his elbow. The child held out an arm that was covered from shoulder to wrist in watches, mostly of the plastic digital variety.

Singh turned to Chhean helplessly as balloons, sunglasses and baseball caps were thrust at him, a fat imposing figure in a pointy *krama* defeated by a few persistent children. 'What should I do?' he asked plaintively. 'I don't want any of this stuff.'

'You don't want anything – you keep walking,' she said firmly, shooing away the nearest set of children with a firm hand. They were immediately replaced by another lot, pleased to get to the front of the 'fleece the foreigner' queue.

'But they need the money,' said Singh helplessly.

'Everyone in Cambodia needs money,' she responded tartly. 'Do you have enough for all of them?'

The restaurant had a cheery air with its checked red-and-white table cloths and smell of freshly baked bread. The workers were Cambodian, smiling and young. They must have wondered what an old *barang* was doing, sitting in a French café in Phnom Penh, drinking steadily through their beer supply. Or maybe it was common enough. Perhaps the only unusual aspect of François's presence was that he was not accompanied by a nubile creature, young enough to be his daughter – or granddaughter – like the sex tourists that he had noticed out and about in the city. It was extraordinary that such blatant exploitation went unchecked and unpoliced. Yet another consequence of poverty and corruption, he supposed. Was this the future that his children – probably long dead, such beautiful girls both of them – had avoided?

His mind replayed the image of the painting at Tuol Sleng. For a painful second, it had seemed to him that the figure was that of his wife, the baby being torn from her arms, his baby. It was unlikely that the artist had set about to record events that affected his family. But the part that had caused his knees to give way beneath him and the strength to leave his body was that it *could* have been his family. Not in the painting, but in reality. If his wife had ended up in a Khmer Rouge prison – if the children had been taken away from her – exactly such a scene might have been enacted. He knew she would have fought to keep them, her children and his children. She would have fought while he remained in the safety of his home in Paris.

There was a sudden commotion at the door and a young man swaggered in accompanied by a collection of thugs, some wearing the uniform of the Cambodian police. François, glancing past them, saw a fleet of Mitsubishi Pajeros pulled up outside. He guessed that this was the son of a Government bigwig or powerful businessman. He had heard that these young men in their expensive designer clothing were a law unto themselves in Phnom Penh. This punk was dressed in black: black silk shirt, black suit with thin leg-hugging trousers and black boots with pointy ends. He was wearing shades although it was late evening. Now, he sat down and shouted for drinks. Immediately, the serving staff hurried over with platters of food and bottles of beer. He waved aside the beer and one of his entourage reached into a bag and retrieved a bottle of Johnny Walker, Gold Label. Only the best for daddy's boy, thought François snidely. His disdain must have been visible on his face because one of the men leaned over and whispered into the ear of his paymaster.

The young man swivelled slowly in his chair until he was facing François, his eyes still hidden behind sunglasses. He was a handsome youth with a slightly dissipated air and midnight-black hair swept away from a narrow forehead.

'What are you staring at, grandpa?' He spoke the fluent French of an overseas-educated youth from a well-heeled family.

François shook his head to indicate a negative.

'I saw you staring. Do you deny it?'

'I really was not looking at you,' explained the Frenchman.

Responding to an unseen signal, a large man wearing the green of a military policeman came over and picked François up by the scruff of his neck so that his feet were barely touching the ground. He shouted something in Khmer and there were loud guffaws from his audience. Gaudin noticed that the waitresses were watching the scene with trepidation. He hoped one of them would call the authorities and then remembered that it was a policeman that had him by the collar.

The youth had a swig of whisky. He said, 'I hate the French. See what they have done to my country.'

François did not respond. He didn't even really disagree. Tired of his weak prey, the antagonistic youngster gestured with a languid hand. The large man dragged François outside and threw him to the dusty ground. He kicked him a couple of times in the ribs with a heavy boot and said in a guttural voice, 'Next time you don't look at my boss if you don't want to get hurt.'

François waited for him to go back in, sat up slowly and painfully and threw up suddenly all over his shirt.

'You must be careful in Phnom Penh,' explained the driver of one of the Pajeros in a not-unfriendly tone. Apparently they did their master's bidding but did not feel obliged to entertain his prejudices.

François nodded, his breath coming in painful gasps. So, this was the Cambodia of today – a place where young males commanded the loyalty of policemen with their father's wealth. He tried to wipe his shirtfront with a handkerchief and abandoned it as a waste of effort. The pain and adrenaline had cleared his head of the alcohol and he stood up slowly, holding on to a concrete pillar.

'If you got cash, you're the boss – you understand?' The driver was bored and talkative. He added helpfully, 'In Cambodia, money can buy you anything.'

To François's ears, he sounded almost proud of this feature of Cambodian society, as if it was an attribute to attract tourists: Cambodia, Kingdom of Wonder – where money can buy you anything.

'Anything?' he asked.

'Anything you want,' responded the other man cheerfully.

Six

The dead man lay on his back, arms flung out on either side, hands hanging limply at the wrists. The position reminded Colonel Menhay of the stylised depictions of the crucifixion. The policeman, standing at the open doorway, was reluctant to step in, as if he knew that once he had taken ownership of this body, this room, this crime – he would be in over his head. He had no difficulty identifying the victim. Cheah Huon's head was turned to one side so that the scar tissue that had distinguished him at the trial the previous day was clearly visible. If that was not enough, his wooden leg was at right angles to his body. The clasp had probably snapped as he fell to the ground. The wooden leg looked farcical. There was to be no dignity in death for this poor fellow. The colonel's shoulders hunched, foreshortening his thick neck. It was only the previous day that he had listened to Huon's testimony and felt the old memories bob to the surface like a week-old corpse in a muddy river.

He saw that Huon's eyes had rolled back into his head. Menhay felt a frisson of pure superstitious fear. He was a teenager again, a novitiate at the *wat*, dressed in saffron robes and feeling the presence of otherworldly elements in the rituals of the monks. The vacant eyes of the dead man were terrifying, as if the vision of his own impending death had robbed him of his sight.

Menhay sighed and walked into the room slowly. He had to focus on the dead man, not the ghosts pushing at the periphery of his imagination. He poked the victim with his foot. Huon was stiff – he'd been dead for at least a few hours. He knelt down and felt the skin of his forehead, his fingers brushing against the furrows of scar tissue. The corpse was cold, so much colder than he ever got used to, the skin clammy in the morning humidity. He tried to move the victim's arm – rigor mortis had set in but the process was not yet complete. The pathologist would narrow the time for him but it seemed likely that Huon had been killed the previous evening and grown cold over the course of a long cool night. Menhay was quite prepared to back his own preliminary judgment as to the time of death. He was a middle-aged Cambodian man – he had seen his share of killing and death. He had an instinct for it. It was why he had become a policeman – to channel his memories into something positive. He looked down at the victim again. There was not a whole lot of positive right now. A witness had been killed on the grounds of the war crimes tribunal. There would be hell to pay when it became known. He toyed with the idea of trying to keep the killing under wraps. Surely it was better not to taint the ECCC?

To let them get on with the business of seeking justice for past atrocities? This man lying dead had already been a victim so many times. He would not want his death to impede his revenge.

The colonel stepped out of the room into the corridor and hurried through the side door that led to the outside. He needed to get out of that small room with its grisly contents – he was sick of violent, untimely death visited upon innocents. And yet, it was Cambodia's destiny, it seemed, to be always steeped in blood.

The bright early morning sunshine on his face was warm and restored him slightly. He tried to think coherently, squinting against the glare. He had to decide the best way forward. In the daylight, he knew already that there could be no cover-up. Practically, the cleaning woman who had found the body and the guards she had notified – none of them could be silenced except with tactics that he refused to use. He remembered the quiet voice with which Cheah Huon had spoken the previous day as he sat upright in the witness box. Menhay would not think of the big picture, about justice for Cambodia as embodied in the war crimes tribunal. He would focus on justice for the man lying in the room with a knife buried in his chest. Huon deserved no less and Menhay could not do less. The policeman straightened his back and pulled back his shoulders. He whispered to an aide to inform the judges that the trial would have to be postponed that day – the whole compound was a crime scene.

Looking up, he caught a glimpse of a portly figure wandering towards the courtrooms. An instinct which he would later question and sometimes regret caused him to shout, 'Inspector!'

The fat man looked around in surprise – he had been cocooned in the anonymity that came of being in a strange country, enjoying the knowledge that he was far away from Superintendent Chen and his monthly 'you're a disgrace to the Force' lectures. The loud yell pierced his isolation and caused him to stop and scan the horizon in puzzlement. He saw the colonel in the distance – what was his name? Menhay? The honest cop according to his difficult-to-please minder, Chhean, which probably meant that the fellow deserved a medal and a promotion. Why was he beckoning with such intensity?

He hoped the Cambodian wasn't looking for some sort of 'fellow copper' bond like they had on the television. Two cops covering for each other, watching each others' backs, falling for the same girl – he'd read the script but always been fairly sure that a cop-buddy would soon grow tiresome in real life. In this particular instance, it would probably end in a diplomatic incident. The Sikh detective sauntered towards the Cambodian policeman anyway. Perhaps there were more biscuits in the offing. His need was not quite so great that morning – he had been careful to ensure that he ate a massive breakfast: bacon and eggs washed down with lukewarm sweetened milky coffee. He had to prepare for the eventuality that the lunch menu hadn't improved. He was determined not to go with Chhean on any more food forays for skewered stick insects either. Singh had always approved of the philosophy of camels, storing up victuals for when resources grew scarce. He grinned suddenly – perhaps his overhanging gut was his hump.

He noted absently that Colonel Menhay had not responded to his broad smile. Something was up. Perhaps a twelfth body had been found. Fat lot of good there was waving him over if that was the case. What did he know about Cambodian serial killers bumping off ex-Khmer Rouge? He, Singh, having listened to the testimony of victims of the Khmer Rouge, already felt sympathetic rather than censorious towards this unknown but efficient killer. He disapproved of murder on principle, of course. But those bastards had it coming to them.

As he got closer to the Cambodian policeman, Singh realised that the man was pale and agitated. He stared hard at Singh as if trying to will him over more quickly with the force of his gaze alone. The Sikh inspector quickened his step, feeling his thighs in their light-wool dark trousers chafe against each other.

'What's the matter?' he asked as he got closer, subconsciously lowering his tone. Menhay had a furtive air, as if he was a keeper of secrets.

The other man didn't answer. He beckoned to his tubby counterpart with an urgent gesture and led him into one of the outlying buildings on the premises. Looking round, Singh guessed that the rooms had been set up as hostels – clean, Spartan and not justifying the clandestine behaviour of Colonel Menhay.

He followed the policeman through a door but didn't even have to look past him to know what lay within. The slightly protruding nostril hairs in his broad nose quivered slightly. He had picked up the scent, that familiar cloying rich odour that his years of experience on the Singapore murder squad had taught him to identify immediately. He pushed past Menhay. The other man was blocking his view and his way, perhaps having second thoughts about allowing another cop and a foreigner to boot onto his turf.

Singh stopped short in the doorway. He had smelt death, expected death and was now confronted with death, but he was still surprised. 'Why in the world would anyone kill this guy?' he asked, pulling at an earlobe that protruded from under his tightly wrapped turban.

'What do you mean?' demanded Menhay.

'This place is crawling with people with enemies – Samrin, that chap who was a prison guard, I've forgotten his name – Ta Ieng? They're still alive but someone killed the grave-digger?'

Moving closer, Singh noted that the man had been stabbed at point-blank range. He would have seen his killer, met him face to face. The knife hilt was still visible in his chest. The policeman shook his big head. In a way, Cheah Huon had been unlucky. It was not as easy to stab someone through the heart as popular literature suggested. The point of the blade was often deflected by the sternum resulting in a lung wound which, while potentially fatal, would not result in immediate death. There might have been time for Huon to call for help or crawl out of this small room so that he might have died in the open, with a view of the sky. But this killer had been determined or lucky, probably both, and the knife had penetrated the heart. If the metal was not buried in the dead man like a cork in a bottle of rich red wine, he would have bled profusely. As it was, except for a stain on the front of his white shirt – which looked like a red bloody mouth, decided Singh – there was not much blood on the victim, which meant not much blood on the murderer.

Singh knelt down next to the body, peering at the knife hilt. 'Different MO from your serial killer . . .'

'Besides which this guy was hardly Khmer Rouge,' retorted Menhay.

'Nice gold chain,' remarked Singh, noticing a thick rope of gold that was visible around Cheah Huon's neck. 'I don't think he was wearing that in court yesterday.'

'Cambodians often keep their savings in gold – they don't trust the banks.'

Singh could see from the way he was shifting his weight from foot to foot that Colonel Menhay was feeling edgy. It was more than the presence of the dead man that was bothering him. His Cambodian counterpart had almost certainly seen more death than a detective from Singapore. Say what you liked about the rigidity of law enforcement and the sheer boringness of Singapore's law-abiding citizens, they killed each other with less frequency than their ASEAN counterparts. Singh guessed that Menhay regretted summoning him. He didn't really care, not when there was a dead body in the vicinity. The inspector peered at the knife hilt like a butterfly collector looking at an exotic sample under a pin. He could see that the handle, a black plastic grip with indentations for ease of grip, was smudged. 'Might have prints,' he pointed out.

'I just pray to all the deities that we find some reason for this that has nothing to do with the tribunal!' exclaimed the colonel.

'Why? What's the issue?' Singh squinted at his counterpart. It was too early in the morning for elliptical references.

'We finally hold a tribunal, thirty years after the killing fields, and a witness is murdered? Most Cambodians are still fearful – this will convince them that the Khmer Rouge still pulls the strings . . .'

'That doesn't make sense. He's already testified.'

'Do you think our people are going to think rationally? Besides, he was going to testify further today. Who knows what he might have said – whom he might have implicated?'

'So you think this has something to do with the Khmer Rouge?'

'Who else?'

That was the question, certainly. The other question was what the hell was he doing in a small windowless room with a one-legged dead man and an unhappy Cambodian policeman? Curiosity had kept him here – the adrenaline charge of a fresh body distracting him from the realities. But this was well outside his remit. It was time to devise an exit strategy. Singh's tone was abrupt. 'Why did you call me in here? What do you want from me?'

'No idea – I saw you when I stepped out, remembered that you were Singapore's top murder cop. Maybe I was hoping you would come in here, look around and tell me immediately who had done it!' Menhay managed a rueful smile at the end, exposing his teeth which were worn to stumps.

'I'm afraid I have absolutely no clue who did this,' confessed Singh.

Menhay slapped him on the back, an unexpected gesture of camaraderie.

'This is a Cambodian problem. We will find a solution.'

Singh nodded in agreement but quietly hoped that this solution would not be thirty years in the making like the war crimes tribunal. This victim, Cheah Huon, had survived such horrors as would have destroyed a lesser man, and yet the fates had not been content to leave him alone. Singh glanced down at the dead man and there was pity in his dark eyes as he took in the dislodged wooden leg and the furrows of scars like a paddy field after harvest. It seemed that Huon had been killed in a place where it was still possible to get away with murder.

Judge Sopheap was getting dressed. He laid his gown over a chair, brushing it with his hands to remove any lint and dust. He liked to look his best, to present a picture of Cambodian justice that was neat and well-kempt, even though he was not looking forward to the day's trial at all. It was bad enough listening to the testimony of torturers and reading the statements of survivors, but he was also acutely aware that there were spies ensconced in the audience. He could imagine them, though he could not identify them, listening to every word, looking out for danger – making sure that he, Sopheap, was doing his job. Well, he had done his best for the boss, and he hoped they would realise that and leave him alone.

The original request to him had seemed so reasonable. He was being considered for the war crimes tribunal, a gruff voice had explained over the phone, despite his relative youth and lack of experience. After all, who in Cambodia had experience? Almost every professional, including lawyers, had been killed thirty years ago. Almost by definition, there were no elderly legal sages in the Cambodian judiciary.

I can make sure you make the bench, the caller had explained reassuringly. He knew the people who counted. Indeed, he was one of the people who counted. The judge had felt his hands turn clammy. The pounding of blood in his ears rendered the speaker almost inaudible. He took a deep quiet breath. He was being offered a chance to crown his career – he needed to grasp it with two greedy hands.

What do I have to do? He had injected a note of enthusiasm into his voice so that the caller could hear and understand his interest in the post. *Nothing at all, now*, the man explained easily. During the trial, if there was any testimony that could prove an embarrassment, someone would ask him to steer the conversation in another direction – that was all. He had demanded to know who was on the phone – who was behind the offer. The question had provoked a giggle at the other end. He was much better off not knowing, the man had insisted, and something in his voice, an implied threat, had convinced Sopheap that the caller was right.

But it is important that I do my job if I'm selected, he had insisted.

Of course. The man sounded surprised and a little offended. His job was to preside over the trial of Samrin – they were just giving him an extra role, to limit any damage to the caller, the government and broader Cambodian society. As a patriot, he could have no objection to that? Sopheap had agreed at once, apologising for his unwarranted doubts.

And now look where he was – up to his neck in trouble and sinking further with every second. The irony was that, unlike so many Cambodian judges, he had never taken money to determine an outcome or changed his decision based on the status of a defendant. He had avoided the low-hanging bounty only to be tempted by robes as red as the rambutan fruit. He fingered the cloth. He had been shaking like a schoolboy with excitement when he had first been given the ceremonial robes of a judge of the ECCC. Now, if anyone ever found out about him, prison garments would be all that he wore for the rest of his life.

The peal of the telephone on his desk interrupted his train of thought. He picked it up nervously but the voice on the other end was full of good humour.

'Good work, Sopheap.'

'I beg your pardon?'

'I admit it. I didn't think you would have the guts. But you have surprised me – and made me very happy indeed.'

'I'm sorry but I have no idea what you're talking about.'

'Cheah Huon, of course. You have solved the problem once and for all. I heard he was stabbed with a kitchen knife.' There was a guffaw of laughter at the other end. 'That was very clever of you to find a weapon on the premises.'

'Huon has been stabbed?'

'Why are you acting the innocent with me?'

Sopheap was holding the phone so tight that his fingers were cramping. He heard a gentle knock on the door and saw a note slipped under it. He walked over and opened it hurriedly. The trial had been postponed indefinitely – all the judges were asked to convene for a meeting with the police so that they could be briefed on recent events.

'Judge, are you there? Why aren't you answering?'

'I didn't do it.'

'Don't be ridiculous . . .'

'I swear – I had nothing do to with the death of Cheah Huon.'

The other man replied in a knowing voice, 'Ah, I understand . . . you do not wish to admit it *even to me* to protect yourself in case of trouble. You are right to be cautious – the walls have ears. And we all know that the Cambodian police have unpleasant ways of discovering information.'

Sopheap started to deny his involvement again but his voice petered out in the face of the other man's iron-clad certainty.

'Understand this,' remarked the caller, 'you have done a service to me and I will not forget. You have my thanks.'

The line was cut. Sopheap stared at the phone in silence. He noticed that he had crushed the note in his clenched fist. He looked at the glossy robes hanging on the back of his chair. He would have no need of them for the foreseeable future.

'I'll help if I can,' said Singh despite his earlier determination to avoid being embroiled in the murder investigation. He gave himself a mental kicking. What was the matter with him? He realised he felt sorry for Menhay. There was something about his isolation that appealed to the Sikh detective. It reminded him of his own leprous quality within the Singapore police. He remained a policeman under sufferance, his bosses always looking for an excuse to get rid of him. He suspected that deep down they feared someone whom they could not control, who valued a victim's right to justice more than the rules and regulations of the Force. He grunted, causing Menhay to look at him in surprise. If he was being honest, it was just as likely the higher-ups couldn't stand him because of his long lunches. He tucked him thumbs into his trouser band. The fact that he could substitute his belt with a hula-hoop probably didn't reflect that well on the Singapore police force either. The Cambodian policeman on the other hand was the real thing – someone who came up against his peers and his superiors because he was determined to do the right thing despite being part of a largely corrupt police force. Only that morning the inspector had read about some military police big shot who had been acquitted, in a highly dubious decision that was being mocked by human rights groups, of throwing acid in the face of the husband of his young coerced lover. Singh reached for his packet of cigarettes. He disagreed with his bosses on process and protocol, Menhay on results. He was not so lacking in self-awareness that he didn't know which one of them was the real hero.

'I'm not sure what you can do,' replied Menhay. 'Probably it would be better if you remain an ASEAN watching brief.'

His doubts were put on the backburner as a sharp knock on the open door drew their attention to the forensics team. As he pressed up against a wall to avoid getting in their way, the inspector noted with interest that they were unexpectedly professional. He said in a low tone, 'These chaps seem to know what they're doing.'

If Menhay was offended by the surprised note in his voice, he did not show it. Instead, he said regretfully, 'We have had great need for forensics experts in Cambodia over the years. This team was trained overseas.'

Singh watched as they took photographs from every angle and started dusting the room for fingerprints. So far, they had refrained from examining the body.

'They're waiting for the doctor,' explained the colonel.

On cue, a young man with slicked-back hair and a supercilious expression sauntered in. He looked around, thrust his hands deep into his pockets like a recalcitrant teenager and asked, 'Who's in charge?'

He spoke in English which surprised Singh.

Menhay stepped forward and barked, 'Colonel Menhay.' It was a response but also a challenge.

The young man nodded and a lock of his over-long black hair tumbled across his forehead. He did not take his hands out of his pockets. Singh eyed him thoughtfully. Was he trying to offend the colonel or merely oblivious to the courtesy the older man expected? A vein throbbed on Menhay's forehead like a worm just beneath the surface of the earth. He growled, 'Who are you?'

'Kar Savuth – I'm the pathologist.'

'Well – get on with it then . . .'

Savuth turned to the body and became quickly professional.

'I'll wait outside,' said Singh hurriedly, as the doctor pulled out a thermometer. He had no desire to watch him insert it into the dead man's rectum to establish the temperature of the corpse. Singh knew full well it was imperative in determining time of death to know how cold the body was. A good pathologist would be able to estimate, based on the temperature of the surrounding area, how much time had elapsed since the killing. But he was content to read about it in the autopsy report. Menhay nodded a curt farewell. Singh knew he was wondering how Singapore's top cop could be so squeamish. The Sikh detective wondered at it himself. He was notorious for his cast-iron stomach and had been known to go straight from an autopsy to a curry lunch to the dismay of his less-hardened colleagues. But there was something much more disturbing about the place of death. If he were a religious man he would have said that he could sense the presence of the victim, his last drawn breath, his soul perhaps still tethered to that location – staying long enough to whisper in a corpulent Sikh detective's ear that he wanted justice so that he could rest. Out in the open, Singh took a deep breath and rubbed his eyes with the heels of his palms. He was getting fanciful in this land of death. What was it the advert on television said? Cambodia, Kingdom of Wonder? That wouldn't have been his chosen moniker.

Colonel Menhay was angry and it showed in his mottled skin and clenched jaw. He was standing up, both hands splayed on the table in front of him, glaring at the man who sat primly on the edge of a chair across from him. The colonel remembered the policeman from Singapore who had occupied that same chair the previous day. Say what you liked about Singh's predilection for his biscuits, Menhay preferred him any day of the week to this career paper-pusher who was busy ensuring that a day which had started badly, very badly indeed, was only going to get worse.

His aggressive posture, which had his underlings cowering with fright, seemed to have no effect whatsoever on the other man.

Mr Adnan Muhammad from the United Nations said carefully, 'I'm sure you understand our concerns.'

'No,' snapped Menhay. He did, of course. It was understandable that the UN were sceptical about the Cambodian police force. Everyone was – and with good reason. This lack of faith in the institution had even led the international body to bring in foreign bodyguards for the foreign judges. It had been a slap in the face to the police force but difficult to gainsay. Who would want their safety to be in the hands of a police force with such an unsavoury reputation?

'You're being unreasonable, Colonel Menhay.' The voice was priggish and a perfect fit for the man. The tone was quiet but penetrating. Adnan Muhammad was not a physically imposing man but Menhay could see all too clearly that he was used to getting his own way.

The colonel sat down suddenly, the fight going out of him. Life had taught him to pick his battles, to retreat from the fray when there was no hope of victory. He said quietly, 'A man was killed today here at the tribunal. I'm supposed to be in charge of security at the ECCC.' He ignored the faint sneer on Adnan's face. He knew he had failed but he didn't need to read it in the other man's expression. He had seen the evidence of his failure lying in a small room with a knife buried in its chest. He continued doggedly, 'I want to head the investigation. I *know* this country, this town, these people.'

Adnan Muhammad was not mincing words. 'The reputation of the war crimes tribunal hangs in the balance. We need a reputable person with international prestige to manage the investigation.' He added thoughtfully, 'Perhaps someone from our peacekeeping unit.'

'No one you bring in will have the background to investigate a murder in Cambodia,' barked Menhay. 'Besides, where are you going to find some top policeman at short notice? If you wait too long, the trail will go cold.'

The UN chef de mission to the ECCC said coolly, 'We are determined to seek this murderer, of course.'

Menhay looked at him sharply. Their eyes met and he read the truth in the muddy brown irises. It was obvious that this man was 'speaking out of the side of his mouth'. He didn't give a damn about Cheah Huon or finding his killer. He was just panicked that his precious war crimes tribunal was going to be tainted by association. The UN needed a quick solution that looked credible. That was why they couldn't leave it to the Cambodians. Any result, any arrest, would be suspect. They weren't looking for a competent policeman. They were looking for window dressing.

Adnan continued, 'It was probably some madman anyway – the trials have brought back a lot of memories. Maybe someone snapped.' He uttered the word 'snapped' with relish.

It had been the colonel's own theory until he heard it from the mouth of this bureaucrat. He wasn't so sure any more. 'That's just ridiculous. Why would someone "snap" and kill Huon of all people?'

The UN man shrugged delicately – presumably to indicate that he was not in a position to understand the thought processes of the criminally insane. He reverted to the subject, the only subject which was of interest to him. 'We need to get someone in – we will issue a press release that you are jointly in charge. I have already obtained the agreement of your government for this procedure as long as there is no loss of face for Cambodia.'

Loss of face. A man lay dead no more than a hundred yards away. The country had indulged in a comprehensive national bloodletting less than thirty years ago. And yet all anyone seemed to care about was losing face. What about losing life, honour, integrity? Menhay looked across his desk and spotted the corner of a name card sticking out from under a pile of papers. He extricated Inspector Singh's card and slid it across the table with a flick of his fingers like an expert *caroms* player.

'I think I know just the man you need,' he said.

Adnan was looking down at the card with interest so he did not see a slow smile spread across Colonel Menhay's harsh features.

Seven

Singh was loitering. Without intent. He didn't quite know what to do with himself. He watched a succession of officious-looking individuals – he guessed they were part of the forensics team and police hierarchy – wander in and out of the block. Probably contaminating the evidence, decided Singh, with a petulant pout. Two guards had been posted at the entrance to prevent the ingress of those without a reason to be there. One of them had been eyeing him for a few minutes. Singh knew that a certain type of criminal returned to the scene of a crime to watch the proceedings with a voyeur's interest. These guards probably thought that he was in the frame for the murder now. One of them would soon come and tell him to 'move along' or whatever the Cambodian equivalent was for shooing people away for no other reason than that they looked suspicious. Or perhaps they'd arrest him. That would certainly make Superintendent Chen's day. He really *was* behaving most peculiarly. It just felt odd to have a murder occur and not be in the thick of the action. He was isolated, a bit-part actor – perhaps just an unnamed extra – in a movie in which he should be the star. After all, wasn't he Inspector Singh, famed for the way his broad nose, a few hairs sticking out of the nostrils, could follow the scent of a killer and apprehend him, when all others were stymied?

He needed to stop believing his own propaganda. The reality was that he was delighted not to be involved in a crime which was probably insoluble in a country where the powers-that-be would make Singapore's authoritative figures look like teddy bears. That poor bastard, Menhay, already had a serial killer on the loose. Now he had an unrelated – or was it? – murder. The victim would soon be a political football for the competing interests involved in the war crimes tribunal. He, Singh, was well out of it. He should stay out of trouble, enjoy this break from policing and hone his detective instincts in the pursuit of more palatable meals. He might try French food. The French hadn't spent much time *governing* their colony if they were to be judged by results. Perhaps they'd left a culinary legacy. Having decided firmly that he wanted nothing to do with the investigation, Singh continued to loiter in the vicinity of the crime.

He heard his name called in the same gruff voice as earlier that morning. He glanced up and saw Menhay waving to him with windmilling arms. Singh's skin prickled uncomfortably with a sense of déjà vu. Then he noticed differences from the earlier summons. This time, Menhay was smiling broadly. And he was not alone. Next to him, wearing a three-piece suit that was devastatingly inappropriate for the steamy weather, stood a slight man with a naturally disdainful expression which he was trying with difficulty, and very little success, to rearrange into a more welcoming visage.

'What's going on?' asked Singh, panting slightly. He addressed his question to Menhay and ignored the other man.

'This is Mr Adnan Muhammad, UN liaison to the war crimes tribunal.' The colonel gestured at the fat man. 'And this is Inspector Singh of the Singapore police force whom I was just telling you about,' he explained further.

Both men shook hands. Adnan's hands were small and dry, like a woman's hands, thought Singh dismissively engulfing it with his clammy paw. His grip, however, was firm.

Menhay led the way to his office, made his way around the big desk and nodded his invitation to the two men to sit down. They did so, one carefully, the other collapsing into the seat as gravity took over.

Singh repeated his earlier question. 'What's going on?'

It was Adnan who answered, indicating with the way he drew his chair around to face Singh that he saw himself as the major force in the room. 'This murder is a disaster,' he said, the extreme words contradicted by his impassive face.

'Especially for the victim,' remarked Singh and was rewarded with a glare.

'We need to get to the bottom of this crime quickly and with credibility to protect the reputation of the ECCC.'

Singh waited, his impatience signalled by the fingers drumming on his thigh.

'The Cambodian government and other relevant parties have agreed that we appoint a third party to assist in the investigation in order . . .' For the first time the other man was at a loss for words. '. . . in order to ensure that the process meets international standards.'

The Sikh policeman glanced at his Cambodian counterpart. Menhay's face was expressionless but his eyes were turbulent. He didn't like this one bit but had been presented with a *fait accompli*.

'I've had a look at your résumé and made some quick phone calls.'

Singh stiffened as if bracing for a body blow.

'You'll undoubtedly be pleased to know that the Singapore government has agreed that you are now, with the colonel here, in charge of this murder inquiry.'

Adnan left, his machinations complete. The atmosphere in Menhay's office lightened considerably although there was still a sense of constraint between the two men. The situation reminded the Sikh policeman of breakfasts in the Singh household the morning after a particularly tetchy argument, usually involving his refusal to attend a tedious family wedding or funeral of some distant relative whom he had never heard of until their nuptials or demise. Circumstances on the home front were only capable of improvement through his complete capitulation to the wishes of his spouse. But that was Mrs Singh. This was only a Cambodian copper. Such extreme measures were not called for – not yet anyway.

Singh eyed the other man. 'So what do you think?'

Menhay shrugged. Singh knew that the colonel understood what he was asking in this oblique manner. How did he feel about having a policeman from Singapore trample all over his turf at the behest of a United Nations bag carrier?

'What do you want me to say?' Menhay was not going to grant him absolution.

'If you don't like the idea, I can refuse the assignment.' As he said the words, Singh knew he would be very disappointed to walk away from this case. His depth of interest in the inquiry surprised him. However, he would not proceed without the agreement of the other man. He owed him that much, out of courtesy for a fellow policeman and a certain respect he had developed for Menhay.

The square-jawed Cambodian policeman smiled suddenly. 'I don't think you were given a choice.'

Singh cracked his knuckles together, a fat man ready for a fight. 'I can find a way out if need be.'

'If you refuse to do this – they'll just give me some other' – he consciously altered his first choice of words which Singh suspected had not been very polite – '*person* to boss me around. It might as well be you. In fact,' he added, throwing Singh a bone, 'I suggested you.'

The policeman from Singapore was well aware that he was not going to receive a more fulsome welcome than that. He didn't blame Menhay for his muted reception to the plan. He would have been livid if some starched-up pencil sharpener had pulled the rug from under his feet the way Adnan Muhammad had done to the colonel. He wondered at his own willingness to accept an assignment in such fraught circumstances. What was he thinking? This was a no win situation. He should be running as fast as his short legs would carry him away from the scene of the crime, not licking his lips in anticipation at getting immersed in its complexities.

Singh realised suddenly that it was his role as a *bystander* that he had not enjoyed these last few days in Phnom Penh. It was one thing to be between murder inquiries in Singapore with nothing to do except ignore the paperwork on his desk and keep a watchful eye out for his superiors, but it didn't suit his personality to be a 'watching brief', unless it was for a cricket match on television.

He screwed up his face. There was something about the present situation that seemed familiar to him – violent death in unfamiliar surroundings accompanied by a reluctant local policeman. It came to him. This case reminded him of the Malaysian murder he had been embroiled in some time ago. Singh perked up noticeably. If there were parallels between the two cases, a beautiful woman would soon be accused of Huon's murder.

'So – where do we begin?' he asked cheerfully.

'You tell me,' said Menhay with only a faint thread of sarcasm in his voice. 'You're the expert.'

This developing mutual understanding was interrupted by a hurried knock on the door to Menhay's office followed by the entrance of a uniformed policeman. He looked flustered. A tall, thin man was hard on his heels.

'What is it?' snapped Menhay.

Singh suppressed a smile. He might be jointly in charge of this investigation but the Cambodian's sense of authority was undiminished.

The response from the junior man was in Khmer and sounded apologetic. Singh caught the name François Gaudin which he assumed referred to this panting elderly man with gangly limbs like an angry scarecrow. Whatever was said, it

109

caused Menhay to turn to the Frenchman and ask brusquely, 'What do you want? We're quite busy this morning.'

He spoke in English. It was an interesting choice given that Menhay was of a generation that still spoke French. Probably it was an instinctive reaction to the presence of Singh. It was an irony that the three men, a Khmer, a Frenchman and a Sikh, should choose English as their *lingua franca*.

'Is it true what I hear? That there is a dead man?'

Singh straightened up in his chair and exchanged a glance with the other policeman. Did this fellow know too much? More likely, the inevitable leaks had sprung and word of Huon's untimely death was spreading like a cold virus. The newspapers would soon be circling like vultures over a carcass. There was a large crew of foreign journalists encamped at the ECCC who would be quick to see the potential in the murder for a career-making byline.

'Who is it? What happened? You *must* tell me.'

The Frenchman looked familiar. Singh stared at him fixedly, trying to work out the connection.

'There is an investigation ongoing, sir. Any information about it is confidential. I cannot tell you anything.'

There was a sudden sharp sound that punctuated Menhay's brusque explanation like an exclamation mark. It was Singh slapping his hand triumphantly on the desk. They both turned to him. Menhay's expression was mildly inquiring. The Frenchman was staring at him wildly, as if struggling to understand the role of a turbaned Sikh man in the greater scheme of things.

'You were at the trial of Samrin,' said Singh. 'I noticed you during the testimony of Ta Ieng.'

Gaudin spat at the ground but his lips were dry and chapped and the saliva merely left a thin streak on his unshaven chin. 'You speak of that animal by name?'

Singh was taken aback by the aggressive response. He played back the scene in his mind's eye – this man with tears streaming down his cheeks, Ta Ieng glaring at the gallery as if daring anyone to question his choices, his decision to follow orders to save his own skin. Even since yesterday, the condition of Gaudin had deteriorated. His skin had an unhealthy pallor that spoke of a lack of sleep and there were new bruises as well. His shirt was stained with food hurriedly eaten. The stubble on his jaw was the same dirty grey as an elephant's hide, the skin underneath creased with age and worry.

Gaudin returned to the subject closest to his heart. 'I heard a witness is dead. Is it true? You have to tell me!' The voice had reached the pitch of a scream. Echoes bounced off the whitewashed walls and caused the Sikh inspector to wince.

François Gaudin must have read the answer to his question in Menhay's eyes. His shoulders curved as if only the tension within his body had held him upright. His eyes were bright with tears but they remained nestled along his bottom lids like pearls in an oyster. Singh had seen his expression before on other men and a few women, a gradual dawning of knowledge that the death of an enemy was not a panacea to the feelings of hatred that had gone before. Sometimes the sense of emptiness that the death of an adversary caused was similar and more intense than from the loss of a loved one.

'He deserved to die a thousand times.'

What in the world could Huon have done to arouse such passion in this man?

'Why do you say that?' asked the colonel curiously. His line of thinking had obviously followed a parallel path to that of Singh and he too wanted to know why the dead man had provoked such vitriolic emotions in this cadaverous Frenchman.

'You heard him yesterday – about the children, about the killing tree – and yet you can ask me that? What sort of people are you?'

'That was Ta Ieng,' explained Menhay, his tone almost kindly.

It was left to Singh, no respecter of emotions in the midst of a murder investigation, to interrupt with the most salient piece of information. 'It's not Ta Ieng that's dead. It's Cheah Huon!' And as Gaudin looked at him blankly, he embellished impatiently, 'You know, the chap with one leg!'

Eight

'Well, that was more than a little strange,' remarked Singh, reaching for a biscuit. The colonel, who was receiving high marks from the Sikh inspector for his ability to anticipate the fat man's inclinations, had placed a small paper plate on the table with an assortment of cookies. Singh, after some thought, chose a floral-shaped chocolate confection with a jam centre.

François Gaudin had been led away by a young uniform with instructions to take him to the medical centre. The old man had been unable to stand up upon the news that it was Cheah Huon who was dead, not Ta Ieng. Only quick thinking from Menhay, who had noticed him sway on his feet and rushed over to place a steadying hand at his elbow, had prevented him from collapsing.

'Do you think that Frenchman had anything to do with it?' asked Menhay.

'The murder? It's hard to see why. It seems clear enough that he's only interested in the death of Ta Ieng.'

'You mean he meant to kill Ta Ieng but stabbed Cheah Huon instead?'

Despite the gravity of the situation, both men chuckled. It was difficult to imagine a situation where one could have mistaken the gnome-like amputee for the tall and emaciated Ta Ieng.

'No harm checking up on him anyway,' said the inspector, returning to the subject at hand. 'He's certainly capable of doing something unexpected – I have rarely seen such intense hatred, even if he hasn't committed a crime yet.'

The colonel reached for the telephone on his desk and dialled a number. In a moment, he was speaking fluent French, his tone persuasive.

Singh was multi-lingual like so many Singaporeans of his generation. He had been educated in English, spoken Punjabi at home growing up and picked up enough Malay at school to be comfortable in that language. His Hokkien and Cantonese, the two most common Chinese dialects in Singapore, were limited to swear words picked up from gang members he'd arrested. And he had effectively ignored the government's 'Speak Mandarin' campaign for a number of years. Unfortunately, he spoke neither Khmer nor French. Singh realised that he was going to need a competent translator if he was to play an active part in this investigation. Otherwise, most of the information received was going to be incomprehensible to him. Even with an interpreter, he was quite likely going to miss the sort of nuance which often gave him the first hint as to the identity of a murderer.

Menhay hung up and said, 'I spoke to a contact at the French Embassy. He'll see what he can dig up on Gaudin.'

'I need Chhean,' said Singh, changing the subject abruptly.

'Who's that?'

'The minder provided to me by ASEAN. She can help me with interpretation. Otherwise,' and he nodded at the phone to indicate the recent conversation in French, 'I'll have no idea what's going on most of the time. I don't speak any Khmer or French.'

'Can she be trusted?'

Singh leaned back in his chair and folded his arms across his ample belly. Could Chhean be trusted? She was dogged, snappy and officious but had an unexpected sense of humour and a keen sense of justice. He said baldly, 'Yes!' and hoped he would not be proved wrong.

Menhay walked to the door of his office and issued an order in Khmer. He came back in and said, 'Someone will find her for you. In the meantime, we're back where we started before that mad Frenchman came in. What do you want to do first?'

'When will the autopsy results be back?'

'I told them to hurry but tomorrow is the earliest for preliminary results.'

'I guess we should start at the beginning – with Huon's family, friends and workmates.'

Menhay looked sceptical.

Singh could see that his faith in the advanced methods of the Singapore police had taken a knock. He didn't blame the man. It was difficult to believe that some personal matter, unrelated to Huon's role as a witness at the trial, had been at the root of the murder.

'A murder investigation is a process of elimination,' pointed out Singh. 'And statistically speaking, most people are murdered by someone they knew well – strangers wielding knives are mostly found on the television or at the movies.'

'The statistics for Cambodia paint a different picture,' remarked Menhay dryly.

Singh nodded a belated agreement. Most countries did not have genocide in their recent history to skew the numbers.

Chewing on his bottom lip so aggressively that Menhay pushed the plate of biscuits closer, the inspector added, 'We'd look like a bunch of clowns if we ignore the nearest and dearest and it turned out his wife hunted him down because the one-legged man was a serial adulterer!'

He was distracted by a loud knock on the door. Chhean marched in without waiting for an invitation. She addressed Singh, ignoring the Cambodian policeman. 'You were looking for me?'

'Yes,' said Singh. 'I have another odd job for you.'

She smiled at this reminder of how she had characterised her role looking after Singh.

'I've been asked to look into the death of Cheah Huon with the Cambodian police and I need an interpreter. Can you help?'

'Cheah Huon? You mean the witness from yesterday? He's dead?'

Singh nodded curtly.

'How did he die?'

'Stabbed,' he said succinctly. The young woman's face drained of blood. However, her first thought was not for the dead man. Singh had to admire her single-mindedness.

'How will this affect the war crimes tribunal?'

116

'We've had to postpone the hearings for the time being,' said Menhay.

'Postpone? The defendants are all so old, Samrin may die before he is found guilty.' She continued, 'It isn't fair that he might be able to cheat justice by dying. I don't trust the gods to punish him.' Her voice was strident as she finished the sentence.

'That's why I'm asking for your help,' said Singh. 'The sooner we get to the bottom of this the better.'

'Yes, in that case I would like very much to help you with this investigation. The trial *must* continue.'

Colonel Menhay said something to her in Khmer, his tone harsh. She turned to Singh and explained, 'The colonel is warning me that this is a serious matter as the future of the war crimes tribunal hinges on it. If I care about that as I claim to do I must work hard to assist you and keep my mouth shut.'

'And can you do that?'

'Of course!' She added quickly, 'But wait here now. There is something I need to get for you.'

With these words, she hurried out of the room, leaving two bemused policemen behind.

'Is she always like that?' asked Menhay.

Singh nodded glumly. His minder rarely waited for agreement or approbation before embarking on a course of action. He fervently hoped that she would settle down and do as she was told but he rather doubted it. Perhaps he should have asked Menhay for a less determined character to interpret for him. A respectful young Khmer man would have been nice.

In a few minutes, his newly appointed interpreter reappeared, flushed from her energetic display. The inspector noticed that she was carrying a thick folder under her arm. 'More reading material for me?' he asked, a hint of sarcasm in his voice.

She shook her head vigorously and her glossy short hair swirled across her cheeks. 'I thought that the police might not realise that there is a file on each witness at the tribunal documentation centre. This is Cheah Huon's file. I just retrieved it.' She held it out to Singh, and then as an afterthought, changed her mind and passed it to Menhay.

Singh nodded approvingly. Perhaps his doubts about Chhean were unfounded. This was a smart woman. She knew that any hostility to her role or suspicions about her *bona fides* would emanate from the colonel. So she was ensuring that she treated him with the appropriate respect, placing him higher in the pecking order than Singh, to win him over.

'All the documents are in the Khmer language,' explained Chhean.

That was the other possible explanation.

Menhay was leafing through the file, occasionally licking his thumb to gain traction on the smooth paper. And leaving a trail of DNA evidence, thought Singh snidely. 'How come the documentation centre has so much information?' he asked curiously.

'All the witnesses were checked – just to make sure that they had no issues which would reflect badly on the tribunal.'

'What sort of things?'

She shrugged – 'Connections to politicians, money problems . . .'

It made sense, decided Singh. After all, a little background checking might be sufficient to save the tribunal a lot of embarrassment if it turned out that a witness was subject to outside influences.

'To be honest,' explained Chhean, 'there was only a small budget. I was part of the team and we could not always dig as deep as we would have liked. It does not mean that all the information on Huon is in the file. Cambodia,' she paused for a moment, 'Cambodia is a land of secrets.'

There was something in her tone that caused Singh to look at her sharply. He noticed for the first time that there were shadows under her eyes that looked as if they had been administered with a dirty piece of charcoal.

'Why do you look so tired?' he asked.

'I was awake the whole night looking through papers.'

'Why? For the trial?'

Her words were accompanied by a small sigh. 'I am trying to find some trace of my family.'

No wonder she looked exhausted. His interpreter was burning the candle at both ends. He noted that even her eyes were bloodshot with tracings of fine red veins like country roads on a detailed map. He couldn't help feeling sorry for her but he was also concerned that her fatigue might affect her work for him. He was about to question her further when Menhay drew his attention back to the case.

The colonel, who had been scrutinising the file, shouted for a minion and handed the documents over. 'Getting a photocopy for you,' he explained, 'but I can already tell you that there was no angry wife in the background – Huon was a widower. Also, he did not have a job. He sold postcards and books at tourist sites on behalf of a charity that cared for the disabled – mostly landmine victims.'

Singh had only been in Cambodia a few days but had already been accosted by a number of amputees, their misshapen stumps exposed – some on crutches, some in wheelchairs – selling books and cards from cardboard boxes. The juxtaposition of idyllic pictures of rural Cambodia (the postcards) and the harrowing subject of the books (mostly first-hand accounts by survivors of the genocide) had been disturbing, even for a hardened policeman. So far, he had purchased Philip Short's biography of Pol Pot and a book by Vann Nath, an artist who had survived Tuol Sleng prison. He suspected he would buy quite a few more before he left Cambodia.

Singh stood up slowly, feeling his knees creak with the effort. He held out his hand to the junior policeman who had walked in with the photocopies. The young man, upon receipt of a nod from his boss, handed them over. Singh hefted the file in his right hand; it was a weighty mass. The policeman adopted his most pontificating tone. 'The best way to track down a killer is to get to know the victim. Most murders are rooted in the character of the deceased. There might be something in here which will point us in the right direction.'

'Something from his past, you mean?' asked Chhean eagerly.

'Yup,' said Singh. He was pleased with her enthusiasm despite her apparent tiredness. With some good fortune, she would graduate from interpreter to sidekick and do his legwork for him.

'Thank you for your assistance to the Cambodian police, Inspector Singh,' said Menhay.

Was he being sarcastic?

'Tomorrow, we will receive the autopsy report. Perhaps even more so than the "character of the victim", this will allow us to track down the murderer.'

Now he was definitely being sarcastic. Colonel Menhay was clearly from that school of investigators who preferred blood-spatter patterns and DNA-covered cigarette butts to the less certain, but in Singh's eyes equally important, evidence of lifestyle and relationships.

'They told me when I went to get Huon's file – Samrin's hearing has been postponed for a week.'

Chhean's words were a stark reminder of what was at stake beyond the death of a man and the apprehension of his killer.

'We'll just have to find this murderer in a week then,' was Singh's terse response. In his heart, he really hoped that this was justified confidence, not hubris. Either way, it was time to sniff around and see if he could pick up the scent.

'I think we should have another look at the room where he was killed and then go over his personal file with a fine-tooth comb,' suggested Singh.

'I will set up a headquarters here and have my men sweep the area for physical evidence as well as interview everyone with any connection to this place from cleaners to lawyers,' added Menhay.

Singh nodded. The minutiae of a murder investigation – that would have to be handled by the Cambodians. It demonstrated the flaw in Adnan's thinking in appointing Singh top dog. There was no way he could supervise a team of non-English speakers. Menhay would have to conduct the nitty gritty of the investigation. Singh would operate like a freelance private eye – but one with whom the buck stopped. Maybe Adnan Muhammad wasn't so dumb after all. 'What are we waiting for then?' demanded Singh, trying to shake the feeling that the UN man had pinned a note saying 'kick me' to his back and he was the only one who didn't know it.

'First we see the judges.'

The fat man pouted like a small child denied an ice-cream cone. 'Why in the world do we have to talk to a bunch of men in skirts?'

'Robes, not skirts – and one of them is a woman.'

Singh glared at the colonel, whom he suspected was being intentionally obtuse. 'You know very well what I mean – we need to look for a murderer. We're hardly going to find him amongst the judges.'

'Adnan wants us to brief them about what has happened and explain what we intend to do about it . . .' Menhay was tapping his foot on the ground impatiently.

'Well, that shouldn't take long,' said the inspector flippantly. 'Man killed, looking for killer. There. It's done. Why don't we just send the justices a note?'

Menhay ushered them out of the door, ignoring the fat man's reluctance. He said, as they stepped out into the open, 'You've been appointed to the case by Adnan. I guess you need to follow his instructions as well.'

Singh looked amused. 'Adnan Muhammad might be in for a surprise,' he said prophetically as they walked across the grass to the judges' anteroom. He suspected that Adnan's research into his background had been superficial. He'd probably just Googled him and found glowing newspaper reports from the sycophantic Singapore press. He hadn't spoken to Superintendent Chen, that was for sure, or he would have given the Sikh policeman a wide berth. The inspector stopped abruptly in his tracks – unless they'd conspired to set him up to be the fall guy. Singh gritted his teeth. He needed to find this killer and fast.

'Do we have any information on these men – the judges, I mean?' asked Singh.

Menhay handed him a double-sided sheet of paper with brief biographical sketches of the judges. Singh noted that it was a flyer for the general public – further attempts by the ECCC to keep the people informed about proceedings. He wondered whether there would be a flyer about the murder as well.

There were three Cambodian judges, a Frenchwoman and an Australian man. The foreigners appeared to have spent their careers on a circuit of failed states trying to deal with bloody pasts: Sierra Leone, Kosovo, Rwanda. Not a life he would choose, decided Singh immediately. Dealing with Cambodia's past was quite enough for him.

The educational background of the Cambodians surprised the fat man.

'Kazahkstan, Ho Chi Minh City, East Germany, Moscow – what happened to Oxford and Cambridge?'

'Cold War politics,' replied Menhay.

Singh nodded his head with sudden understanding. All these people had studied to be lawyers while Cambodia was still a pariah in the West because of its Vietnamese-backed government and Russian ties. It had not been easy to seek a higher education from poverty-stricken Cambodia. These individuals had qualified as judges and had the added eminence of being chosen to preside over the war crimes trial of Samrin. He would treat them with the respect they deserved.

The five judges sitting around the table were not interested in his respect or otherwise. Singh had forgotten the gimlet eye and crisp voices of most members of the bench – whatever their background and qualifications. The Frenchwoman was particularly aggressive. She spoke in French and Chhean translated in hurried whispers.

'You are in charge of security at the ECCC, Colonel Menhay?'

'Yes, ma'am.'

'And yet a man has been killed? A crucial witness at the trial of Samrin?'

'I'm afraid so, ma'am. It is most unfortunate.'

Singh winced. It was the wrong choice of words.

'*Unfortunate*, colonel? I would not describe it as unfortunate – incompetent, maybe, but not unfortunate.'

The colonel shuffled uncomfortably but did not respond.

'Do you have any suspects?' The question was from one of the Cambodian judges. Looking at the flyer surreptitiously, Singh identified him from his receding hairline and reading glasses as Judge Sopheap. He vaguely remembered him from the trial.

'Not yet, sir.'

The judge leaned back in his chair and Singh was puzzled that he sensed relief from the man rather than disappointment.

'We have just begun the investigation. The autopsy report will not be out until tomorrow.' Menhay sounded defensive.

The Australian butted in and Singh noted his broad shoulders and barrel chest. A man capable of dispensing justice – as well as rough justice – by the look of him. 'We have been forced to postpone this trial for a week against our wishes. There are many who would like to see this trial fail and the accused go free. Are you one of those people, Colonel Menhay?'

Singh breathed a sigh of relief that they had not been informed by Adnan that he was jointly in charge of the investigation. He had no desire to be at the sharp end of this interview. These justices were worse that Superintendent Chen.

Menhay shook his head decisively. 'No, sir. I am a supporter of the trial. I believe that these men should be called to account for what they did to *my* country.'

Had there been an emphasis on the 'my'? Was this policeman trying to provoke the red-haired, short-tempered Australian?

To Singh's surprise, Menhay appeared to have drawn the sting out of the judges. There were friendlier expressions all around except from Justice Sopheap, who was staring out of the window with a worried expression on his face.

'Very well, Colonel Menhay. We wish you luck with your investigation. Please keep us informed of progress.' It was the Frenchwoman – she looked like the headmistress of a girls' boarding school – who was all smiles now.

One of the Cambodians – Judge Phanit – leaned forward. 'Colonel, we need you to get to the bottom of this as quickly as possible for the sake of the ECCC. Cambodia depends on you,' he added and his voice quivered with passion.

Great, thought Singh, lay on the pressure, why don't you? If he was Menhay, he would retire to bed with a pillow over his head. He stole a glance at his counterpart. He was obviously made of sterner stuff. His back was ramrod straight and he saluted smartly. 'I will do my best, sir.'

Nine

'So, what's this?' asked Singh, looking at his plate will ill-concealed distaste. The inspector, accompanied by Chhean, had embarked on a hunt for some food and to peruse Huon's file.

'Try it. You won't regret it, I promise.' Chhean could not help smiling at the tubby inspector's expression. She had persuaded him to give Khmer food one last chance, insisting that the canteen food at the tribunal and the roach kebabs had not been a reasonable trial. Singh was reluctant. He had, through a careful perusal of the tourist map handed out at the hotels, identified two Indian restaurants in Phnom Penh and was desperate to try at least one of them.

'It might not even be run by Indians,' she pointed out. 'Could be Khmer-style curry. Very watery. Just like soup.'

Singh had blanched – he could not face any more soup, stew or watery curry. Finally, he had agreed to try an up-market Khmer restaurant. 'You will like it, for sure.' Chhean was reassuring. 'All the corrupt business people eat there. Must be good.'

And now the policeman was staring at his plate, an expression of utmost suffering on his face.

'Pickled green vegetables with chillies.'

Singh's drooping jowls received a non-surgical face-lift at the reference to chillies. He poked the dish with a finger and licked the tip tentatively. 'Spicy *kang kong*,' he said appreciatively and tucked his fork in with enthusiasm.

She supposed that he must be referring to the leafy vegetable on his plate. She didn't know what it was called but was pleased to have found a dish that appealed to the fat man's taste buds. Or what was left of them. He had smoked all the way to the restaurant, puffed vigorously as they crossed the flagstones, passed the stone Buddha and made their way over the decorative *koi* ponds. He probably didn't have much sensation left on his tongue and she wouldn't have thought his lungs were in good condition either. As if to reinforce her opinion of his state of health, the Sikh man broke into a paroxysm of coughing.

She waited until he had recovered his breath and replaced the snowy white napkin over his expansive thighs. She reached for the folder on Huon and asked, 'Do you want to know what's in here?'

Her dinner companion's attention had wandered. Chhean sighed and beckoned a waiter. Unfed, this policeman was as useless as the usual crooked Cambodian variety.

A platter of rice accompanied by a fish dish was laid before them.

She pre-empted his questioning by indicating the fish. 'Fish *amok*.'

'What?'

She explained impatiently, '*Amok krei* – national Cambodian dish. It is cooked with *kroeung*, you know – spice paste with turmeric and chillies and other things. Also, coconut milk. Everything steamed in banana leaf. Very tasty. And,' she gestured at the other plate, 'vegetarian spring rolls.'

The inspector ate quietly for a while, spooning white rice and fish into his mouth and chewing contentedly. At last, he leaned back, beckoned a waiter, ordered a bottle of Angkor beer and said, like an indulgent parent, 'Now you can tell me what's in the file.'

She opened the folder and slipped two photographs across the table. One was a recent head shot in colour, the travails of experience visible on Huon's half-smiling face. The other was an old black-and-white picture of a young man in baggy pleated trousers and a long-sleeved shirt. He was leaning against a pillar, arms folded and broad smile for the camera. It was almost impossible to imagine the life that had turned the smiling youngster into the ravaged old man.

Chhean turned the photo over and read the date out loud. 'April 1975 – just before the fall of Phnom Penh.' Her tone was subdued. The photo that she carried about with her – which he assumed was of her family – had probably been taken around a similar time. So many smiling faces, none of them with any inkling of what the future held.

She continued to flick through the file while Singh stared at the pictures.

'Nothing much new in here,' she said. 'We heard it during his testimony at the trial.'

Singh nodded.

'Colonel Menhay was right – no family. His wife disappeared when Pol Pot was in charge. He never married again. No children.'

'I'm not comfortable with learning about the victim from a file,' grumbled Singh. 'I want to talk to *people!*'

Chhean said, rifling through the papers to confirm her surmise, 'There is not much information on Huon between 1975 and 1978. In 1978, there is a record of him being admitted to Tuol Sleng. As you know, Duch kept good records of admissions and confessions.'

'It sounds like your people were scattered to the four winds when the cities were emptied by Pol Pot.'

'Huon must have been sent to one of the villages, maybe moved around a few times as the food ran out.'

'Anonymous until he annoyed someone and ended up at S21,' said Singh.

They were both quiet, listening to the low sounds of a busy restaurant; voices, laughter, tinkling glasses and cutlery scraping against crockery.

Chhean had a quick look around. The place was filled with the prosperous of Cambodia. Older men with coarse features were accompanied by young heavily made-up women. The men were uniformly overweight. It was a sign of prosperity in the poverty-stricken country – and in Chhean's view, an indicator of the level of corruption. The fatter you were, the more you had stolen from your countrymen. She looked across at her dinner companion and grinned. It was possible that the same formula did not hold true in Singapore.

'What are you smiling about? Have you thought of someone we can speak to about Huon?'

She racked her brain for an answer. It would not do for the policeman to realise that her mind had been wandering. 'Usually the landmine victims who sell postcards and books stay at the same spot.'

'So?'

'So, maybe other sellers in that place might know him,' she retorted.

'It's possible, I guess. Where did Huon ply his trade?'

She didn't understand the expression and looked at him blankly.

'Where did Huon sell his books and postcards?' The fat man's tone was impatient.

She looked down at the file. 'National Museum.'

'That big red building in town?'

'Yes.'

Singh's phone beeped loudly. He held it up some distance from his face. He was getting long-sighted, she guessed. He needed a pair of those reading glasses to perch on the end of his large nose.

'The autopsy report will be ready at noon tomorrow. Good, that means we have time to stop at the museum on the way to the tribunal.'

'We were patriots,' said Samrin, 'and this is our reward.'

Menhay and the man accused of crimes against humanity were in a small room within the fortified bungalow that was home to Samrin and the other defendants. Duch had been held there as well until he had been transferred to a prison at an undisclosed location. Policemen, wearing the insignia of wardens, stood at the door and the window, the only two exits to the room. It was as if they feared an escape attempt by the eighty-year old man sitting across from them. A nurse sat in a chair in the corner, watching proceedings with a blank face.

'Why am I on trial? What about the Vietnamese? What about the French, what about the Americans?' He spat on the ground. 'Especially the Americans.'

This was an old argument. There was Cambodian blood on so many hands: the French for propping up Sihanouk, the Vietnamese for arming the communists and the Americans for carpet bombing Cambodia from 1969 onwards, killing thousands of civilians and driving the terrified population into Pol Pot's arms. Why, the question was asked, had all these criminals, from Kissinger onwards, escaped justice while a small group of old Cambodian men – and one woman – were hauled before some multi-million dollar UN tribunal?

'We were trying to save Cambodia,' insisted Samrin, fixing his gaze on the colonel.

Menhay remained silent. He had come to see Samrin on a hunch. After all, who more than the man accused of crimes against humanity would benefit if the war crimes tribunal fell into disrepute because of Huon's murder? But now he found himself unexpectedly intimidated by the dapper figure with the hot eyes. It was that sense of shock when coming face to face with evil and discovering it was housed in the body of an ordinary man, a frail old man who was accused of being Duch's henchman – more accurately, Duch's hatchet man – the commandant of the killing fields at Choeng Ek.

'What do you want anyway?' demanded Samrin. The voice of command still came naturally. 'I am tired, I need to rest.'

Menhay stole a glance at the nurse. He was under strict

instructions not to exhaust the old man for fear that he might cheat justice by dying before his trial concluded.

'There was an incident at the compound,' he said carefully.

Samrin cackled like an old hen. 'That ridiculous one-legged man was killed.'

'How do you know about it? Did you have anything to do with it?'

The man accused of mass murder looked offended at being accused of killing an individual. Perhaps it seemed a petty crime compared with this man's grandiose efforts. 'Don't be ridiculous,' he snapped. 'You think I snuck out at night and stabbed that fool?' He held up his hands to show that they were shaking with a mild form of Parkinson's disease. 'I'm just an old man waiting to die.'

Menhay's expression was grim. 'How do you know about the killing?'

Again, the dry chicken cackle erupted from Samrin. 'You think just because you lock me up I don't know what's going on? The walls have ears and a tongue to reveal all your secrets.'

The colonel ignored the hyperbolic language. It was possible that Samrin had picked up the gossip from the kitchen staff or one of the policemen, even the glowering nurse in the corner.

'I think you're like the queen bee with many servants to do your bidding,' retorted Menhay. 'And if I find you had anything to do with this . . .' He trailed off uncertainly.

The old man, sometimes known as the 'butcher of Choeng Ek' – to distinguish him from the Khmer Rouge military leader, Ta Mok, who was known merely as the 'Butcher' – was gleeful. 'Well, what are you going to do?' he demanded, a

133

broad smile exposing teeth that sprouted in all directions like an untended garden. 'Charge me with murder?'

Menhay glanced out of the window. The statue of the Lord of the Iron Staff, *Lokta Dambang Dek*, a Khmer spirit who administered justice, was just visible within the ECCC compound. He noted that the statue was facing away from the court buildings and wondered whether this guardian too had turned his back on Cambodia. He made a silent vow that for as long as the blood ran red in his body, he would not abandon his country.

The colonel leaned forward and placed his hands on the table. Out of the corner of his eye, he saw the nurse fidget nervously, afraid perhaps that he was about to attack her patient.

'Did you know,' Menhay asked quietly, 'that there is someone killing Khmer Rouge? Eleven dead so far in only three months.'

The old man was alarmed and it showed in the whites of his eyes. 'What are you trying to say? Who is doing it?'

Menhay shrugged. 'You should know it's a dangerous world for old men with blood on their hands.'

'I want my protection increased. It is your obligation as the police to protect me.' Samrin was pounding the table angrily like a small child deprived of a treat.

It was Menhay's turn to laugh. 'My men are busy hunting murderers, not protecting them. You should watch your back, Comrade Samrin,' he whispered and walked out of the room.

The following morning, Singh, fortified with a large breakfast of pancakes and maple syrup, decided to walk to the National

Museum. It wasn't too far, he was sure of it. A brisk, health-giving walk would clear his head of the conspiracy theories that had raged through the morning's English-language papers. God only knew what the Khmer-language dailies were saying. He didn't doubt they would run the gamut from shock to outrage. The murder was out and everyone from government to ex-Khmer Rouge and from big business to the United Nations had been implicated by insinuation and innuendo.

There had been a lot of criticism of the security at the tribunal as well – Colonel Menhay would not be enjoying his breakfast. Neither for that matter would that hideous starched-up creature from the UN. A few newspaper editorials had demanded that the trials go ahead immediately – unbowed by the setback – and a number of others had insisted equally firmly that the ECCC hearings be put on hold indefinitely until the safety and integrity of the institution could be guaranteed. Of Cheah Huon himself, very little was said. Singh decided, feeling mildly heroic, that it was his role to look out for the interests of the dead man.

Ten minutes into his walk, the sun beating down on his head from a cloudless blue sky and his nose wrinkled against the stench euphemistically known as the smell of 'drains', he had forgotten any laudable aspirations and was concentrating on putting one sneaker-clad foot in front of the other. He wished he had sunglasses for the glare but he never carried a pair, disliking slipping the glasses under his turban and around his ears.

Young men wearing baseball caps shouted offers of rides and he was tempted to accept but decided, with a combination of stubbornness and courage, to persist. Old women tried to sell him brightly-coloured foodstuffs and small children offered him bottles of water. He turned them all down and the vendors shouted in a regular chorus, 'You remember me, OK?' as if he could be trusted to make his way back to an individual whose product he suddenly desired.

The Mekong River that looked so inviting from his hotel room was stinking, muddy and slow-moving at ground level. Singh tried not to breathe too deeply and wondered whether he should light a cigarette to cocoon himself in a layer of smoke. At last, he reached an enormous square of dry grass and stopped to stare at the Royal Palace on the other side. Here, inspired no doubt by the picture of Mao in Tiananmen Square, a large portrait of Prince Sihanouk looked down benevolently as his people tried to make a living selling transportation opportunities to unwary tourists.

He wheezed his way across the square – there wasn't any shade from the morning sun here either. Singh was quite sure from his map that the National Museum was behind the extravaganza of gold and glitter that formed the palace compound. He had read somewhere that the palace housed floors of solid silver and diamond-encrusted Buddha statues. The policeman wasn't impressed. He waved away a small child trying to sell him trinkets. They'd be better off selling the royal collection and providing some income to these kids. On the other hand, if Chhean was to be believed, someone would pocket the proceeds.

He reached the museum and breathed a sigh of relief. The red-brick building with fish-scale roof tiles made a pleasant change from all the palatial gold and yellow. There was no sign of Chhean so he bought an entry ticket – priced in US dollars, why in the world had he changed any money into *riels*? – and wandered through the high-roofed building constructed around a square forecourt dotted with charming lily ponds in which stood unlikely plastic egrets. There was no point looking for anyone to question – they wouldn't speak English. The cool, almost deserted interior with its dark wooden roof beams and whirring ceiling fans was restful and he sauntered past the enormous stone statues, relics of Angkor mostly, with mild interest.

He was contemplating a statue of the elephant god, Ganesha – Angkor had been a Hindu kingdom – when Chhean found him.

Glancing at him and then the statue, she burst into sudden loud laughter that drew surprised glances from an old woman selling canned drinks and a small boy with a mop, the only other people there.

'What's so funny?' demanded Singh.

'You – *you* look like that statue!'

Singh scowled but turned to peruse the artefact again. The elephant god had a long trunk which nestled comfortably on a pot belly of enormous proportions. He couldn't help smiling, there was certainly a resemblance. 'Maybe he likes Angkor beer too,' remarked Singh and provoked another outbreak of laughter.

The inspector from Singapore decided he'd had enough of being the butt of the joke and asked grouchily, 'Where do we find out about Huon?'

Immediately the Cambodian woman was all business. 'I saw booksellers at the entrance,' she announced and led the way back.

There were indeed a couple of men, both in wheelchairs, each with a leg amputated at the knee and boxes of books on their laps.

'Ask them if they knew Huon,' whispered Singh.

Chhean glared at him. 'What do you think I was going to do?'

She wandered over to the men, Singh a plump shadow in her wake, and commenced her inquiries. There was a lot of excited hand waving in response and Singh was on tenterhooks waiting for feedback.

'Well?' he demanded in a lull in the conversation.

'Oh – they say that you look like the Ganesha statue as well!'

Singh's eyebrows met over the bridge of his nose.

Chhean smiled and added, 'They knew Huon. He kept to himself and didn't like to talk about the past.'

'Is that all?'

'He sold more books than the rest because of the marks on his face – he got more sympathy from tourists. Oh – and he didn't have any enemies.'

Singh considered kicking a large phallic stone that was apparently of historical interest as it stood rigid in the museum's gardens. 'They must know something more than that! I just walked here from the Cambodiana, for God's sake.' He thought hard for a while, desperate for some sort of opening. At last, he said, 'Ask them if there is anything at all about Huon that was unusual, anything at all. I don't care if it was about his toilet habits. I want to know the man.'

She repeated the question and he wondered if she had censored the lavatory angle. Her scepticism was apparent in her voice despite the curious language that made everyone speaking it sound as if they had a strong lisp.

There was silence accompanied by much shrugging and hand wringing. Finally, one of the amputees muttered something and Chhean's face brightened noticeably.

'A big car – Mercedes – stopped here a few days ago. The windows were dark so he could not see inside. The passenger in the back wound down the window and called Huon . . .'

'By name?' interjected Singh harshly.

Chhean relayed the question and nodded at the answer. 'Yes, by name. Huon went over. They talked through the window.' She listened and then continued, 'Huon was angry at first, but then excited.'

Singh noted that the other wheelchair-bound man had taken up the tale. Whatever had happened, and regardless of whether it was important, these men were corroborating each other's story.

There was a pause and Singh asked, 'Is that all?'

'It is very strange – Huon gave the man his whole box of books and postcards. He told the others that he had sold everything.'

One of the men gestured at Singh and pointed at the cardboard box on his truncated lap, formerly a condensed milk tin carton, now a repository of stories. Singh knew the time had come to cough up for their cooperation. He selected two books each, more tales of survivor horror, and nodded his thanks – he really needed to ask Chhean how to at least say 'thank you' in Khmer.

One of the amputees gestured at Singh and said something to Chhean. The policeman fervently hoped it was not another joke at his expense. Chhean however was sombre. 'This man's name is Som. He says you should find the killer. Huon did not deserve to die like that.'

The other wheelchair-bound man leaned forward and patted his companion on the arm. It was a gesture that Singh found oddly touching from this infirm pair sitting in the shade of a tree and selling books to foreigners. Drawing from life's abundance of short straws, they still had the ability to show kindness to each other and seek justice for their friend. Unlike the newspapers and the politicos, these two men – Som and his friend – were genuinely concerned about Huon. He instructed Chhean to say something reassuring, anything really, to the men and hurried out of the gates.

Their car, with its chain-smoking driver, was waiting outside and Singh slid into the back seat with relief. He let the desultory air conditioning cool and calm him down.

Chhean leapt in after him, athletic and youthful despite her short stocky frame. 'What do you think it means?' she demanded. 'A big car, a rich man . . . it must be important.'

Singh leaned back against the plastic seat, abandoned his hunt for the long-since-dismantled seat belt and closed his heavy lids against the enthusiasm of amateurs. 'Perhaps the rich man was merely a lover of good books?' he suggested.

He didn't need to open his eyes or look at his companion to know her reaction – her snort of derision was evidence enough.

'A generous tycoon who felt sorry for a man with one leg and a scarred face to boot?' suggested Singh.

'Who knew his name?'

The inspector pursed his lips into a thoughtful pout. 'There, indeed, young lady, is the rub.'

140

Ten

Colonel Menhay was sitting behind his desk, a gloomy expression on his face and the morning newspapers spread out before him. His office was a quiet escape from the hive of activity going on in the adjacent rooms. Singh tactfully ignored the headlines demanding that the head of security for the tribunal be sacked but Menhay was not in the mood for such subtleties.

'Look at this,' he said, gesturing at the newspapers. 'They're blaming me.'

'Everyone needs a scapegoat at a time like this,' said Singh comfortingly. 'They'll forget in a week and things will get back to normal.'

'You forget that we also have unsolved serial killings on our hands. The journalists will soon bring that up too.'

'Have there been any other developments with that?' asked the Sikh policeman.

'No,' replied Menhay tiredly. 'I'm still looking for connections between the victims – I need someone competent to look into their pasts. My policemen are useless. They spend their time smoking and playing cards. Hopefully the documentation centre will lend me a clerk.'

'I've been researching documents every night,' Chhean said tentatively. 'Should I look into this for you at the same time?'

'Why?' It was Menhay with the quick question. 'Why have you been researching documents?' Singh had already queried her nocturnal activities on a previous occasion but Menhay's attention had been elsewhere at the time.

'I look for some information about *my* past,' she answered rather sadly. 'I hope to find some trace of my family.'

Menhay stared at the interpreter, chin resting on his entwined fingers. He reached into a drawer and took out a sheet of paper with a list of names. 'Take this,' he said, handing the document to Chhean. 'Tell me if you find anything.'

She nodded, unable to hide her pleasure at this new role and the implied approbation of the colonel.

Forgetting that he had been the one who brought up the serial killings, Singh suggested sarcastically, 'Shall we get back to Huon's murder then?'

The Cambodian glanced at his watch, a large dial which superfluously kept time in several cities at once, and said, 'Autopsy report should be here in a few minutes . . .'

'Anything else turned up?' Singh jerked his head in the direction of the adjacent offices where junior policemen appeared to be very busy if the ringing telephones and active photocopy machines were anything to go by.

Menhay snorted. 'A show to impress Adnan Muhammad. We're not going to solve this murder chatting to cleaning staff or handing out flyers.'

Singh reported what they had discovered about Huon and the mysterious wealthy stranger but Menhay merely looked despondent when he was told that, aside from a general description, they didn't have sufficient information to track down the man or his car.

'How am I supposed to find this rich man?' he demanded.

'Perhaps you could send some photo-fit chaps to talk to the booksellers?'

The colonel grimaced. 'This is Cambodia, not *CSI Miami*. Where would I get such a person?'

The Singaporean policeman had the grace to look sheepish. He knew very well that the best way to annoy a cop from a small town was to throw modern policing methods – or modern police force budgets – in his face. Not that he, Singh, was a proponent of modern policing methods. Superintendent Chen had once informed him that he was the dinosaur of the Singapore police force and it hadn't been a compliment about his aggressive T-Rex-like instincts.

'Maybe you can find the Mercedes,' suggested Chhean.

Menhay's expression suggested that he believed that interpreters should be seen and not heard except to translate accurately the words of their superiors and betters and occasionally do a bit of research on the side. Singh was fairly sure he was in agreement with the colonel's point of view. Chhean's willingness to lead the questioning of the two amputees instead of merely interpreting for him indicated a streak of insubordination as wide as the Tonle Sap after the rains.

'You know as well as I do that for a poor country we have a lot of big cars,' growled Menhay in response. 'You think I can find one Mercedes? Or should I set up a roadblock on

Rue Sihanouk and ask every fat rich man in the back of a Mercedes whether he likes to read books?' He pointed at the newspapers with an angry thumb. 'You don't think I am in enough trouble already?'

Chhean subsided in the face of this verbal onslaught. Singh, watching her face, didn't think she was in the least cowed by the Cambodian policeman's ire. More likely she was keeping her powder dry for more important battles.

'I did hear from the embassy,' Menhay added, perhaps feeling apologetic for his surliness.

Singh scratched his beard with a puzzled frown and then remembered the overwrought Frenchman. The colonel had said he was going to call in some favours and find out what he could about François Gaudin. That was quick work if Menhay had already heard back. It seemed that he had leverage at the embassy. Singh knew how these things worked – the colonel had probably picked up some drunken minor functionary with a call girl and now that person owed him a favour.

'His wife and children are . . . were, Cambodian. They disappeared in 1975 after they were evicted from the French embassy. You know, just before the foreigners were evacuated to Thailand.'

'And he only looks for them now?' Chhean's voice was accusing. Singh guessed she was thinking back to her own abandonment in the aftermath of the war. His interpreter's wounds seemed as fresh as the day they were inflicted.

'Gaudin caused a scene at Tuol Sleng a couple of days ago. He started screaming and then fainted in one of the rooms,' added Menhay.

'Why?' Singh's brow was furrowed. Something must have triggered the episode although it could also have been an accumulation of horrors.

'Don't know. We can find out if you think it's important? The prison staff might remember – or I can have Gaudin questioned.' He finished on an aggrieved note. 'Although I still don't see what this has to do with Huon's murder.'

'There's no such thing as too much information.' Singh was getting a sense of how his colleagues felt when dealing with him. A harassed policeman with a short fuse – it seemed that he and Menhay had quite a lot in common. It was strange to be the one wearing kid gloves – and out of character as well. On the other hand, he was willing to tread warily, until such time as he and Menhay were no longer going in the same direction. That would be the moment to remind the colonel that the UN, in the form of that toothpick of a man, had left them both in charge.

Menhay beckoned to a policeman and issued a few curt instructions.

Singh assumed the young man had been told to look further into François Gaudin's activities. He had to guess what was said because his interpreter was too busy staring out of the window, chewing on a thumbnail thoughtfully, to do her job.

He was prevented from indulging in a bit of sarcasm at the expense of Chhean by the entrance, without knocking, of the young pathologist who had attended the crime scene the previous day. The doctor sauntered in with his usual cockiness and flourished a file at them as if it was a magic wand. He was grinning from ear to ear and even his too-long hair was standing on end with excitement.

'Dr Savuth,' said Menhay in the sort of forced, even tone that suggested he was inches from losing his temper at the insouciance of the youngster.

'I have the autopsy report,' said the pathologist, somewhat unnecessarily, as he was still brandishing the file.

'Well, what does it say?'

'Cause of death – stab wound that penetrated the left aorta. Death would have been almost instantaneous.'

'Tell me something I don't know,' snapped the colonel.

'Weapon – ordinary wide-blade, single-sided knife.' He added as an afterthought, 'Probably stolen from the cafeteria kitchen.'

'I think you can leave the investigating to us,' said Menhay but Singh's ears had pricked up. It made sense that the weapon was from the premises. It would not have been easy to sneak one through the metal detectors at the entrance to the compound. Did that suggest that this murder had not been planned in advance? That it had been a spur-of-the-moment decision – grab a knife, stab a man? He wondered again whether the killer had been an expert or merely lucky to have penetrated a vital organ.

'There is bruising on the jaw.'

Singh looked up at this. He hadn't noticed that when he perused the body – the bruises had probably been obscured by the scar tissue. 'Post-mortem or pre-mortem?' he asked.

'You mean did someone smack him on the chin or did he hit his face on the way down after being stabbed?'

'Exactly.'

'Hard to say really – the bruising was not severe and not very old. Pre-mortem, I would have guessed. But before you

146

get excited, he could have fallen and hit the floor after being stabbed – but before dying.'

'He might not have died immediately?'

'He wouldn't have lasted more than a couple of minutes with that wound . . .'

The fat man fell silent, considering what he'd been told.

Dr Kar Savuth was still beaming like a child on Christmas Eve.

'There's something else, isn't there?' Singh asked abruptly. 'What haven't you told us? Spit it out, man.'

'Fingerprints!' announced the doctor with the air of a medical man who had just discovered a cure for cancer.

'Fingerprints? On the murder weapon?' Singh's tone combined hope with doubt. Was it really going to be this simple? Problem solved, case closed?

'Yes.'

'Well, go on!' Menhay was standing up now, reaching for the autopsy report. The pathologist skipped back, unwilling to relinquish his prize until he had milked the moment further – he was the man of the hour and he knew it.

'A lot of smudges – two sets of clear prints,' he said importantly, miming a more serious expression.

'Identification?' demanded Singh.

'Unfortunately, Cambodia does not have a comprehensive data base of fingerprints,' explained Savuth in response.

'So you mean that we have to find the killer before you can do a comparison?' Singh acknowledged that this would be good evidence at any trial. Juries – did they have juries in Cambodia? – loved fingerprint evidence. It was easy, it reminded them of stuff they had seen on the telly and, fortunately for the appeals courts, it was often decisive. It took a cunning killer indeed to plausibly explain away fingerprints on a murder weapon.

'One set of prints belongs to the deceased.' Savuth grabbed a chair, twirled it round and sat down with his arms resting on the back.

Singh could see the lines creasing his forehead mirrored on that of Colonel Menhay.

'The deceased? Huon?'

'How could that have happened?' asked Menhay. 'Was it suicide?'

'I thought I "could leave the investigating" to you?' replied Savuth.

For possibly the first time in his life, Singh missed Dr Maniam, the grumpy old pathologist at the Singapore General Hospital who was wont to make personal remarks about Singh's health based on the organ condition of his autopsy subjects.

Chhean interrupted. 'Shall we concentrate on working together for a moment?'

All the men except Singh looked sheepish.

'Not suicide,' said Singh dismissively.

Menhay nodded. 'Possible hypothesis – Huon had the knife before the killer grabbed it and killed him with it?'

The Sikh inspector's face wrinkled like an old bed sheet. He tried to picture the scene in his mind. It was possible that Huon had been expecting trouble, armed himself and then discovered that he had bitten off more than he could chew. But surely there would have been some defensive markings on the dead man's hands in the circumstances?

Like an echo to his thoughts, Savuth said, 'There was no evidence of a struggle. Nothing under the nails. No scratches.'

When he was concentrating on the issue at hand rather than playing up his own importance, Kar Savuth had a competent air which was persuasive. It persuaded Singh anyway. Although, truth be told, he was always easily convinced by explanations that matched his own initial thinking. It was a habit which occasionally amounted to a weakness if he did not test a hypothesis sufficiently rigorously. That was why he needed sceptical sidekicks. He glanced at his sturdy young interpreter.

Chhean duly obliged. 'Even a one-legged man could put up some defence if he was attacked with his own knife!'

'Especially since the killer was a *woman*,' said Savuth.

There was no sound in the room except for the rasping of the overworked air-conditioning unit.

'What in God's name are you talking about?' demanded Menhay.

'Why in the world would you think it was a woman?' asked Singh in a tired voice. He wondered what far-fetched theory the young fellow had for his assertion. The strength of the blow? The angle of the wound? It would all be nonsense, whatever it was. This was what happened when you let a pathologist who was still wet behind the ears at a dead body. They wouldn't be satisfied without some insight that was wildly speculative, indeed absurd. It was a pity. He had been on the verge of trusting the boy's judgment.

Kar Savuth had placed the file on Menhay's table. Now he opened it, straightening loose pages as he did so, and took out a sheet of paper, a computer print-out.

'What's that?' asked Menhay.

'You just got lucky,' Savuth said cheerfully. 'The ECCC collects fingerprints from all those associated with the tribunal from the accused right down to those providing witness statements.'

Singh cut to the chase. 'Are you trying to say you have a match for the second pair of prints?'

'Yes, your killer is a woman, aged forty-one, by the name of Sovann Armstrong.'

So it was going to be straightforward after all. Menhay muttered a heartfelt thanks to the Buddha. He glanced at the newspapers on his desk. Singh had been right. The mood would turn quickly when he had made his arrest and word got out to the press. Tomorrow, he, Colonel Menhay of the Cambodian police, would be a hero.

The square-jawed man smiled at the other members of his team. A short while earlier, he had viewed them with emotions ranging from irritation at the ornery interpreter to downright anger at the uppity pathologist. Now, he was prepared to beam at them and share the credit. He was not a selfish man – he would give thanks where it was due. Kar Savuth had done a fine job. It was a good day at the office when the forensic evidence did a policeman's job for him. The fat man from Singapore had agreed to share the poisoned chalice – albeit at the behest of the UN – and had been unexpectedly tactful while doing so. He deserved some kudos for that. He must be just as relieved that this matter was going to be resolved quickly with credit enough for each to have a share.

'I picked up Sovann's statement from the documentation centre on my way here,' said Savuth. He handed out copies quickly and they all looked down at the paper as if it was a confession to the murder of Huon rather than the story of a time long since past except in the memory of the victim.

Chhean translated and abridged as she read it out loud. It was a sorry tale of a young girl who had witnessed her father's death at the hands of a Khmer Rouge cadre. The interpreter's voice broke as she narrated the midnight march through the paddy fields, the men, including the girl's father, on their knees, the cadres with shovels, a vicious blow to the head and an eleven-year-old thinking about the spectacles, secreted in the hollow of a bamboo pole, which her father would no longer need.

Menhay rubbed his eyes. Pol Pot had died in his own time and in his own space while his legacy was a pile of witness statements with stories, different in the detail, but identical in substance, to the one that Chhean had just recited. And these represented just a fraction of the actuality. So many were dead, mute, illiterate, ignorant – but they had suffered as well, were still suffering because memories like these could not be suppressed. Cambodia was a nation that had to reinvent itself from scratch, from ground zero, as Hun Sen and others called it. To some extent, like a phoenix rising from the ashes, they were succeeding. But sometimes the past reached out and tapped one on the shoulder, reminding Cambodians of what had gone before.

'I wonder why she did it?' wondered Menhay out loud, although it was a largely rhetorical question. A part of him didn't care about the answer. The copper who needed a quick result to appease the government and the UN and had fingerprints on a murder weapon didn't care what had driven this Sovann Armstrong to murder. But the man – who had fled into the jungles and arrived in Vietnam half-starved and delirious and then taken part in the invasion of his own country to remove the Khmer Rouge – was interested to know what had led this forty-one-year-old woman to kill. She had seen death as a child and inflicted it as an adult. But why Cheah Huon? After all, he was innocent too.

'With a story like that,' Savuth said, tapping the statement with a long finger to indicate what he meant, 'she might have just snapped under the pressure of her memories.'

'I can understand that – no one can be entirely sane who has lived through such an event,' said Chhean in a subdued voice. 'But why did she kill Huon? He had suffered too. Why didn't she attack one of the others – like Ta Ieng?'

Menhay pressed his hands firmly together at chest height, trying to undo the knots in his shoulders. He thought about the serial killer knocking off ex-Khmer Rouge one by one. So many people, in their conversation, implied that they would have sympathy with the murderer of such men.

'If she had killed Ta Ieng instead of Cheah Huon – it would still be murder and I would still be planning her arrest.' Menhay spoke sharply in response to Chhean's remark, more sharply than she deserved.

The air-conditioning unit on the whitewashed wall, struggling to cool the room, began to drip water on the carpet. He watched the stain grow in size – slowly yet inexorably. The dark patch reminded him of blood. The same size and shape as the stain on the front of Huon's shirt. He felt a shudder run through his squat frame – it was like an omen.

'Are you confident of getting her?' Savuth turned to the colonel and asked the question in a polite voice.

Menhay grinned suddenly, exposing his brown stumps for teeth. He nodded at the witness statement that he was clutching in his hand like a lucky charm. 'According to this – she is staying at the Raffles Hotel in Phnom Penh.'

Savuth smiled back with the even white teeth of a modern-era Khmer. 'Nothing but the best for our murderers, eh?'

The pathologist had a point. Very few Cambodians passed through the luxurious Raffles Hotel. It was a place for wealthy tourists and foreign investors – foreign *exploiters* he preferred to call these businessmen from South East Asia who were happy to come and pay a few cents for all of Cambodia's natural wealth, aided and abetted by some of his own greedy countrymen. 'Armstrong . . .' he muttered under his breath.

'So this Sovann person married a foreigner,' said Chhean.

'One with money,' suggested Savuth.

Menhay nodded. 'That must be the explanation. It says here that she was resettled to the United States from a refugee camp on the Thai border.'

'American husband – they all have plenty of money,' explained Chhean with the simple certainty of someone who had been brought up to believe that other lands are bountiful, literally flowing with milk and honey.

'And they know how to make trouble.' Menhay's tone was worried. Better than anyone, he knew Cambodia. Here, money talked, and only the very rich and the very poor ignored what was spoken. He turned to look at Singh, seeking someone with experience to allay his fears that there were still bumps in the road ahead. He wanted – no, he needed – a smooth ride from this point onwards.

As he looked at the Sikh man's pensive expression, he realised with a start that the entire conversation, since Chhean had translated the witness statement, had been conducted in Khmer. The fat man would not have understood a word and yet he sat quietly, his bearded chin resting in the palm of his hand, his elbow supported by the table that separated them.

'Singh?' questioned Menhay.

The other two occupants of the room turned to look at the fat Sikh as if remembering for the first time that the usually assertive man had been absent from the discussion. A silence followed Menhay's attempt to attract his attention.

At last, Inspector Singh turned to face the others. He said simply, and with conviction, 'I know Sovann Armstrong. I don't believe she did it.'

Chhean had come along, doing her best not to draw attention to herself so that she would not be ordered away. She followed in Singh's shadow, obscuring her own solid figure behind the ample form of the angry detective. The policeman from Singapore was irate that no one was prepared to entertain his doubts over the guilt of Sovann Armstrong. When quick questioning by Colonel Menhay, operating on overdrive, had elicited that Singh had met the woman *once*, a chance encounter over lunch, he had been more than dismissive, he had been angry.

Chhean couldn't blame the colonel, although she thought his accusation, that Singh was trying to prolong the investigation in order to seek more personal glory, had been harsh.

They were on their way to the Raffles Hotel Le Royal, she and Singh in an unmarked car that followed the lead car, the Toyota four-wheel drive of Colonel Menhay. Behind them was a convoy of police cars with sirens blaring and flashing lights.

'What are they expecting?' Singh demanded of his companion, on seeing their colourful noisy escort. 'That she's going to make a run for it?'

As all Chhean knew of the woman was that her fingerprints were all over a murder weapon, she was not as sceptical as Singh. What else could she do but run for it? There was not going to be much sympathy in Cambodia for her – she had not just killed a man, she had almost destroyed the ECCC. Chhean hardened her heart against the stranger they were pursuing in such theatrical style. Closure was essential if the trial of Samrin was to get back on track.

'Where is this hotel anyway?' demanded Singh.

'In the European quarter – near the French embassy,' she answered in a soothing voice.

Singh subsided into grumpy silence. She wondered if her tone had indeed calmed the beast. If so, she would keep talking. 'Oldest hotel in Phnom Penh,' she explained with the forced cheerfulness of a tourist guide. 'Very famous, very expensive, Jackie Kennedy stayed there.'

'Really?'

'Yes, on her way to Angkor. Later Khmer Rouge attacked the building and used it to store rice and fish.'

Singh slumped back in his seat, chin resting on his chest

and hands resting on his belly with the same tenderness Chhean had previously only seen with pregnant women.

In a few moments, they were pulling into the driveway of the hotel, past well-tended gardens with an abundance of frangipani trees and fan palms. The lead car drew up and Colonel Menhay leapt out. Chhean followed suit and noted that Singh could move quickly for a man of his size. His white sneakers were hard on the heels of the colonel. As they walked into the foyer, light bulbs flashed and she realised that Menhay had notified the press that an arrest was imminent. She stole a sidelong glance at the inspector. He was livid, his face discernibly red even under the dark skin.

Menhay, surrounded by an armed guard, demanded to know the room number of Sovann Armstrong.

The receptionist, thoroughly intimidated by the show of strength, said hurriedly, 'I can tell you the room number, sir. But you don't need it. She is sitting over there!' Using his thumb, he pointed at the conservatory to the rear of the lobby where a number of guests were staring at the commotion with wide eyes.

All except for one woman who had her eyes firmly fixed on a newspaper, although the large Caucasian man across from her was sitting on the edge of his seat.

'Which one is she?' Menhay asked the question of Singh.

He reluctantly trained his turban on the woman with the newspaper and Menhay marched up purposefully.

The large Caucasian man stood up and barred the way.

'Looking for someone?' he asked, and Chhean heard an underlying tremor that was incongruous in such a big man. Was he so afraid for his wife – she guessed this must be the wealthy American husband – or was there something that he feared for himself?

'We are looking for Sovann Armstrong,' said the colonel.

'What?' His ruddy face had grown pale.

So he had thought that this police invasion had something to do with him. In Cambodia, that could mean anything – underage girls, or boys, drugs, kickbacks. Jeremy Armstrong was in a panic because, unlike the usual circumstances involving a rich *barang*, consequences seemed about to flow from his wrongdoing.

'I am Sovann Armstrong.' The woman stood up. Immediately she became the centre of attention, drawing all eyes and cameras. She was thin and elegantly dressed in a rich silk *sampot*, her hair swept up in a chignon. Chhean felt a stab of envy. No wonder the fat man was convinced that this gorgeous creature was innocent. Her own lack of height and stocky figure was suddenly uppermost in her mind and she chastised herself firmly for thinking about anything so trivial. What sort of idiotic female was she anyway to feel resentment towards someone who was about to be arrested for murder?

Sovann looked around at the mass of policemen and press with a bemused expression. She did not look afraid, which surprised Chhean. Even the innocent were entitled to look fearful in the face of the AK-47-toting police. Sovann's gaze fell on Inspector Singh and her face creased in a smile of recognition. Chhean, darting a quick glance at the policeman, noted that he did not return the mild salutation. She was surprised that the inspector from Singapore had ignored Sovann's overture. The cock has already crowed once, she thought, and found that she was unreasonably disappointed in her fat friend.

It was Menhay's turn for centre stage. He spoke clearly and with only a hint of self-importance. 'Sovann Armstrong, you are under arrest for murder.'

Back at the Phnom Penh police headquarters, the woman accused of murder confounded them with her opening statement.

'He deserved to die, of course,' said Sovann.

'What's that supposed to mean?' demanded Menhay.

Singh wondered whether the colonel was seeing a real flesh-and-blood woman or just a feather in his cap. A part of him knew he was being unfair. He had developed a healthy respect for the colonel before this arrest. Just because they disagreed on the guilt or innocence of Sovann Armstrong wasn't a good enough reason to change his mind. After all, the evidence was with Menhay.

Sovann did not mince her words. 'I believe that Cheah Huon deserved to die – but I am sure you know that.'

The interview was being conducted in English. Sovann had insisted, as a courtesy, she had said, to the visitor from Singapore. Menhay's grinding teeth had been almost audible at this display of *sang froid* from his murderer. Singh nibbled on a fingernail and then stuck his hands in his pockets. He decided firmly that it was not the beauty of Sovann Armstrong that had him convinced of her innocence but the resilience he sensed in her. Women who had shown fortitude over a long period of time at the vicissitudes of life did not chuck it all in suddenly and stab someone.

They were in a small interview room that smelt of piss and stale cigarette smoke and felt crowded despite being of a reasonable size. There were only four people in the room: Singh, Menhay, Chhean and the accused. The entourage from the Raffles were kicking their heels outside the building somewhere, no doubt filing reports with their various news agencies, all claiming the scoop for themselves. Quite a few of them would have greased the palms of officials, hoping to get an inside line on the story. Singh doubted they would have much success. So far at least, only the four people in the room and the pathologist were privy to all the information. Mr Jeremy Armstrong was elsewhere carrying through his various threats and promises to call everyone from the American embassy to the United Nations to protest the wrongful arrest of his wife.

Singh decided that the sense of claustrophobia was a result of their gravitation to the centre of the room and away from the dirty stained walls. This was Cambodia and he didn't need more evidence than the streaks of blood and snot and God-knows-what-else to know that it was frontier country as far as law and order went. He had been surprised that Menhay did not offer Sovann legal assistance. Singh had intervened but Sovann had refused representation in the same quiet, faraway voice with which she had responded to the entire escapade.

'I recognised him.'

Singh's ears pricked up. He looked at Sovann directly for the first time. She was sitting neatly, feet and knees together, on a plastic chair. The only concession to circumstances was her position on the edge of the seat. Although that might just have been fastidiousness – the seat too was stained like a piece of modern art.

Menhay, who had been doing the questioning, looked like

a drenched cat, surprised and uncomfortable. The questions and answers were not proceeding as he had intended or expected. Singh lit a cigarette, sucked in a lungful of tobacco-laden smoke and waited to see how Menhay was going to deal with this piece of information.

'You recognised him?'

'Yes, during his testimony to the tribunal.'

Confronted with confounded silence from the investigator, Sovann obligingly took up the tale again. 'Not immediately – he had changed a lot. When I knew him he didn't have those injuries.'

The inspector exhaled smoke rings, needing the concentration that the blowing of white circles required.

'But when he turned to face the judges, I noticed a birthmark on his neck, a rose-coloured oval shape the size of a palm . . .'

Singh remembered how Sovann had fainted towards the end of Huon's appearance. If she had recognised him, it would explain the sudden loss of control. He couldn't stop himself butting in. 'Who was he then – this man with the birthmark?'

She met his eyes unflinchingly. 'The Khmer Rouge cadre who killed my father.'

Eleven

'What did you just say? Huon killed your father?' Singh's tone was incredulous.

All of them remembered the witness statement. Sovann Armstrong's father had been bludgeoned to death by a Khmer Rouge cadre when she was eleven years old. But to suggest that it was Huon? Singh shook his head regretfully. The pathologist had been right with his far-fetched theories about individuals being pushed to breaking point by the dredging up of old memories. To believe that Huon had killed her father – that was madness, surely.

Sovann spoke in a perfectly reasonable tone. 'But you must know all this already. I filed a police report when I recognised him as a murderer and not the victim he pretended to be.'

'You made a police report?' demanded Menhay angrily.

She nodded briefly. 'The policeman who took my statement didn't look very convinced. I'm not sure I blame him. I could hardly believe it myself.'

The colonel stormed out of the room, his face the colour of a thundercloud. They could all hear him screaming at his underlings although no one gave any overt sign of it.

'He's asking for the report,' whispered Chhean.

Sovann gazed down at the hands folded in her lap and then looked up at all of them, finally fixing her gaze on Inspector Singh. Did she suspect, had she guessed, that he was the soft touch? The policeman blinked rapidly a few times; his eyes felt grainy and tired. Didn't Sovann Armstrong realise that by revealing that she believed Huon had killed her father, she was providing them with a motive? She was damning herself out of her own mouth.

'Listen,' he whispered urgently to the woman accused of murder, one eye on the door to watch for Menhay's return, 'I'm not convinced you killed Huon. So just try and be calm until we figure this out.'

Chhean, who had been rifling through her papers like an angry accountant, found what she was looking for. She waved it in the air like a lion tamer with a whip and a collection of frisky lions. 'Autopsy report – Huon *did* have a birthmark as described by Mrs Armstrong.'

'Yes,' said Singh impatiently. 'Unfortunately we only have the word of Mrs Armstrong that such a birthmark was also on the neck of the cadre who killed her father. That's evidence of nothing except her keen eyesight.'

Chhean looked miffed but did not deny Singh's point.

Menhay walked back into the room. He held out a handwritten report to Chhean who ran through it quickly for Singh. It was the police report that Sovann had made fingering Huon as the killer of her father. Only the deep indentations of pen on paper revealed the internal turmoil of the writer. The information itself was succinct and clearly expressed. No wonder Sovann had been surprised that her interrogators knew nothing of her motive.

'Apparently we're getting a lot of reports of this nature – my boys didn't realise the importance of this one.' The policeman was apologetic, hinting at the many Cambodians who were imagining Khmer Rouge cadres behind every bush now that the war crimes tribunals had commenced.

Singh turned his attention back to the accused but was pre-empted by his impatient interpreter. 'What did you *do*?' she asked Sovann. Chhean was speaking out of turn but no one shut her up. Instead, they turned to Sovann as one, waiting for the answer. The hands folded on her lap balled into fists. Singh noted uncomfortably that for a slight creature, the thin fingers looked strong, certainly strong enough to stab a man with a bit of luck and a sharp kitchen knife.

'I decided to confront him. To ask him why he had done it. Even if he lied to me, I would know the truth if I could watch his face when I asked the question.'

She paused, as if gathering her thoughts – or her strength – for what was to come next. They all waited like children at a storytelling, knowing the climax was coming, guessing what it was, but breathless with anticipation anyway. Singh tried to tell himself that it was all over bar the sentence of life imprisonment. It was ironic that this woman faced the same penalty, no more, no less than Duch and Samrin. Sometimes, the law really was an ass. Singh pinched the bridge of his nose firmly, trying to ward off a migraine. His famous instinct for guilt and innocence had been completely out of kilter. It was

Cambodia with its bloody past and beautiful women that had thrown him off balance. How was his antenna supposed to operate accurately in such a strange land?

'I went to find him, late that evening. It was quite dark, perhaps about eleven? I can't remember. It was a very confused time for me. I hadn't eaten or drunk anything for hours.'

Singh nodded. It was as good a time as any to lay the groundwork for a plea of temporary insanity or whatever the equivalent was in Cambodia.

She glanced at him and the inspector was rewarded with a small smile for his support.

'I went towards the wing where I knew some of the witnesses were staying. As I grew closer, I heard voices shouting. There was a lot of anger. I kept going . . .'

Her audience had almost stopped breathing.

'I heard the sound of footsteps, someone running – but whoever it was did not pass me. I reached Huon's room. I was terrified. Part of me wanted to run away . . . I know it sounds strange but I felt as if I was eleven years old again.'

She stopped. The fortitude that she had shown from the beginning was showing signs of wear and tear. There were tears in her eyes and the hands on her lap were clasped together tightly to stop them from shaking.

'Go on,' said Singh in a gravelly whisper.

'His door was ajar – I opened it and saw Huon – the man who murdered my father.'

'Did he say anything?' It was Chhean again, forgetting her role as translator and turning into an inquisitor.

Sovann looked up with an expression of astonishment on her face.

'What do you mean? I saw him lying on the floor. He was dead!'

'Dead?' Menhay was mystified and it showed in his raised eyebrows and round eyes.

'Yes. So you see, I didn't – couldn't have – killed Huon. I didn't realise he was dead at first. He was lying on the ground. His artificial limb was lying across him.'

Menhay noticed a small nod from Singh. The description of the position of the body matched what they had seen. The colonel did not see where this approbation was from – of course she would be accurate about the details of death. She was the murderer.

'Then I saw the hilt of the knife . . .' Sovann shuddered like a leaf in a gust of wind.

It was a good performance, thought Menhay sceptically. It needed to be if they were expected to swallow this ridiculous tale.

'What did you do?' Singh asked the question, indicating with his words that he was not treating the story with the outright disdain it deserved.

Menhay was fast coming to the conclusion that the leading murder investigator from Singapore was a gullible idiot. It seemed that he had a better nose for stale biscuits than a blatant falsehood.

'I knelt down by the body. I touched him.' She pressed her own forearm to indicate where she had put her hand. 'He was still warm, like a living person.'

'Very cool behaviour,' remarked Menhay. Unexpectedly, he hit a nerve.

'How old are you, Colonel Menhay? About fifty?' Sovann had risen to her feet. She was literally trembling with anger. 'Then, as a Cambodian, I think you would have seen a lot of death. I was fifteen when I left for the United States. By then, I had learnt to walk past a corpse as if it wasn't there, to ignore the screams of the dying and to be indifferent to the pain and suffering of children. Do you think that sort of training disappears after a few soft years in the land of plenty?'

She was leaning forward, waggling a finger in his face like an angry schoolteacher with a student who had forgotten the lessons of history.

'Every night, every *single* night, I relive those memories. Seeing another body . . . this was just a waking nightmare, but not that much different from the rest.'

Menhay put his hands out, palms flat and facing her. He said, and he meant it, 'I'm sorry.' His voice was husky. 'I get the nightmares too sometimes.' He drew a deep breath, he was a policeman again, not someone who shared a common past with the accused. 'But the fact is that nothing you have said explains why your fingerprints were on that knife.'

She sat down suddenly as if the strength had gone out of her legs. 'I had this idea that I should remove the knife. I wasn't even sure if he was dead.' Sovann was miming her actions, leaning forward, her fingers curled as if she had her hand on the dark, rubbery hilt of the kitchen knife.

'You were trying to save him? This man you believe killed your father?' It was Singh who had spotted the inconsistency between word and deed.

'No, but I wanted to ask him why he had killed an innocent man. I wished to know what was in his mind.'

166

Singh nodded as if he was satisfied and she continued. 'The knife was stuck fast. It wouldn't move. I looked at his face. As I watched, his eyes rolled back into his head so I knew he was dead.'

'What did you do next?'

Menhay let the Singapore policeman speak uninterrupted. Sovann was more likely to respond to the man she perceived as the 'good cop' rather than to his 'bad cop'.

'I left the room and returned to my hotel. A part of me, a large part of me, was very, very *happy* that Huon was dead. The man who killed my father was dead.'

'And *that's* your story?' demanded Menhay with unfeigned disbelief.

'That's the truth,' said Sovann Armstrong.

A knock on the door was a welcome distraction. The colonel was about to blow his top and start haranguing Sovann. Even Singh needed a few moments to regroup after her revelations. He had been certain Sovann was innocent. But he had not imagined that she would present them with a motive for murder as well as a rather peculiar explanation for her fingerprints. As to the former, he supposed she had no choice. She couldn't have anticipated that her police report would have been lost, even temporarily, in a pile of paperwork. As to the latter? Well, her fingerprints were on the knife. If she hadn't killed Huon, it was as good an explanation as any.

The policeman who came in whispered something to Menhay. The short powerful man rose to his feet, nodded curtly to Sovann and then beckoned to Chhean and Singh to follow him out of the room.

Once outside, he locked the door carefully, as if Sovann was some sort of desperate killer bent on escape, thought Singh irritably, and pocketed the key.

The rookie handed him an envelope and Menhay opened it with a fingernail, one of the few he had left. He stared at the picture and then handed it over to Singh. Chhean stood on tiptoe, peering over his shoulder to see what he was looking at.

It was a vibrantly coloured reproduction of a painting.

'By Vann Nath,' explained Menhay.

'One of the seven survivors from S21,' added Chhean.

Singh looked at the picture of a baby being snatched from her mother by a Khmer Rouge cadre while other children looked on, the expression of terror on their faces causing Singh's heart to turn over with a combination of intense sympathy and profound helplessness.

'Why are you showing me this?' he asked, swallowing hard to clear the lump in his throat.

'That was the painting the Frenchman, François Gaudin, was looking at when he collapsed.' Without another word the colonel marched down the passage.

Singh stared at the picture for a moment longer, committing it to memory although he feared that it wasn't necessary, that the image would return to him often in the cold hours of the morning. He slipped it into his shirt pocket and hurried after Menhay.

'Where are we going now?' he demanded, puffing in his effort to keep up. The colonel was not much taller than Singh and almost as broad, but his width was densely packed muscle, not the flabby evidence of a few too many curries.

'*I* am going to my office. You can do whatever you like!' Perhaps regretting his rudeness, he added by way of explanation, 'I thought it would be good to give that woman some time to rethink her lies.' He glanced at the winded Sikh. 'And I think we need to make a progress report to Adnan Muhammad as well.'

'What are you going to tell him?'

Menhay stopped in his tracks. He turned to face the Sikh man, his expression one of weariness. 'What am I going to tell him? That I have my murderer, what else?' He continued, 'And I hope you're not going to make this difficult.'

'You heard her – that was a plausible explanation for the fingerprints!'

'Are you trying to be funny? She tried to pull the knife out? Give me a break.'

'People behave in strange ways when they are confronted with violence. It's possible.' It sounded lame even to Singh's ears. He needed to come up with something more convincing if he was to sway the colonel.

'All I know is that she's presented us with a motive,' enunciated Menhay clearly. 'That was the one weakness in my case. I mean, why would some rich woman from America stab the star witness at the war crimes tribunal? Now we know, she thought he killed her father.' He shook his head. 'She must be mad.'

Singh had no idea how to break down this man's wall of certainty, buttressed as it was by compelling evidence. Even he was doubtful as to the veracity of Sovann's story. But they had to test it, they had to investigate. That was their job as policemen, not reaching for the suspect nearest to hand and chucking them in jail for the rest of their lives. 'Look – let's look at it the other way. Let's assume she's telling the truth,' he said, trying to inject a note of patience that he didn't feel into his voice.

Menhay snorted.

'Just listen to me for a moment. If she was right, Huon was a Khmer Rouge killer. It opens up entirely new avenues of investigation.' Avenues as wide and as long as Phnom Penh's French boulevards, thought Singh excitedly, pleased with his own reasoning.

'Like what?'

'Well, your serial killer for starters! Huon would have been the perfect target, escaping justice by pretending to be a victim.'

'Those men were shot – a single bullet to the head. There is no similarity between the killings at all.'

Singh swatted away the argument as if it was an irksome fly. 'It would have to be different here. Too difficult to smuggle a gun into the compound with the metal detectors and things . . .'

'Take my word for it – it wasn't the serial killer.'

'Huon's story at the tribunal was true – about being the gravedigger. Some of the others remember him.' Chhean spoke with understandable tentativeness. It took courage to insert herself, even conversationally, between these two angry men locking horns in a narrow corridor.

Singh emitted a deep sound from his throat, like an aggressive dog. This woman worked for him, he thought, conveniently forgetting his preference for sidekicks who were prepared to play devil's advocate. Shouldn't she be on his side?

Chhean redeemed herself. 'But do you remember I mentioned that there was a gap in his file before he was sent to Tuol Sleng? Maybe he was Khmer Rouge and they decided he could not be trusted and sent him to prison.'

'That's quite possible,' exclaimed Singh. 'I read in one of those books that most of those in S21 were ex-Khmer Rouge anyway. They were purged from the party for whatever reason.'

'Usually their crime was only in Pol Pot's imagination,' added Chhean.

'His is not the only active imagination,' said Menhay pointedly.

'Look, colonel. All I'm trying to suggest is that we look into this a bit further. I agree with you that the evidence points to Sovann and she most likely did it.'

Menhay visibly wavered.

'Just let me keep sniffing around,' urged the fat man.

The colonel slammed a fist into the palm of his other hand. Singh didn't doubt that Menhay would rather have made aggressive contact with Singh's bearded chin. He waited, holding his breath, deeming it prudent to keep out of Menhay's internal debate, reflected in his flickering eyelashes.

'OK, Cambodia has seen too much arbitrary justice. You may keep investigating. I won't tell Adnan that we have a suspect – he'll read about it in the papers tomorrow anyway. If he asks, I'll say we need to keep "sniffing around" for a few days to shore up the evidence.'

Singh's usually grouchy expression was transformed by a broad cheek-to-cheek grin. He slapped the colonel on the back. 'You won't regret this,' he said reassuringly.

'I already do,' was Menhay's snide response.

Twelve

Singh crooked his finger at his interpreter and set off towards the main entrance to the police station. 'We'll see you a bit later,' he muttered over his shoulder to the colonel. He hurried away before Menhay could call him back or ask him his plans. He didn't have any but he was sure that, as and when he formulated a strategy, the colonel wouldn't like it. It was best to plough his own furrow – ideally in parallel to the efforts of the Cambodian police but if necessary at cross purposes. Singh was suddenly happy. A murdered man, a beautiful woman wrongly accused (he amended the description in his head, *possibly* wrongly accused), the bosses against him – this was a murder investigation as he understood it. If only the food in Cambodia was more to his taste, he would have everything his heart could desire. He glanced at Chhean, walking purposefully by his side, short legs taking long strides – a slightly less crabby sidekick would be an improvement as well.

'So where are we going?' the crabby sidekick demanded.

'Your job is to follow me around and translate all these airy consonants and suppressed vowels into an intelligible language, not ask questions. *I* will ask the questions.'

She groaned and he glowered at her. He deserved some respect for his seniority at least. Weren't Cambodians taught to respect their elders like the children of other Asian societies? He grimaced – the reality was that there just weren't that many Cambodian elders. Thanks to the killing fields of the Khmer Rouge, Cambodia had one of the youngest populations in the world.

He shook his great head, all smiles gone. He was investigating a murder in the early twenty-first century. But every aspect of the killing indicated that it was a crime born of events thirty years ago. It was probably the first time in his life that an investigation of his had invoked history in this way. In a sense, he supposed, it wasn't history at all – what was that expression, *the past is prologue*? It was a useful phrase to keep in mind when looking at the grubby reality of present-day Cambodia. Despite Hun Sen's efforts to model himself on the other strong men of Asia – Suharto, Mahathir, Lee Kuan Yew – and drag his backwater into the future, the long cold fingers of times gone by would not release Cambodia.

They stepped out into the fierce sunshine and Singh mopped his brow with a large white handkerchief. He peered down at his shoes past his overhanging belly. They were no longer the pristine colour of his facecloth. He neatly folded his hanky and put it back in his trouser pocket – it wouldn't take much exposure to the dust and grime to transform it into the same grubby beige as his sneakers.

'Doesn't it ever rain here?' he asked irritably.

'It's the dry season,' explained Chhean. She looked the fat man up and down. 'You would not like the monsoons. Most Phnom Penh streets become rivers and the Mekong and Tonle Sap flood. People drown and you can find fish in your living room.'

Singh tugged at an earlobe peeping out from under his blue turban. She was probably right that he would not enjoy wading through flood waters but this town looked like it could use a good wash. He remembered, with an unexpected wistfulness, Singapore in the aftermath of a thunderstorm. The air would be sweet with the smell of rain and the trees would glisten in the half-light of the sun breaking through the clouds. It had never occurred to him that the entire spectacle depended on good drainage.

'Have you decided what we're going to do now?' It was back to business for Chhean. She was not the sort to indulge in long conversations about the weather.

Her mobile phone interrupted his curt reply. She answered it with the same snappy authority that she brought to all her tasks. Singh hid a smile. If this kid was in charge, the streets would soon be spic-and-span, the children in school and the corrupt in jail.

She placed a hand over the mouthpiece and whispered, 'It's one of the men from the museum.'

Two vertical lines formed above Singh's nose when he remembered the handicapped booksellers. He had told Chhean to pass them a card with her phone number and not thought much about it since. It appeared that his forethought was about to provide dividends – either that or they had new titles that they were keen to flog.

She was still speaking in Khmer and he pointed at a hairy ear, indicating to her that he would appreciate some interpretation.

She motioned with her hand as if she was patting an imaginary, albeit large, dog. He assumed she was telling him to be patient and he shifted his weight from one foot to the other, trying to comply with her instructions but without much success.

At last, she held the phone away from her small ear and whispered, 'He – the one called Som – wants to see us. He says that he has good information but we will have to' – she was clearly quoting – '"buy a lot of books to get it".'

'How do we know he's telling the truth? I'm not interested in setting off on some wild-goose chase.' He meant it as well. It had suddenly occurred to the Sikh policeman that a cold Angkor beer would provide his brain cells with the necessary lubrication for an investigation.

She spoke into the phone briefly and then muttered the translation to Singh. 'If we do not like the information, we do not have to pay. We can be the *judge* – not him.' She added, her small nose wrinkled in confusion, 'He sounded very afraid but now he's laughing as if he has told a very funny joke.'

'Does he want us to come to the museum – now?' Singh reluctantly decided that he had nothing to lose by following up this lead. It was a starting point. Otherwise, Chhean would ask him what his plan was again and he would still be bereft of ideas.

'He is too afraid to see us at the museum. He will meet us at the killing fields in an hour.'

'Which one?' demanded Singh tartly.

Chhean snapped the phone shut and explained amicably, 'Choeng Ek. In Phnom Penh, when we say "killing fields", we mean Choeng Ek. Of course there are almost four hundred sites around Cambodia and more are found quite often.'

'Is Choeng Ek the one where Cheah Huon buried the dead? Where Samrin supervised the executions?'

She nodded.

'That's good. It will be useful to see the place. It might give us more of an understanding of the dead man. How long to get there?'

'Around forty-five minutes.'

'Well, let's get going then,' he snapped as if his companion made a practice of delaying him.

In the car, he leaned back and shut his eyes, wishing that there was less hooting and screeching and shouting in Cambodian traffic.

'Are you going to sleep?' asked Chhean suspiciously.

He raised one heavy eyelid and swivelled the eyeball to look at her. 'I'm thinking,' he said firmly.

She had a certain tenacity when it came to cross-examination. 'About what?'

If he was honest, he had been pondering whether to wait until he returned to the Cambodiana for his beer or if he dared stop at one of the small cafés that littered the side of the roads. He had no intention of being honest. 'It's none of your business,' he answered.

'I think she did it – Sovann, I mean. I think she murdered Huon.' Chhean was trying to be provocative but Singh was too sleepy to rise to the bait.

'It's possible,' he agreed.

'Did you see the body?'

He nodded, eyes still firmly shut, hoping it might dissuade further conversation.

'Was it – was it, you know, disgusting or scary?'

Suddenly his interpreter was a voyeur? 'Why do you want to know?' he asked sharply. The policeman always treated the dead with courtesy. With more courtesy than he treated anyone alive, Superintendent Chen had once remarked in disgust.

Chhean was looking at him as if he was mad. 'To see if it is likely that someone would touch the knife.' She shuddered. 'I don't think I would.'

Singh nodded thoughtfully. It was an interesting line of analysis, dealing as it did with the psychology of those involved. 'The wound was neat, not much blood. Someone like Sovann – with her experiences during the Khmer Rouge years – it's possible she might have had the courage to touch the knife. Especially if she thought he was still alive.' He continued, 'I still can't believe she thinks Cheah Huon murdered her father.'

'Do you think it's true?'

'We might never know,' responded Singh. 'In a sense it doesn't matter. Whether she was right or not – it still gives her a motive.'

'I never knew my father,' said Chhean quietly. 'I don't know who he was or what happened to him.'

Singh could find no response to this. His thoughts turned to the burly Sikh with the snowy white beard, his own father. That man had been such an enormous presence in his life – whether it was the ambition he had centred on his only son or feel of the back of his hand when Singh had failed to meet his expectations. There had been the rough edge of his tongue and the rare, almost endangered, words of praise. He had been cut down suddenly, a stroke caused by the fondness for beer that Singh had inherited. But it took only an instant to conjure him up in his mind's eye. Singh Sr was very much alive in the memory of his offspring. It was difficult to imagine growing up without such a presence, without a father.

Chhean sniffed and battled her way back to the matter at hand. 'It's very hard to guess what someone like Sovann would do. I don't understand her.'

Singh nodded – Sovann was certainly adept at playing the inscrutable oriental. He asked, 'Do you have the pathologist's number?'

'Of course.'

'Ring him, will you – I want to have a word with him.'

Chhean dialled the number while he considered his best approach to the rebellious young man. She handed him the phone and he took the small device in his large paw and held it to his ear.

'Kar Savuth, this is Inspector Singh from the Singapore police.'

'What can I do for you, inspector? Found another body?'

How did the fellow achieve such a flippant tone with so little effort? 'I want to talk to you about the autopsy report.'

'What about it?'

'Sovann Armstrong denies killing Cheah Huon.'

He cackled loudly, dismissive of even the possibility of innocence. 'You're kidding me, right?'

Did Savuth watch too many American movies or had he

been trained in the United States? 'No, I'm quite serious,' the policeman replied, injecting a note of gravitas into his voice to convince the disbelieving pathologist.

'She's obviously lying. Her fingerprints were all over that knife. They were a perfect match as well.'

'She claims to have found the body that night, the night of the murder. She says her fingerprints are on the knife because she tried to pull it out.'

'She's taking you for a ride, brother.' Gangster films, decided Singh. It was time to cut to the chase.

'I'd like you to re-examine the forensic evidence to see whether there is any possibility that her version of events might be true.'

'Tell me something, Inspector Singh – is Sovann Armstrong a beautiful woman?'

The policeman used his driest voice. 'I have no idea what you're insinuating, young man.'

There was a shout of laughter at the other end. 'Really *hot*, huh?'

'Are you going to look at the evidence again or do I have to inform Colonel Menhay that I do not have your full co-operation?'

'Colonel Menhay?' asked the doctor. 'I'd be surprised if he knew anything at all about your attempt to poke holes in his precious case.'

Kar Savuth was a smart kid as well, acknowledged Singh ruefully. 'Look, I agree she probably did it. All I'm asking is that you have a second look. You don't want an innocent woman to suffer any more than I do.'

'Especially if she's good-looking,' agreed Savuth.

Singh wondered if he was about to have a stroke like his father before him. Certainly, he could feel a vein pounding in his neck as his blood pressure went through the roof.

'All right, old man,' chuckled Savuth. 'Hold on to your hat – turban, I mean – I'll have another look.'

Singh had learnt to take the language of Cambodia in his stride. He used words like 'genocide' and 'crimes against humanity' easily. He knew 'S21' and 'Tuol Sleng prison' were one and the same. He talked of 'almost two million dead' as if he understood the numbers although his career had involved treating dead bodies as individuals, each one with an identity, a history and a right to justice. Now, their taxi was drawing up outside Choeng Ek, the 'killing fields' near Phnom Penh, and the evocative name did nothing to upset the policeman's composure. He had been in the country for no more than a week and he'd already come to terms with mass murder. Or so he thought.

The inspector scrambled out of the low-slung taxi with difficulty and glanced around. The muddy parking lot didn't have many cars in it. The tourists wandering towards the gates, clutching water bottles and badly-folded maps, were mostly white backpacker types. No surprise there. He didn't think there were many Asian visitors who would add a trip to a mass burial site to their itinerary – they were more likely to be scouring the markets looking for cheap silk and bargain-priced gemstones.

Chhean was paying the entrance fee – US dollars again – while Singh gingerly made his way across the muddy surface, avoiding an aggressive cockerel en route. He didn't know what to expect, hadn't put much thought into their destination except as the place where Huon had 'worked' and as their rendezvous point with the amputee. Now, as he stepped through the gates, his eyes were drawn inexorably to the massive white and glass *stupa* in the foreground. He took a few steps forward and almost bumped into a few Khmer women squatting on the ground, *kramas* tightly wound, feet politely folded away from him. They gestured at him to buy an incense stick. He breathed deeply; the scent was intoxicating.

'This *stupa* was built to commemorate the dead,' said Chhean.

He nodded. That was fairly obvious although he wasn't certain he liked the choice of structure. There was something of that familiar communist-meets-Khmer architecture about it – straight lines with a pointy gold roof.

As they got closer, Singh's breath caught in his throat. 'What are those things in the *stupa*?' he asked and his voice was hoarse with shock.

'Skulls,' replied Chhean succinctly. 'Skulls found on this site. About ten thousand so far.'

Singh stared up at the six-storey-high building, craning his neck so that he could see to the top of the glass structure. It was crammed with skulls. Most were damaged and cracked – Singh identified a few bullet holes and a lot of blunt instrument trauma; most of the victims had been clubbed to death. He sat down suddenly on a step. He was a murder investigator. He had seen it all before but never like this, on this scale.

'It is a shock to see this place for the first time,' agreed Chhean sympathetically.

'I don't know how Cambodia has survived.'

'That's why the war crimes tribunal is so important.'

Singh nodded – he could understand her point of view. These people needed some closure, some justice, perhaps some forgiveness if such a thing was possible.

'And that's why we have to find this murderer,' Chhean added.

Singh cracked his knuckles together. Did she think that he didn't understand the importance of finding the killer before the whole incident tainted the reputation of the tribunal? He could almost feel the weight of history on his burly shoulders.

The fat man got to his feet with difficulty. 'All right, where's this informant then?'

Chhean scanned the horizon carefully. 'Not here yet – or hiding. Let's walk about so that he can see us.'

There were tracks through the area and she set off at a slow pace along one of them. Singh lumbered after her like a bear on a lead. The whole compound was shady and quiet with a few sombre individuals drifting along the paths, stopping from time to time to read a small signpost describing a particular horror. The policeman looked around with interest. 'Where are the mass graves anyway? Under those sheds?' He indicated a couple of wooden constructions in the distance that were cordoned off with rope.

'Where are the graves?' she repeated in confusion.

'Yes.' He didn't understand Chhean – some of the time she was so quick off the mark she made him feel like an old man. At other times, like now, she stared at him blankly when he asked her a simple question.

She gestured with a broad sweep of her arm. 'All around you – these are all graves.'

Singh followed the arc of her arm with his eyes. They were in the middle of grassy undulating fields, dappled in sunshine. Huge rain trees spread their protecting branches overheard. It was quiet except for the underlying sound of insects; bees humming, crickets strumming and bird calls from the trees. The compound was sufficiently far from the main road that the ubiquitous third-world traffic noise of angry horns, two-stroke motorbike engines and screeching tyres was absent. Enormous numbers of black and orange butterflies were flitting about, adding to the sense of peace. With a sinking heart, Singh realised that what he had assumed was undulating ground, smooth round verdant cavities separated by grassy knolls, were actually excavation sites. The graves, having been exhumed, had quickly been reclaimed by the spreading grass. Quite possibly, the meadow was so lush because human remains had fertilised it over the years.

'Over that way they are still digging.'

A minor building site with exposed ground and earth-moving machinery was actually an exhumation in progress, realised Singh.

'Where in the world is Som?' he asked, his angry tone a thin disguise for his distress.

'There!' shouted Chhean, attracting a few surprised, annoyed glances.

Singh saw that the man from the museum was making his way slowly towards the main entrance, placing his crutches with care so as not to fall over on the uneven surface. He had not seen them yet. Singh decided a more circumspect approach was merited. A full-frontal assault might have one of two undesirable consequences: either Som would be frightened into having second thoughts about divulging his information or he would jack up his price when he sensed their enthusiasm. This was assuming that he had something to tell them in the first place and hadn't just needed to make a fast buck from innuendo and falsehood. Still, what was it that Som had told Chhean – they could be the judge of his information? It sounded like he had something and, furthermore, from his choice of meeting point, that he was afraid. Singh led the way, taking a circular route that kept them out of the informant's direct line of sight. Chhean followed him, almost treading on his heels in her hurry to get to Som.

A large four-wheel drive with blacked-out windows drove into the car park. An unusual visitor, thought Singh – he wouldn't have expected many, or any, of Cambodia's elite to make pilgrimages to this site. The vehicle headed closer to the entrance. Singh almost smiled. It was such a *kiasu* approach, as one might have said in Singapore, eschewing wide open spaces to try and find a parking lot closest to the destination.

Som had noticed the vehicle as well because he paused to let it pass. Everyone in Cambodia knew intuitively who took precedence in everyday life.

The vehicle stopped a few feet away from the amputee. Singh, who would have trusted his instincts with his life, felt a sudden overwhelming sense of foreboding. He abandoned his surreptitious approach and hurried forward, shouting to Som, waving his arms, trying to attract his attention. He realised what had filled him with intuitive dread. The four-wheel drive didn't have number plates.

Everything after that happened in slow motion. Som turned to face Singh. He leaned on a crutch and waved a hand in acknowledgement, his face splitting into a broad grin. The policeman broke into a run, moving quickly for a man of his size. Behind him, he heard Chhean calling after him, surprised by his sudden movement.

The front left-hand tinted window of the four-wheel drive wound down with the even pace of an electronic device. A swarthy man in dark sunglasses leaned out, an elbow resting on the edge. He called – Singh heard him – 'Som!'

The amputee turned around. The man slung an AK-47 – even from a hundred metres away Singh recognised the wooden stock and curved ammunition cartridge – over the sill. Without pausing, ignoring Som's sudden panicked cry for help as he realised what was about to happen, the man opened fire. Within seconds, although it felt a lot longer to Singh, who was still running, hadn't stopped running, the man retreated into the vehicle and sped off, spitting gravel into the air.

Singh reached the spot. The amputee was lying on the ground, his body a network of bullet holes. Blood flowed from Som's body through the cracks and crevices on the ground like minor tributaries from a great river.

He was quite, quite dead.

Singh squatted down on his haunches next to the body. He covered his face in his hands. He could hear screaming but it seemed to come from a long way away. It appeared that Som's information was very valuable indeed. It had just cost him his life.

Thirteen

'You were only gone for a couple of hours,' complained Colonel Menhay. 'And you managed to get some poor bastard killed.'

Singh felt a sudden childish urge to stick his fingers into his ears – to block out the criticism from the colonel. More importantly, to try and shut out the echoes of Som's screams when he had seen the machine gun, screams that were first drowned out and then silenced by the rapid fire of the weapon. The policeman feared that it would take quite some time before he could put that animal sound of terror behind him.

He tried to focus on the here and now, to put Som's death out of his mind except as a case to be solved. He was a policeman – he needed to pull himself together. Unfortunately, the cold hard reality was that he, Singh, murder expert, had never actually seen anyone killed before. His role was to arrive at the scene of death in the aftermath, ready to take charge and play the hero. To be there at the kill had been a stomach-churning experience and one he didn't want repeated – ever.

His thoughts turned to Sovann and how she had explained her composed behaviour when confronted with Huon's corpse; that she had seen too much death, too much dying, to be knocked out of kilter by such a discovery. Well, he had seen death, but seeing the dying was a quite different experience. He dragged himself back to the matter at hand. 'Som must have had important information about Huon.'

'Possibly,' agreed Menhay. 'But even informants have enemies.'

'You're suggesting he might have been killed for something unrelated to the Huon investigation?'

'We should not ignore any possibilities.'

'Really – do you want me to take into account the possibility that he was killed by little green men from Mars?'

Menhay appeared unmoved by the lame attempt at sarcasm. 'Your eye-witness testimony seems to exclude that possibility,' he remarked.

Singh had described as fully as he could the dark vehicle with the tinted glass, the missing plates and the swarthy man, his features in shadows, his eyes hidden behind shades, his hands gloved. It had been hopeless and he knew it. On the quiet drive back to the police station, he had counted half a dozen vehicles and even more men who fitted that description. 'Som called us, we agreed to meet,' he insisted stubbornly. 'Someone killed him before he could divulge what he knew. There's a connection to this case, I guarantee it.'

Menhay steepled his fingers and peered at Singh over the

top. 'Even if I agree,' he said, 'what do you want me to do about it?'

'Trace the weapon?'

Menhay laughed out loud, a sudden crack with no humour in it. 'This country is awash with AK-47s. That gun is in a ditch somewhere, not resting by our killer's bedside table.'

There wasn't much Singh could do to contradict Menhay's analysis. He glanced at Chhean. She was sitting on a chair in a corner of the room, her eyes huge and dark in a pale face. She had been violently sick when she saw Som's body, riddled with holes like a sieve. Apparently, bullets were no longer scarce in Cambodia. Fortunately, she had the good sense to make a dash for the bushes beforehand and hadn't contaminated the scene. Not that there appeared to be much information to be derived from the body or the vicinity of the crime.

'I'm sure it was a contract killing anyway,' added the colonel. His jaw clenched. 'Probably, it was an off-duty policeman. Anyway, there won't be any traceable link between the killer and whoever ordered the hit.'

No traceable link. A small part of Singh was convinced that Menhay wasn't trying hard enough, throwing up obstacles instead of thinking of ways to further the investigation. Mostly, he understood that the colonel was just being honest with him. The inspector scratched his beard directly under his lower lip – it always itched when he was feeling the pressure. There were no leads. That was the reality. Som had been killed and it looked like whoever did it was going to get away with murder. His only hope was to prove a link to the killing of Huon – and trace the murderer, and his master, that way.

'Where is Sovann?' he asked.

'Still in the lock-up.'

'And you don't think that Som's death changes anything?'

'I don't think it wipes her fingerprints from the murder weapon – no.' Menhay added in a resolute voice, 'Tomorrow, I'm going to charge her with Huon's murder. That's it. Case closed. The Cambodian police force would like to extend its thanks to our ASEAN colleagues from Singapore for their assistance.'

Singh ground his teeth with frustration. He wondered whether it was audible to the other man. At this rate, he'd soon be down to yellow stumps like the rest of the population. This Cambodian colonel was like a piece of granite, immovable from his position. But if Menhay thought that he was going to accept his diktat, he was in for a nasty surprise. A sudden recollection of his secondary school physics gave the inspector some comfort. What was it the cigarette-smoking, chalk-throwing Mr Wong used to say – moving an object was not a question of mass but of leverage? Very well, he knew what he was looking for now – some, any, leverage. He spared a last thought for Som. The killing fields of Choeng Ek – what a place to die.

The next morning, Singh was awoken from a troubled sleep by his telephone ringing. He dragged himself upright with difficulty, propping the pillow up behind him. His muscles were stiff with shock at the events of the previous day: a disconcerting similarity to the dead man, thought Singh, who was presumably in an advanced state of *rigor mortis* by now. The hotel room was in pitch darkness but that could be a consequence of the heavy curtains which excluded all light. He was so disorientated by recent events that it could be high noon for all he knew.

Singh fumbled for the phone while glancing at the luminous digital clock on the bedside table. It was only seven a.m – who would call him at that hour? He really, really hoped it wasn't his wife with news of the death, from natural causes, of some distant elderly relative by marriage. He wasn't in the mood to give a damn about peaceful deaths at an advanced age. Not here in Cambodia.

He picked up the receiver reluctantly. The voice at the other end was young and excited. 'Inspector Singh – is that you? Are you awake?'

What sort of question was that to ask a person after ringing them at dawn? wondered Singh. He snapped, 'Who is this?'

'Kar Savuth – the pathologist on the Huon case.'

He should have recognised the high-pitched voice at once. It was the absence of the usual underlying snideness which had thrown him off the scent. Perhaps Savuth's customary bad attitude, like Singh's powers of deduction, only kicked in after his third cup of coffee.

'What do you want?' he grunted. He was a fat, turban-less man who had slept badly. Savuth had better have a good reason for calling so early or he was going to get an earful from Singh. The inspector was not a morning person at the best of times, his wife would testify to that.

'You remember you asked me to have another look at the fingerprint evidence?'

'Yes.' He tried to inject a note of regret into the single

191

word. He certainly wouldn't have asked for a second opinion if he had known that it would arrive with the sun.

'The fingerprints belong to Sovann Armstrong. I double-checked.'

'Tell me something I don't know,' he growled.

'Angle of entry!'

'What?'

'The angle of entry of the knife – the knife went straight in. A horizontal line.' Savuth's voice was no more than a squeak of excitement now.

'What in God's name are you talking about?' Singh scratched his head with blunt fingers since he hadn't put his turban on yet. It made a change from scratching his beard but it still reflected a state of increased aggravation.

'The deceased was five feet and five inches tall. I would estimate that Sovann Armstrong is about five foot and two inches tall.'

'Is this a height competition? If I take part am I allowed to wear my turban?'

The pathologist greeted this remark with a gale of laughter. Singh held the receiver away from his ear and missed the rest of Savuth's explanation on the relevance of height differentials. He was waking up slowly although his eyes were almost caked shut with early-morning grime, a sure sign of a very disturbed sleep. He suddenly remembered his recurrent nightmare – it was him that had been shot instead of Som, the pattern of holes on his body like a constellation of stars at night. However, instead of blood, he had oozed disgusting yellow sticky fat from the wounds. He had woken up in a cold sweat with the voice of Dr Maniam ringing in his ears – the

Singapore pathologist explaining to his giggling colleagues that he had feared what would happen if the inspector didn't go on a diet.

Singh shuddered and turned his attention back to Savuth. 'What's that you said? I missed it,' he barked.

He listened to the pathologist with growing interest, nodding his head repeatedly, forgetting his unpleasant dreams. 'That's very interesting,' he said at last. 'I'll explain to Menhay and call you at some point – I suspect he'll think I made the whole thing up.'

Singh put the phone down, clambered to his feet, tied his sarong more tightly around his waist and walked to the sink where he splashed cold water over his face. He needed to be sure that he was awake and not in the throes of another bizarre dream. He thought about what the young man had said – it was a fascinating theory, capable of any number of alternative explanations, of course, but still suggestive. Singh was prepared to rely on a bit of conjecture if it supported his paradigm. Often it came to nothing, but once in a while it was the loose thread from which he could unravel an entire mystery.

His teeth brushed, his shirt pocket well supplied with pens, his turban tightly wound around his head, Singh presented himself at Colonel Menhay's office like a schoolboy looking for approval. The colonel was unprepared for good cheer from the Sikh inspector whom he had last seen dragging himself back to the hotel; shaken by Som's shooting and angry at Menhay for refusing to see the incident as an indication of Sovann's possible innocence.

'Why are you in such a good mood?' queried Menhay.

'Another day, new ideas, new avenues for investigation . . .' explained Singh with a broad smile.

'Let's hope some of your "new avenues" live long enough to see "another day",' said Menhay and then felt a stab of guilt at the shadow that flitted across the fat man's face. It was unnecessary to remind this desk jockey masquerading as a murder cop of the events of the previous day. Menhay had first seen someone gunned down in cold blood so long ago that the memory of that incident had faded. It dated from when he had heeded Sihanouk's call and fled into the jungles to join Pol Pot's revolutionary forces. He had been an idealistic young man, real fire in his belly for taking on the American puppet government in Phnom Penh.

In some ways, he was still puzzled by the fact that he had not been swept away by Brother No. 1's revolutionary ideology. He had been precisely the sort of young man who soon lost sight of the cruelty of the means in a zealot's conviction of the worthiness of the ends. Looking back, he decided that it had been the simple kindness his Buddhist mother had always shown to all creatures: four-legged, two-legged, winged. He had never been able to see his fellow Khmer as just ciphers in a grand strategy. They had been people to him, individuals, and he had seen their pain and felt their suffering. So he had risked death and torture to flee to Southern Vietnam and join the small band of exiled Cambodian soldiers, biding his time, waiting for an opportunity to avenge his people. And his moment had come. He had been part of the army that liberated Phnom Penh. It had been too late to save his mother or the rest of his brothers and sisters. They had all perished of disease and starvation. Seven of them. A neighbour had told him that his mother had always believed that he would return in triumph to save them. She had waited as long as she could but he had not been in time.

'What are you thinking about?' demanded Singh. 'Have you had any leads?'

Menhay shook his head, hoping the other man could not see that his eyes were wet. That would be very embarrassing indeed, especially as he had just been mentally mocking the Sikh for not being sufficiently hardened, despite his job title, to the reality of murder. He said firmly, 'I thought I told you it was "case closed"?'

'I had a call from Savuth this morning.'

'The pathologist? What did he want?'

'He looked at the forensic evidence again.'

'Why would he do that?' Menhay's glance was as sharp as a well-honed knife.

'Er . . . I asked him to – just to be on the safe side.'

'You're still trying to save Sovann – even though she gave us the motive out of her own mouth?' Menhay felt a sudden weariness sweep through his body. How dogmatic could this policeman be?

'Savuth says that the angle of entry of the knife was horizontal – it went in perfectly straight.'

'So?'

'Sovann Armstrong was only slightly shorter than Huon. If she stabbed him, her arm would have been higher than his chest. To inflict a wound to the heart, the angle of entry would have been sharply downwards.'

195

Menhay, elbows on the table, buried his face in his hands.

The fat policeman stood up and mimicked a downward stabbing action. 'You see? Her blow would have been much less straight.'

'Or he slipped, or his false leg fell off, or he stood on tip-toes or he was lying on the ground or she jumped at him.' Menhay was gob-smacked that the policeman from Singapore was prepared to rely on such tenuous evidence. This was less credible than the wisdom dispensed by Cambodian witchdoctors.

'Look, I agree there are a hundred alternative explanations,' said Singh. 'But what Kar Savuth has done is given you one that is consistent with Sovann's innocence, not her guilt.'

Menhay was silent and the other man read it as an invitation to continue. 'I don't know Sovann Armstrong very well. But my instincts tell me that she is not the sort to commit murder. She's more like one of those long-suffering types with enormous quiet strength of character.'

The colonel was suddenly thoughtful. The way Singh described Sovann Armstrong reminded him of his own mother of whom he had been thinking just a few short minutes ago. She had not been beautiful like Sovann, a plain-faced sturdy woman carrying the produce of their small plot of land to market every day. But she too had been a kindly woman with quiet strength. She would never have murdered someone – not in cold blood.

'Maybe you're right,' he admitted grudgingly. 'You should keep sniffing around.'

Singh smiled broadly.

'But no more bodies,' warned Menhay and received an

agreeable nod as if it was within the Sikh's powers to prevent any further killings.

The telephone on his desk rang and the colonel answered it. In a few seconds he hung up and crossed his eyes at the inspector, feeling much more charitable towards him upon the appearance of a common enemy. 'It's Adnan Muhammad, he wants to see us.'

Adnan Muhammad had been placed in a small waiting room with slightly cleaner walls than those in the interview room. Despite this, his expression was that of a fastidious man who was offended by his surroundings. The appearance of Singh and Menhay did not seem to improve his mood. Chhean, who had caught up with the policemen after another few thankless hours trawling through documents, was not sure she entirely blamed him. The two men together reinforced the first impression of each – that they were stubborn men who found it difficult to knuckle down before authority, especially as represented by the mouthpieces of multi-lateral organisations.

Adnan attempted a smile which reminded Chhean of the expression on a child's face when it bites into something sour.

'How is it going, gentlemen?'

The quick shrug of the shoulders from both men, in unison like heavy-set synchronised swimmers, appeared to annoy him. His nostrils flared slightly but he persevered. 'I heard you made an arrest yesterday.'

That was not exactly a secret, thought Chhean dismissively. The morning's newspapers were filled with details of the colourful raid on the Raffles Le Royal the previous day. The editorials were in two minds whether this was a spectacular success by the Cambodian police or a spectacular cock-up. She glanced at the two policemen – they represented both viewpoints.

Menhay nodded woodenly in response. 'Yes, we have arrested a woman – a Cambodian American. We are considering pressing charges.' He glanced at the inspector, who was looking at him pleadingly. 'We need a bit more time to tie up loose ends.'

Chhean sensed rather than saw the tension go out of the fat man. He was still hoping there was another solution.

If Adnan was impressed that the investigation had already resulted in an arrest, he hid it well. 'Interesting,' he mused. 'I would not have thought this was a woman's crime.'

Menhay read criticism into his words and bristled. 'A woman could have struck the blow, the pathologist confirmed it.'

Chhean noticed that Singh had shuffled backwards until he found himself leaning against the far wall. He lit a cigarette and watched proceedings carefully. He reminded Chhean of a bouncer in a karaoke lounge keeping an eye on a situation that had the potential to escalate into trouble.

'I don't doubt you . . . or the pathologist for a moment,' said Adnan, his thin smile suggesting exactly the opposite.

'What is it that you want?' interrupted Singh.

Chhean guessed that Singh was tired of the game, whatever it was, that the UN man was playing. As was she – Adnan Muhammad was like a card sharp with an ace up the sleeve of his expensive striped shirt. Scrutinising him from head to foot, Chhean decided that she had never previously seen such a well-dressed man in Cambodia. Cambodia's wealthy preferred their girth, rather than their clothes, to show their affluence. The children of the well-heeled adopted a flashier look altogether – black suits and black silk shirts.

'Inspector Singh – I am so pleased to see that you have taken your assignment to heart and are assisting the Cambodian police in their efforts.'

Chhean decided she liked his accent. He sounded like a newsreader from the BBC.

The fat policeman grunted and the thin line of ash at the point of his cigarette broke off and fell to the ground. Singh scattered it carefully with the toe of his sneaker, adding an indistinguishable layer to the grimy floor. She was sure he was being intentionally gross in his habits to offend the fussy bureaucrat.

'I have heard more about you from the Singapore authorities and realise how lucky we are to have you on board.'

Adnan wasn't even pretending that he meant it. He hadn't liked what he had heard and he was letting the inspector know it.

Singh grinned suddenly, like a satyr. Chhean guessed that he wouldn't have expected glowing reviews from his bosses so he wasn't disappointed. 'It's always good to know that the higher-ups are on the same side as the grunts.'

Chhean looked at the two men curiously. There was a power struggle going on but it was impossible to tell who was winning or what was at stake. She glanced at Singh. He looked indifferent to the barbs of the other man but she sensed an underlying tension. He too knew that this was more than a courtesy call by Adnan.

'There was another killing yesterday.'

Chhean was reluctantly impressed. The UN man had his ear to the ground if he already knew about Som's murder. It had not been in the newspapers that morning. She wondered where his information was from – a policeman or a journalist?

'Does it have anything to do with this case?' he continued.

'Yes,' said Singh. 'No,' said Menhay almost simultaneously.

Adnan's already thin lips formed a single straight line. 'It's good to see that cooperation between ASEAN nations is its usual triumph.'

Silence greeted this remark while the policemen glowered at each other like two bullies seeking mastery of the playground.

Adnan changed the subject abruptly. 'Do you think this woman killed Huon?' The question was snapped at Singh.

'It's possible. I think the situation merits further investigation,' replied Singh evenly under Menhay's watchful gaze.

'And you?' This time the question was directed at the colonel like a guided missile.

'The evidence is clear – but we will keep looking into it.'

'The evidence is clear – that's good to know. Has there been a confession?' Adnan asked the question as if he was seeking the time of day from a stranger – courteous yet distant.

Menhay shook his head. His short neck meant that his chin appeared to swivel on the mid-point between his shoulders. It was the robotic gesture of a man trying, and failing, to keep his antagonism from showing.

'That's just as well really . . .' Adnan smiled thinly, 'as someone *else* has confessed to the murder.'

Fourteen

Adnan Muhammad's face was impassive but all of them sensed his satisfaction at their combined incredulity.

'It's the husband,' he explained. 'Jeremy Armstrong.'

'The husband? Of Sovann?' Menhay's face was creased like an over-ripe mango.

'Yes,' said the UN man with an air of great patience which was patently false.

Singh was blunt. 'He's trying to protect his wife.'

Menhay nodded immediately, quick to seize an explanation that did not exonerate Sovann. 'Of course, that's it!'

'Not that we are convinced that Sovann is the murderer,' said Singh warningly. 'We're still examining the evidence.'

'Armstrong knew that this would be your attitude. That's why he came to me. Also, he was afraid of the methods you might use to force him to recant – or to compel his wife to confess.' Adnan had resumed his usual patronising tone but for once neither of the cops was offended. They were both grappling with the suggestion that Jeremy Armstrong was the killer. Singh turned the idea around in his head like a cricketer examining the state of the ball.

Menhay was defensive. 'The suspects have been treated with great respect.'

'I'm not accusing you of anything, Colonel Menhay. Everyone knows you try and follow the letter of the law. Some of your colleagues are not so . . . procedurally stringent.'

Why did Adnan speak as if his reading pleasure was derived entirely from dictionaries? 'What exactly did Jeremy Armstrong say?' demanded Singh.

'This is his statement, which he has also released to the press.'

He handed over a neatly typed sheet to Singh. Singh read it quickly and gave it to the colonel, who was champing at the bit to get his hands on the document.

'I, Jeremy Armstrong, hereby confess to the murder of Cheah Huon by stabbing him to death at the war crimes tribunal premises.' It was signed and dated in black ink with a firm hand. There was nothing equivocal about the decision to confess if the handwriting was any evidence.

'This is completely unconvincing,' said Singh firmly. 'There is no explanation as to why he would take it into his head to kill this man. I've seen it before – a confession to a crime that a loved one is accused of committing. This is a complication, not a solution!'

'He's waiting for us outside,' said Adnan unexpectedly. 'He knew you would take this attitude so he has come to convince you himself. He just needs reassurance that some of what he tells you does not get back to his wife.'

'Nobody tells me what I can say,' exclaimed Menhay.

Singh waved a plump hand at the colonel. 'Let's see what he has to tell us – he might shed some light on the case whether he killed Cheah Huon or not.'

'You're right. If he's confessed to protect his wife – that means he thinks his wife did it.' Menhay jabbed a blunt finger into Singh's chest. 'Which means you are the only person in the whole of Cambodia who believes that Sovann Armstrong is innocent.'

Singh grunted. It was certainly disheartening that even the spouse of this woman was convinced she had done it.

Adnan slipped out of the room and returned a few minutes later with the large American in tow. Jeremy Armstrong shuffled in sheepishly and stood before them with hunched shoulders and big feet close together. His body language suggested embarrassment rather than guilt.

Singh looked at him curiously. It was a big step to take, to confess to murder. He must know the evidence against his wife was compelling – news of the fingerprints had made it to the newspapers. On the other hand, he wasn't giving the police much time to find an alternative suspect. Why was he so convinced of her guilt? Did he know something they didn't? Or had he actually killed Huon?

'You guys mind if I sit down?' asked Armstrong. He spoke with a gentle drawl and his voice was both quiet and soothing. He sounded as if he was asking whether he could join a party of acquaintances at a pub.

Menhay indicated a chair and the husband of Sovann lowered himself into it carefully and ran a hand through his white-blond thinning hair. His face was flushed unhealthily but his pale-blue eyes met theirs without hesitation.

'I'm sorry I went to the UN instead of directly to the cops,' he said politely, directing his remarks at Menhay after a quick puzzled glance at Singh. He did not explain his decision and the colonel did not press him. It was self-evident after all. Armstrong needed people in authority to know where he was – so that he didn't disappear forever into the bowels of a Cambodian prison.

'This is yours?' asked Singh, waving the confession at him as if it was a lottery ticket.

'Yes.' Armstrong cut to the chase immediately. 'I killed Cheah Huon, the witness at the ECCC.'

Singh was almost admiring of his sheer gall.

'I would be really grateful if you would release my wife from custody immediately.' His tone became urgent. 'There is no reason for you to keep her any longer.'

'Why should we believe you?'

Armstrong turned to look at Singh. 'Why shouldn't you? Who would confess to a murder he didn't commit?'

'Someone who was trying to protect his wife, of course,' interjected Menhay.

Armstrong smiled rather sadly. 'I suppose I should be honoured that you think I have such a capacity for self-sacrifice. I'll be frank with you,' he continued, leaning forward as if he had secrets to impart. 'I probably would have kept my mouth shut about what I'd done if you hadn't arrested my wife. But I can't let her suffer for my actions.'

'But why would you kill him?'

'Didn't my wife explain that he was the Khmer Rouge cadre who murdered her father?'

'So you were taking revenge on her behalf?' Singh's tone was highly sceptical. He tried to imagine himself leaping into the breach and killing someone on behalf of Mrs Singh. It was unthinkable. Besides, the only person she occasionally wanted dead was him. He snapped at Armstrong, 'Is that the latest recipe for a happy marriage – one murder before bedtime?'

Armstrong leaned back in his chair and pressed a hand against his cheek as if he had a toothache or his neuralgia was kicking in with stress. 'I knew you'd have trouble believing me. But I swear to you, I killed that bastard – and he deserved to die.'

There was no mistaking the anger in his voice when referring to Huon. Singh remembered that Sovann had expressed the same rage. Could they have worked together?

'Why kill him?' he asked.

'Huon wouldn't have faced any consequences, would he? Only the head honchos of the Khmer Rouge are being tried. Men like Huon and Ta Ieng, who deserve to die a hundred times, are free to live their lives as they choose despite the people they destroyed.'

Singh watched the other man carefully. He was speaking in general terms but his anger was for his wife and it was genuine and intense. Could he really have done it?

'How?' the colonel asked. 'How did you kill him?'

'I went to find him – I stopped at the kitchen and picked up a large kitchen knife.'

'So this was pre-meditated? You meant to kill him?'

'I don't think I'd made up my mind, you know what I mean? I intended to confront the son of a bitch, that's for sure. . . .' He fell silent as if he was remembering subsequent events but reluctant to divulge them.

'What happened next?' demanded Menhay impatiently. Singh glanced at him. His expression was one of irritation rather than interest. He didn't believe this man. He was still convinced Sovann was the murderer. But he knew he had to hear Armstrong out – if for no other reason than that Adnan Muhammad was still in the room, a quiet, brooding presence.

'We had an argument. Huon denied being Khmer Rouge at first. When I persisted, he finally confessed. He laughed at me – can you believe it? He said there was nothing I could do, nothing at all.' Armstrong clasped his hands together as if in prayer. 'I got mad – the knife was stuck into the back of my trousers. I pulled it out and stabbed him.' He shrugged and said defiantly. 'I don't have one single moment of regret.'

The narrative was consistent with the evidence which had been in the newspapers but failed to explain the curious knife angle. Singh scowled. It was one thing to use the unexpected forensic detail as evidence that Sovann was innocent, it was quite another thing to exonerate everyone over five feet in height as a possible killer. He decided reluctantly that there was probably an explanation for the angle of entry that was unrelated to the height of the killer. Perhaps whoever it was played lawn bowls rather than cricket and preferred an underarm action. If this American really was the killer, he probably spent every Friday at a bowling alley rather than playing baseball.

'Does your wife know of your confession?' he demanded abruptly.

There was a brief shake of the head from Armstrong. 'I haven't been allowed to see her.'

'She's going to be very upset.'

'I hope she'll understand why I did it.'

'Which is more than we do,' insisted the fat man. 'Nothing you've said convinces me or my colleague here that you killed Huon. I think you're just protecting your wife. It's very charming, of course,' he added sarcastically. 'Maybe someone will make a film about it but it's just a big waste of police time!'

Armstrong sighed. 'I knew you'd feel this way and I can't say I blame you. But what you don't understand is that I owe my wife – I owe Cambodia – a reckoning. This was my payback. Killing Huon was my payback.'

'What the hell are you talking about?' Menhay's right knee was bouncing up and down with aggravation as he listened to this elliptical justification.

'What I'm about to tell you – can you guys swear not to tell my wife?'

'Why?' It was Singh who snapped the question.

'It would destroy her . . .' There were tears in his eyes. Singh was taken aback by this sudden show of emotion from a man who had confessed to murder without batting an eyelid.

'We can't make a deal like that,' explained Menhay in an almost kindly tone. He must have noted the other man's distress as well and didn't have the heart to exploit it. 'However, we will not reveal the secret if it is not necessary to the investigation. That is the best offer I can make you.'

'And if I refuse to tell you without your promise?'

'If you refuse to tell me, I will charge you with obstruction of justice – and Sovann with the murder. Perhaps, if you are lucky, you might get cells that are side by side.'

Singh nodded approvingly. The colonel had leverage and

he was not afraid to use it. Adnan stirred slightly but did not interfere.

Armstrong folded his arms. It should have indicated solidity of purpose. It came across as defensive. The American was afraid – not of spending the rest of his life in jail but of his long-held secret getting back to his wife. Singh was on tenterhooks.

'You don't know this but I've worked with Cambodian refugees since as far back as 1979. The original trickle to the US turned into a flood and I helped out with resettlement, counselling and now the gathering of witness testimony for the tribunal.'

His words were met with silence. Singh had no idea where this was going but he was prepared to wait and see.

'I met my wife at a refugee centre. When she arrived from Cambodia, Sovann was fifteen years old and could not or would not speak. Not a single word. She had witnessed her father murdered and lost the rest of her family to famine and disease.'

Singh nodded. It was not an unusual tale in this most unusual of nations.

'I worked with her for a long time. Finally, when I had just about given up hope that I would ever get through to her, she learnt to trust me. I guess she started to care for me just a little bit and one day – I still remember the moment – she began to speak again. She told me that her family had fled rural Cambodia because of the American bombings – two of her grandparents and a young brother were killed. They moved to Phnom Penh as refugees, living on the edge of town, until they were kicked out by the Khmer Rouge and . . . well, I think you know the rest.'

'It doesn't explain why you would kill a man for your wife's sake – or for Cambodia's.' The last few words were spoken by Menhay with all the disgust of a true patriot for a foreigner's claim to involvement.

'We were married a few years later – she was nineteen and just about able to begin a new life. You've got to understand, there was no way she could forget the past but at least she saw a future too.'

'What is the secret that you don't want your wife to know?' Menhay smacked the table in accompaniment to each heavily emphasised word. Obviously, thought Singh, smiling slightly, the colonel was not a romantic.

'I was a B-52 bomber pilot with the US Air Force. I flew hundreds of sorties over Cambodia in the seventies, during Kissinger's secret war.'

Adnan had left. Armstrong had been taken to a holding cell to kick his heels and, as Menhay put it, reconsider his decision to commit perjury. He refused to release Sovann despite the confession. Menhay was leaning against a grubby wall, a pensive expression on his face. Chhean sat unobtrusively at the back of the room, watching the policemen and contemplating what Armstrong had said.

'A B-52 pilot,' muttered Menhay. 'By some estimates, the Americans killed over two hundred thousand Cambodians in Operation Menu.'

'Menu?' asked Singh.

'Each attack had a different code, Breakfast, Lunch, Dinner . . .'

The fat man paced up and down like a clockwork toy. It

was an unusually active display from the policeman who preferred to sit like the Buddha with his hands clasped lovingly
over his ample belly. Chhean suspected it reflected his mental
turmoil at events.

'Why?' he demanded. 'Why did they attack Cambodia?'

Menhay gestured with open palms. 'They claimed to be
chasing Viet Cong . . . they lied to the press and the US
Congress.' The muscles in his neck were taut. 'It was years
before the true scale of the bombing became known.'

Singh stopped marching up and down and faced them
squarely although he did not sit down. He raised one hand
and started ticking off suspects on his fingers. 'OK, let's start
at the beginning. We have Sovann – good motive and good
forensic evidence of fingerprints but some doubt about angle
of knife entry.'

Menhay snorted like an angry bull but Singh ignored him.

'Second, the husband, Jeremy Armstrong – based on his
confession.'

'To protect his wife,' insisted Menhay.

'I almost agree with you. But Armstrong's carrying an enormous load of guilt over his role in Cambodia's bloody past. He's
devoted his whole life to making amends to the people of
Cambodia while keeping this secret from his wife. He might
really have felt that killing Huon would give him some sort of
absolution.'

'How he must suffer to think that the woman he loves
might find out that he has Cambodian blood on his hands.'
This was Chhean. She blinked to keep the tears back.

'That's not sufficient punishment for what he did,' growled
Menhay.

'He was just following orders,' said Chhean.

'Funny,' said Singh. 'That's exactly what Ta Ieng said at the trial.'

There was a thick silence in the room like a heavy fog as they each remembered the testimony of Ta Ieng: torturer, executioner, child killer. Just following orders.

'Do you think that he's right? That Sovann would not forgive him if she ever found out about his past?' Chhean was frowning, trying to decide how she would act, or react, in the same position. Jeremy Armstrong had been a young pilot – not a cold-blooded killer. And he had worked his whole life to make up for what he had done.

Singh shrugged. 'He can't forgive himself – I don't suppose she would either.'

'You were a child then, Chhean. If you had seen the flattened countryside, the burning villages, the screaming children and the silent adults – well, I don't think you would forgive either.' Menhay spoke with enormous intensity.

Chhean could almost hear the heavy drone of the bomber engines in the silence after the colonel's description.

It was Menhay who dragged them back to the matter at hand. 'What else do we have?'

'Som – shot to death – who had something to tell us about a rich man in a Mercedes-Benz with a fondness for books.'

'What could it mean?' asked Chhean desperately, trying to forget the past and concentrate on the present. 'There must be some connection!'

The fat man raised his shoulders until they were almost brushing his ears. 'It could be any number of things but my best guess is that Huon was being paid to do something, to say something . . .'

'Or *not* to say something,' suggested Menhay.

Singh's eyebrows shot up with interest. 'Paid to leave something or someone out of his testimony?'

'Quite possibly – he might know of an ex-Khmer Rouge in a position of power.'

'Who paid him to keep quiet about it? And perhaps eventually killed him?' Singh was excited now. 'Any sign of extra money in Huon's bank accounts?'

'He didn't have a bank account,' remarked Menhay, dryly reminding the inspector that they were in Cambodia, not organised Singapore. 'If there was any money lying around the room he stayed in, there was no mention of it in the report.'

All the occupants of the room refrained from pointing out that the cops tasked with searching the premises might have trousered any cash.

'What about that thick gold chain around his neck that Savuth mentioned?' pointed out Singh.

'That could certainly be a down payment,' agreed Menhay.

'Cambodians prefer to keep their savings in gold because of the time when Pol Pot banned money,' explained Chhean.

'What else do we have?' It was Singh with the question.

'I went to see Samrin,' answered Menhay. 'It is possible that he was behind the killing. If the war crimes tribunal is thrown into disrepute – or the trial postponed or cancelled – he might be released. Already there are some who are calling for an end to the ECCC since even the witnesses are not safe. They claim that the whole institution has been degraded.'

'Could he organise a hit from prison?'

'Sure – the shadow of the Khmer Rouge is long and dark. Many people believe that it is wrong to try these men in the first place. Samrin himself told me he was a patriot.'

'What did he say when you accused him of murder?'

'As a man on trial for mass murder, it didn't seem to bother him much that we were trying to pin another killing on him.'

The sharp ring of the old-fashioned telephone distracted them from their speculations.

'It better not be Adnan with some other confession,' grumbled Menhay to no one in particular as he reached for the receiver. He listened for a while, barked a few sharp sentences in Khmer – he is arranging to meet someone, whispered Chhean to Singh – and slammed the phone down. There were white rings under his eyes and around his mouth that contrasted sharply with his ruddy face. 'One of my contacts wants to see me – about this case,' he said.

'Did he say what it was about?'

'No – just that I would owe him a favour and he would not forget to collect.'

Singh was familiar with the world of police informants. The 'you scratch my back, I scratch yours' arrangements that were often entered into and sometimes regretted. These people were an important source of information from an underworld to which the police had no access otherwise. On the other hand, it made for some pretty unsavoury encounters. What was the expression – politics makes strange bedfellows? So did murder investigations.

'Shall we come along?' asked Singh.

'You must be joking,' retorted Menhay. 'Do you think I want this guy gunned down as well?'

Chhean winced – she had almost been able to put the images out of her mind. Now Menhay's words brought back the events of yesterday – Som walking towards them and then shot in cold blood.

Singh was huffy. 'Well, what do you want us to do in the meantime?'

It was clear from his expression that Menhay was biting back all sorts of inappropriate suggestions. At last he said, 'Why don't you go and see Ta Ieng? Maybe someone is bumping off witnesses and his turn is next. Make sure you tell him that anyway. It's nice to think of him feeling some fear for his life.'

'Speaking of which, is there anything new with your serial killer?'

'No, first break we've had since the killings started.'

'I guess he must be busy . . . or on holiday.'

Menhay was sarcastic. 'He hasn't run out of ex-Khmer Rouge, that's for sure.'

The colonel left the room for his appointment and Chhean said, 'Are we going to see Ta Ieng?'

'Yes,' said Singh, 'but we have a stop to make on the way.'

He led the way quickly down the stairs until they reached the holding cells. Despite what Menhay had suggested, the Armstrong couple were some distance from each other and ignorant, Chhean assumed, of the presence of the other.

'Why are we here?' she whispered.

'To tell Sovann about her husband's confession!'

'The colonel won't like it.'

'You heard Adnan earlier – I'm jointly in charge which means I'm entitled to follow a hunch.'

Chhean refrained from pointing out that if he was confident of his authority there would be no need for this cloak-and-dagger approach. Instead, on the fat man's whispered instructions, she asked that they be allowed in to see Sovann. The gaoler, familiar with their earlier visits with Menhay, did not stand in their way.

As they entered the cell, they saw that Sovann was sitting upright in a chair as far away from the stinking toilet as possible. She looked worn, the lines on her face as clearly defined as highways on a map. She greeted them with a tremulous welcoming smile although she did not stand up or offer to shake hands.

'It is a pleasure to see you, Inspector Singh. What can I do for Singapore's finest?'

Chhean suppressed a smile. Singapore's finest was looking distinctly uncomfortable in the filthy cell that housed Sovann.

'I wish they would let you go or find somewhere less awful to lock you up,' he said roughly.

'It's certainly not quite up to the standard of the Raffles,' she agreed. 'Although I always feel guilty staying in such luxurious surroundings when so many of my countrymen are poor.' She looked around. 'I doubt that many of them would envy my present abode.'

'I still don't think you killed Huon,' explained Singh.

'And does Colonel Menhay share this conviction?'

'Not yet – but we have to prove it to him.'

'I'm not sure I blame the colonel,' she admitted ruefully. 'I have a strong motive and my fingerprints are all over that knife.'

'There are other suspects,' said Singh carefully, watching her face. Chhean did the same. Were they supposed to be gauging her reaction? 'In fact,' continued Singh, 'there's been a confession.'

'What do you mean?'

Chhean threw a dagger glance at the inspector. Surely, despite what he'd said earlier, he wouldn't dare divulge Jeremy Armstrong's confession without a go-ahead from Menhay? Her hopes that the Singaporean would have some tact or common sense were immediately dashed.

'Your husband's confessed.'

If she had been pre-warned, she was an actress of Oscar-winning quality. Her face drained of blood so slowly it was like watching the sands run through an hourglass. She whispered, 'My husband? Jeremy?'

'Yes, he's confessed to murdering Huon.'

'Why?'

'To avenge your father.'

'That's just ridiculous!' She looked up so that her eyes were fixed on the inspector. 'You know why he's done it, don't you?'

'Tell me.'

'To protect me. He probably doesn't think I'll survive long in a place like this.' Only the merest tremor ran through her body but it shouted louder than words that her husband was quite likely to be right.

'It's an extreme step,' remarked Singh.

'This is an extreme situation.' Her tone was embarrassed when she said, 'Jeremy loves me and sometimes he gets carried away in his efforts to protect me.'

'Look, Jeremy's a big tough American. He'll last a lot longer than you in here. Why don't you just accept what he's done with good grace and I'll persuade Menhay to let you go.'

Chhean held her breath. It was a good offer. It even made sense. Would she accept it, this woman of flesh and bone who looked more like a spirit creature?

'Are you really suggesting that I let an innocent man rot in jail on my behalf?'

It was interesting, thought Chhean, that she couched the question in the abstract. Sovann was a woman of principle who would not let anyone go to jail for her; the fact that the volunteer was her husband was a secondary issue.

'This is a serious matter – it affects the tribunal. Menhay has to put *someone* away.' Singh sounded almost desperate as he ran out of options.

'Don't you think I know that?' She changed the subject. 'Why don't *you* think I did it?'

He shrugged his fleshy shoulders. 'Not the type!' And then, a small smile exposing the smoker's teeth, he added, 'I've been wrong before, of course.'

'And my husband?'

'No comment.'

Her face hardened – Chhean thought it looked like water freezing into ice. 'If you don't let Jeremy go – I'll confess as well.'

Singh was alarmed and it showed in his widening eyes. 'Don't do anything hasty,' he begged. 'There's no way I'll get you out of here if you confess too.'

'You heard me – if you try and pin this on my husband I'll

217

make Colonel Menhay's job easy for him.' It was her last word on the subject.

Menhay stood by a grubby little stall selling bottled water, kerosene and cigarettes. The glass display cabinet in which the limited wares were housed was on wheels. Menhay assumed that, at the end of the day, the proprietor would attach the whole ensemble to his motorbike and take it to the shack that he called home. The colonel glanced up and down the narrow dusty street. Every entrepreneurial enterprise had the same desperate poverty written all over it. Heaps of second-hand clothes piled on mats on the floor, baseball caps tied with raffia string to a pole, a basket of stale baguettes. He supposed that these were the first fledgling steps of a young nation towards commercial success.

Hun Sen, the Prime Minister, was convinced that Cambodia would turn into a wealthy trading nation with his guidance. No doubt, Malaysia and Singapore had all begun from such simple roots as these. But the independence struggles of these countries had been quiet affairs involving negotiations, not violence. None of the other ASEAN nations had their intelligentsia murdered – although Burma was trying. The massacre of Cambodians with Chinese roots – the backbone of the flourishing market economies in neighbouring countries – all killed because Pol Pot suspected their commitment to the socialist ideal, hadn't helped either. And this was despite the fact that Mao's China had been the only country with which the Khmer Rouge had foreign relations during their entire tenure.

An attack of almost uncontrollable rage caused Menhay's

face to flush and a vein to throb in his temple like an angry snake. No punishment was sufficient for those murderous bastards – the Khmer Rouge. It was just as well he had sent Singh to interview Ta Ieng. The way he felt at that moment he would quite likely throttle him on the spot. The colonel flexed his powerful fingers open and shut. He could almost feel the soft flesh of the throat, the wobbly sac of the Adam's apple and the fragile bones of the neck vertebrae. It would not be difficult to summon up the will to murder someone like Ta Ieng. Unfortunately, it was Cheah Huon who had been killed. And although Sovann Armstrong was convinced that he had been a cadre with the ruling elite, Menhay was not prepared to take her word as conclusive evidence of culpability. That was not the way he operated. There had to be evidential certainty based on witness corroboration, confessions or forensic data before he would reach a conclusion of guilt. It was why he was a misfit within the Cambodian police force where a mild suspicion was usually equated with guilt and reinforced by a confession obtained with a beating. He twisted his head from side to side, trying to release the tension in his neck. Did these people, his fellow cops, not realise that they were no better than Duch or Samrin when they behaved like that?

A tuk tuk swerved to avoid a pothole and Menhay took a step backwards. He had too much to do and too little time to complete his mission to add to the statistics on Phnom Penh road deaths.

A thin man with large ears and a broad grin sidled up to him. 'Colonel!'

Menhay scowled at him. He hated consorting with low-lifes

and this informant was a real bottom feeder. 'This better be good.'

'Oh yes! But before I tell you anything – you must remember that I, Keat, have helped the great Colonel Menhay.'

'I'll remember,' said Menhay curtly.

'Because some day the little mouse might find itself in a trap and need the help of a good powerful friend . . .'

More like a rat, thought Menhay, but he kept his observations private. 'Within reason, Keat. I know you are a petty thief who hangs around with the big boys. They put up with you because you run errands, keep your mouth shut and lick their boots. But if you overstep that line, you're on your own.'

The ingratiating smile on the other man's face receded like a setting sun. He nodded his head. 'I would get away from them if I could but it is too late – I know too much.'

Menhay felt a sudden wave of sympathy. 'How about returning to your village?'

'They would find me.'

There was a silence as both men acknowledged the truth of what he said. It was too late for this young man, drawn to the excitement and security of gang membership, to withdraw. He was in for life – and quite likely it would be a short life. It always was for those at the bottom of the pyramid.

Keat was all business again, the moment of weakness had passed and the smile was back. 'That's why I need connections in high places, my good friend.'

'What do you know?'

'You are looking into the killing of that cripple at the trial?'

'Yes,' answered Menhay. He was surprised that Keat even knew there was a war crimes tribunal ongoing. He had a fairly narrow range of interests: girls, guns and protecting his own skin.

The smile was radiant now. 'I know who the killer is!'

'Where are we going?'

Chhean was huffing and puffing, her pale skin flushed a deep pink as she tried to keep up with the inspector. The fat man, who usually lumbered slowly from place to place like an elephant in white sneakers, could move very quickly when he was of a mind to do so.

And he was of a mind to do so now. 'Menhay might be back at any moment,' he explained. 'We need to hurry!'

'Are we trying to run away from Cambodia? That will be the only safe thing to do after he finds out that we told Sovann about her husband's confession.'

She was behind him so she could not see the fat man's small smile. He would not have admitted it to anyone but he enjoyed his sidekick's rude commentary to his actions. It kept him alert, knowing that she would be quick to point out mistakes and inconsistencies. In a way, he preferred it to the quiet restraint of Sovann Armstong. It was impossible to know at any one time what that woman was thinking. But Chhean wore her opinions on her sleeve.

She was right that it had been a move calculated to annoy Menhay, going in to see his chief suspect and letting a few cats out of the bag to boot. But he didn't have much time to save Sovann from a lifetime in prison. The colonel was not going to give him much more rope. Adnan Muhammad was growing impatient with progress. The trial was due to restart soon. He needed to set a few cats amongst the pigeons and see what would happen. Singh wondered for a moment why all his mental metaphors involved cats. He didn't even like the self-interested creatures – and he was allergic to the fur.

'That Sovann is a smart woman,' he said over his shoulder, still striding forward. 'If she confesses – we're through.'

'She is brave and loyal,' insisted Chhean.

'And beautiful,' answered Singh provocatively. He sensed rather than saw his wilful sidekick grimace. He supposed he wouldn't appreciate it if someone kept bringing up Shah Rukh Khan's good looks. He thought about Menhay. The colonel was pug-ugly too with his square head, drooping jowls and surly expression.

'Is that why you think she's innocent – because she's beautiful?'

'Why does everyone think I'm so shallow?' demanded Singh. 'You sound like my wife.'

There was no answer from Chhean but her silence spoke volumes. They had reached their destination and Singh peered in through a small window with rusty grilles. 'This is it!' he said. He looked at his watch, the strap embedded in a plump wrist. 'We don't have much time – get security to let us in.'

'Who's in there?'

'Jeremy Armstrong, of course! Who else?'

Chhean hesitated, as if she was about to withdraw from her role as interpreter on the grounds that the job had grown too dangerous, shrugged her broad shoulders once and hollered for the guard.

'What about Ta Ieng?' She asked the question as they waited for someone to let them in.

'He can wait.'

Unless that efficient killer of ex-Khmer Rouge got to him first. Singh ran a finger along the rim of his turban. His scalp was itching in that hot damp place that seemed designed to break the spirit of the prisoners incarcerated within. He would soon be a snivelling wreck, he suspected, if he had to spend much time here. The policeman reached for his pack of cigarettes instinctively.

Chhean wrinkled her nose in disgust.

'It's my emotional crutch,' he explained. 'It's either this or religion.'

When they were finally let in – after some hesitation on the part of the guard, a lot of translated yelling on the part of Singh and the exchange of a fistful of *riels* – Jeremy Armstrong was in good shape. He seemed unaffected by his unsalubrious surroundings. The inspector, perusing him as carefully as a scientist with a new form of swine flu virus under a microscope, thought that he had the inner peace of a martyr. Probably Daniel in the lion's den had adopted a similar air of smug self-righteousness.

It was time to burst the bubble. 'I don't think your wife killed Huon.'

'I know that,' he responded calmly. 'I killed Huon.'

'I don't believe you understand,' said Singh in his most patronising tone. 'I didn't think your wife killed Huon *before* you confessed.'

Was that a crack showing in his impassivity? A flicker of interest in the light-blue eyes?

'Who do you think did it then?'

'We had a number of leads . . .'

'What do you mean "had"?'

Singh looked mournful. He turned lugubrious brown eyes on the self-confessed murderer. 'Well, after your confession the police halted the investigation. I've been taken off the case. If you recant,' he added hopefully, 'they'll let me continue my investigations, follow up those strong leads that might get your wife out of jail – *without* your help.'

On the edge of his line of vision, he saw Chhean shake her head at him. She disapproved of the direction the conversation was going. The inspector guessed that she was appalled that he should take such liberties with the truth. The young woman was as straight as a die. In the policeman's view, that was an enormous impediment to being a successful investigator.

Armstrong sat on the edge of his cot. His shoulders were rounded and his long arms hung limply by his side. He looked oddly vulnerable – physically and emotionally. 'I don't believe you,' he said at last. 'The evidence against Sovann is way too strong.' His voice firmed. 'It's like I told the colonel. I killed that bastard, Huon. Please just get my wife out of here.'

The inspector changed the subject. Suddenly, he was a fellow traveller, not a man on the other side of a police barrier.

'So your wife really doesn't know about your Air Force days?'

'No, I've always been too afraid to tell her.'

'I can see why,' remarked Singh in a friendly tone. 'I read somewhere that the Americans dropped more bombs on Cambodia than on Japan during World War Two.'

'They told us we were bombing Viet Cong enclaves in Cambodia,' Armstrong said. The words were defensive but the tone was tired, as if he had rehearsed these arguments in his head over the years and found them wanting.

'At least you've tried to make up for what you did.'

'Make up for what I did? Killing civilians – men, women and children? My Lai after My Lai from the air? Driving the country into the arms of the Khmer Rouge?'

'Well – you had some help,' said Singh dryly. 'It's not *all* your fault.'

Armstrong ignored the sop to his conscience. 'I have to protect my wife. She's been through enough. This is my redemption.'

Singh nodded. He understood what motivated this American with the empty eyes. It was as good a reason as any to confess to a murder one had not committed. Not just protection of a loved one but a personal salvation for past sins. It was the act of a man who did not believe in God or in forgiveness. Perhaps Sovann Armstrong had taught him that. Singh looked at the big bear of a man and felt a profound sympathy.

He sat down on a chair and sucked in a lungful of tobacco.

'You won't tell her, will you?'

Singh pondered the question. He had admired Menhay earlier for using the leverage he had to extract information. He had exaggerated – Chhean would say lied – to this man about the alternative avenues of investigation in the Huon murder in the hope that he would rescind his statement. If he threatened him with disclosure, it might just work. Armstrong was as concerned for his wife's mental wellbeing as her physical condition. The American was sure that the knowledge he had been a B-52 pilot would damage Sovann irretrievably.

She might retreat into the silent cocoon of thirty years ago. He was also – Singh could see it in the man's eyes – terrified of losing his wife. Singh scowled. Whichever way you looked at it, that just wasn't his problem. He was a murder investigator not a marriage counsellor.

He would have to threaten this man with what he feared the most. He saw that Chhean was begging him with her eyes not to say anything. She would never make a murder cop, he thought dismissively, if she was afraid of hurt feelings. The truth was what counted – this man had not murdered Huon and the sooner he admitted that, the quicker the investigation would get back on track. Singh opened his mouth but no words came out.

He tapped his cigarette with a stubby forefinger so that the ash fell to the floor. He looked Armstrong in the eye. 'All right, I won't tell her,' he said.

Fifteen

Singh's brows almost met across his broad nose and his eyes were sunken pools.

'What's wrong with you?' demanded Chhean.

'I should have threatened Armstrong with disclosure.'

'That you would tell Sovann about his past?'

'Yes – I bet he would have recanted his confession if I'd done that.'

'It would have been cruel.'

'Worse than letting him rot in jail for a murder he didn't commit?' Singh spat the words out but she knew the anger was directed internally. He was upset because he believed that he'd been weak. She thought it was compassion rather than weakness but it was useless to argue with a thwarted murder cop, especially if the cop in question was the tubby but determined policeman from Singapore.

'It's his choice,' she pointed out.

'It's my *job*.'

'Fine!' It was her turn to sound cross. 'Do your job. Find this killer and prove that it's not Sovann or her husband.'

The inspector spoke through gritted teeth. 'I'm out of ideas.'

She almost patted him on the shoulder. It was odd to see the usually gung ho policeman admitting defeat. Instead she said comfortingly, 'Ta Ieng might have something to tell us.'

Singh grunted his contempt at the likelihood that the child killer and mass murderer might have something useful to say about Huon's murder.

He changed the subject. 'Have you found out anything about the serial killer's victims? I know you're spending every night trawling through documents.'

'I have a lot of information on most of them.'

'Any links between them?'

'Except for being from the Khmer Rouge? Not so far. But they are all quite well known ex-cadres. Easy to identify.'

'The killer is skimming the cream off the top,' explained Singh.

Chhean ignored this last remark as being too opaque for her language skills and added, 'There is something very strange that I found out as well. For the tenth victim, I cannot find much information. There is a man with the same name – Dith Anh – who was well known for his cruelty in the northeast province. He worked for Ta Mok, the "Butcher". But I don't think it's the same man who was killed – just the same name.'

Singh grunted an acknowledgement. 'Typical of all these bloody vigilante types,' he said. 'Eventually, they make mistakes. I don't see how it will help Menhay find his man though.'

They contemplated the fate of the man killed by mistake. Chhean was worn out by the unending loss of innocent life. And yet, all their efforts were being utilised to find Huon's murderer – and he was probably a killer too if what Sovann said was true. She comforted herself with the idea that they were also trying to save the tribunal – a grander and more noble purpose.

Singh distracted her with his next question, perhaps intentionally. 'Anything on your family?'

Chhean looked at the inspector and could see only a kindly interest on his face. She reached into her pocket and removed a tatty black-and-white photograph.

'What's that?'

She hesitated for a moment and then passed it over, almost wincing as she saw it engulfed in the policeman's hand. It was her treasure – her most precious possession – and she had entrusted it to the fat man on an impulse. He looked at it, frowning slightly as if trying to understand its importance.

'That was in the pocket of my shorts when they found me wandering around Phnom Penh after the Vietnamese invasion.'

'Do you think this might be your family?' His voice was gentle. It surprised her that he had the capacity to modify his usually gruff tones.

She nodded. 'I think so – I hope so. Why else would I have had it?'

'Why are you showing me this?'

'Because I know now that you are a good man – and I would like you to know what I am searching for when I look at documents every evening.'

'Some trace of these people . . .'

She nodded. 'I would like to have a family. Even if there is no one alive, it would be good to know that – once upon a time – I had a family.' She smiled at her own choice of words, fighting back tears. 'I guess I'm looking for a fairy tale.'

They found Ta Ieng sitting glumly in his room at the tribunal compound. Being a free man wasn't worth very much when one had nowhere to go, thought Chhean, eyeing the child killer with a combination of pity and disgust. What was it that she had said to Singh earlier? That she was looking for a fairy tale. Well, she had certainly come to the wrong place.

'What do I know about this Cheah Huon?' Ta Ieng repeated Singh's opening question. 'Nothing! So you waste your time coming here to ask me about him.'

Chhean translated hurriedly for the inspector although she suspected he had got the gist of it from Ta Ieng's body language and truculent tone.

'Who is this fat man with the silly *krama* that you bring here anyway?'

'What's he saying?' demanded Singh of Chhean.

'He wants to know who you are.' There did not seem much point in a literal translation at this point.

'He is not a policeman. I don't have to answer his questions.' The witness waved a dismissive hand in the direction of Singh, who took two angry retaliatory steps forward.

'Er – he is just wondering about your authority to question him.'

'Tell him that he needs to be really, really nice to me or the Cambodian police will put him away for the murder of Cheah Huon.'

She tried to keep the surprise off her face but did as Singh asked.

'What do you mean?' Ta Ieng's tone was less aggressive. Chhean detected a note of fear.

'The police need a scapegoat. Otherwise the trial of Samrin will be affected. Do you think they are interested in who *really* did it? They will lock you up and throw the key away and not one single person in Cambodia will care what happens to a child killer like you.'

'I didn't want to kill anyone. I was just following orders,' whined Ta Ieng. 'I already explained at the tribunal.'

'Were you following orders when you killed Huon? Whose orders? Samrin?'

Chhean translated quickly, keeping her voice even. There was no need to replicate the threat in Singh's voice or in his body language as he walked right up to Ta Ieng so that his grubby white sneakers were toe to toe with the taller man's rubber slippers. Beads of sweat broke out along Ta Ieng's upper lip. Chhean realised to her disgust that she could smell him – the musky stench of a frightened animal.

She glanced at the inspector. Was he really that menacing? She supposed that he was – radiating both anger and authority. It was perfectly credible that the Cambodian police would be looking for someone to blame regardless of actual guilt. Even so, Ta Ieng's terror seemed extreme.

Looking at the witness, she realised suddenly that his fears were based on his own experience. He of all people knew what a man would do, could stoop to, under the guise of following orders – and he was as terrified now as he had been terrified then, of being a victim. Singh was playing on his fears like an expert. For a moment, she too was intimidated by the Sikh inspector.

'I didn't do anything – I didn't kill Huon.'

Singh laughed out loud, a sudden genuine guffaw that filled the small room. 'I guess you'll be singing a different tune once the police have worked you over. Maybe you too will confess to working for the CIA.' He paused for a moment, looking at the rake-thin man with revulsion. 'Don't worry – they will just be *following orders*.'

Ta Ieng was snivelling, trying to form words in his own defence but unable to do so. Chhean was not surprised. At his core, this man was a coward.

'The United Nations appointed me to try and make sure that the Cambodian police do not arrest the wrong man,' explained Singh.

Hope dawned. 'So you must help me – please. I swear I did not kill Huon.' Ta Ieng clutched at Singh's shirt, his hands like claws.

Singh shrugged him away. 'First thing you need to remember, never touch me again. Second thing, I will help you if you help me.'

'What do you want?'

'Tell me about Cheah Huon.'

'He was afraid.'

'Afraid? Of what?'

232

It was an interesting three-way conversation, thought Chhean. Singh watched Ta Ieng carefully but was listening to her quickly translated efforts. She tried to be as unobtrusive as possible.

'He wouldn't tell me exactly.' Ta Ieng was concentrating on his tale, speaking quietly but convincingly. His long thin body was as still as a corpse but his eyes were alert and dancing from one person to the other. 'A few days before he was killed he came in very excited. He said he knew something – and people would pay for him to keep his mouth shut.'

Singh nodded. Chhean realised it fitted with their earlier suppositions about the man in the Mercedes.

'He was very happy – he needed money and he had a good way of getting it. The next thing I knew he was showing off that gold chain. He said that the money he had received was just the first instalment – there would be many more payments before the debt was paid.'

'What changed? When did he become afraid?'

Ta Ieng fell silent.

'Go on!' Singh leaned forward aggressively.

'It was that day – the day he died.'

'What about it?'

'He said that he was playing with the man who paid him – hinting that he might have something more to say during his testimony in court. He wasn't really going to reveal anything – but he thought they might pay even more if he worried him a bit.'

'Who was this man?'

'He didn't tell me.'

Chhean folded her arms tightly. Ta Ieng was suggesting that whoever Huon was blackmailing had the resources to have him watched as he testified. It made sense. This mysterious party also had the resources to keep an eye on Som and kill him when it seemed that he might know too much. There was organisation here – and money. She tried to dismiss a sudden shudder as a reaction to the draught that was blowing in the door.

'I still don't understand why he became afraid?'

'The judge cut him off – wouldn't let him finish. The hearing was postponed to the next day. He told me that evening that he feared they might have decided he was unreliable . . .'

Singh was quick to latch on to this. Chhean's mind was still reeling from the suggestion that a judge might be involved.

'You saw him that evening?'

'Yes – he asked me what he should do.'

'What was your advice?' Singh sounded curious.

Chhean supposed she was too – did mass murderers give good advice?

'I asked him to tell me the secret – the more people who knew, the less point there would be in killing him.'

'Or he would have proved once and for all that he couldn't be trusted.'

'That was what he said too. He wouldn't tell me anything.'

'Consider yourself lucky,' remarked Singh. 'I don't think they would have taken kindly to your trying your hand at a bit of blackmail as well.'

From the quick hooded glance Ta Ieng threw at the inspector, Chhean knew that his surmise had been accurate. Ta

Ieng had hoped to feather his nest too. The man was a coward and a fool.

'Did you threaten him? Maybe with a knife? Was there an accident?' Singh was yelling and the tall man cowered before him, fear flickering in his eyes like a candle in a gust.

'I didn't kill Cheah Huon,' whispered Ta Ieng. 'You said you would help me if I told you what I knew.' He was begging now. 'Please don't let the police blame me for this murder.'

'Have you told me everything?' Singh had moderated his tone – suddenly he was a reasonable man asking a reasonable question.

'Yes, of course – *everything*.'

Chhean looked across at Singh. The fat man's expression was thoughtful. Perhaps he too sensed that Ta Ieng protested too much; that, contrary to his assurances, he was holding something back.

'I really fancy a cold beer.' Singh spoke in a matter-of-fact voice, as if he was discussing a mundane element of the case.

'Me too,' admitted Chhean.

Singh raised a single eyebrow. What had got into his interpreter? He hadn't thought that he had so much influence over the actions of others. It was time to test the theory. 'And a curry,' he asked quickly, 'at one of those Indian restaurants on the map?'

His authority was obviously limited. She shook her head and glossy hair swept her cheeks.

'We haven't time,' she insisted. 'We have to work on this case.'

'What do you suggest we do?' asked Singh. He was curious to see if she had picked up on the most crucial piece of evidence.

'The judge,' she blurted out. 'It sounds like one of the judges is involved.'

Singh sat down suddenly on a bench as if the weight of his posterior could no longer defy the summons of gravity. Chhean sat down next to him. He noticed that her glum expression matched his – she was not a fool by any means. She knew what this could mean.

'I was there when the judge – it was one of the Cambodian judges, Judge Sopheap, I think – called an end to the day's testimony. It did strike me as strange at the time. Cheah Huon was clearly in the middle of a story.' He scratched the underside of his beard like a dog with a flea, quick regular strokes. 'I assumed the judge was tired, or needed the toilet, or had an appointment – or felt like a beer and a curry.'

Chhean's phone beeped – indicating an SMS. Singh nodded approvingly. He liked phones that rang with old-fashioned tones and messages that sounded like electronic warnings. It got on his nerves every time he was forced to listen to a snatch of classical music or an animal sound and it turned out to be the ring tone or message alert on someone's mobile. Why didn't they just have the sound of fingernails on blackboards? he wondered. Or caterwauling cats?

Chhean had read the message and now she slipped the phone back into her sturdy bag. 'That was the colonel,' she said.

'What does he want?' asked Singh truculently. He was not

looking forward to relating the day's findings to the Cambodian policeman. Especially the bit where he had gone to see Sovann and her husband.

'He wants us to meet him at the FCC.'

'Eh?'

'The Foreign Correspondents' Club – on the river.'

Singh was in no mood for further excursions on the crowded, pot-holed roads of Phnom Penh. 'Tell him we're busy,' he insisted. 'Like you said, we have to investigate.'

'The best beer in all of Cambodia is at the FCC.'

Singh looked at his sidekick suspiciously, eyebrows drawn together with doubt. 'Is that true?'

She nodded enthusiastically, her eyes wide open and honest.

'All right! What are we waiting for then? Colonel Menhay needs to see us on a matter of importance.'

In a short time they were in the back of their sedan. The policeman's nostrils flared in disgust. 'I hate the smell of stale smoke,' he complained. The detective wound down the windows with some difficulty and took a deep breath. 'I also hate the smell of drains,' he yelled above the street noise and wound the glass back up.

He leaned back in the seat, mopped his brow with the large handkerchief he kept for these occasions and reached for his cigarette pack.

'You're going to make it worse?' asked Chhean.

'On the contrary, I'm going to make it better.'

Chhean fanned away the cloud of tobacco smoke with staccato waves and asked, 'What about this judge? What are we going to do?'

Singh looked down at his large sneakers and wriggled his sticky toes. 'We're going to tread very lightly. That's what we're going to do.'

If Chhean had any doubts about the ability of the large Sikh with the cavalier investigative methods to tread lightly, she kept them to herself.

Instead she said, 'If a judge is involved, there might be a mistrial.'

The turban bobbed up and down in agreement.

'Samrin will be dead before there is another one . . .'

'Assuming that politics don't take over and the whole ECCC isn't chucked into the waste bin of history.'

Chhean gazed out of the window and Singh could see that she was close to tears. He didn't blame her. She and so many other Cambodians had invested everything into seeing some justice done for the suffering of their people. One crooked judge could destroy it all.

'Do you think that a judge is involved?' she asked in a small voice.

'I very much fear so.' Singh's tone was sombre.

Usually, when looking into a murder, the inspector was concerned only with justice for the victim. Others, especially Superintendent Chen and his ilk, might be concerned about the politics and the publicity but not him. Not Inspector Singh of the Singapore police, justly famous for his devotion to the cause of the deceased. Singh snorted out loud and Chhean turned to look at him in surprise, her eyes still wet. Singh ignored her, lost in his own thoughts. This case had dimensions that went well beyond the usual politicking. What was the use of finding justice for Huon if the end result was the collapse of the war crimes tribunal? Was immediate justice for one man more important than retrospective justice for millions of Cambodians? And who was to decide that question? Surely not Singh or Menhay, or God forbid, Adnan Muhammad?

He muttered his last thought aloud.

'What's that? What's that you said?' asked Chhean.

'I wish I'd never come to Cambodia.'

Half an hour later, Inspector Singh was in a much better mood. The beer was on tap. Angkor, of course, but icy cold and with an inch of froth. The third-floor balcony was open, airy and breezy with dark spinning fans that reinforced the wind coming off the river. The wooden floors were well-worn and whispered of the footsteps of many travellers. The din of traffic and the stench of drains were physically distant, lending atmosphere rather than inducing migraines or nausea. The rich cheesy bready smell of pizza baking in a wood-fired oven was soothing. But best of all, the eclectic paper menu that kept threatening to escape his sweaty fingers and dance over the railings had a single but important reference to chicken curry. The inspector ordered the dish, repeating himself a couple of times although the waitress spoke excellent English, to be sure she understood and he would not be done out of his treat. Singh took a deep swig of his drink, wiped the white froth off his moustache and glanced around. He nodded his head. So this was where the expats hung out, those 'in the know' as opposed to newcomers and tourists. It reminded him of the Singapore Cricket Club. The men at the bar were large, ruddy-faced and tired – but looked at home. A French family sat at a table further along the balcony. The father was a school-teacher, guessed Singh, kindly face and round glasses. There were very few Cambodians in the place – those that were there had the look of the foreign-educated, hair slightly too long, glasses, polo T-shirts. And yet Singh did not get the impression of money. These were probably journalists or local NGO staff – their ambition to inflict pinpricks on the elephant hide of government.

The tubby policeman looked across at his square-jawed counterpart. Colonel Menhay, in his uniform and gold-rimmed Rayban sunglasses, appeared out of place in the old-world charm of the Foreign Correspondents' Club. He sat stiffly in his chair, as if he too was aware of the fact.

'Why did you call us here?' asked Singh.

'We're waiting for someone. Did you find out anything from Ta Ieng?' It was a determined effort to change the subject by the colonel.

Chhean looked at the inspector pleadingly. He guessed she didn't want the judge mentioned. Singh chewed on his bottom lip – a man who couldn't wait for his chicken curry or a man trying to make a difficult decision.

'Well?'

'You know Ta Ieng. "I was just following orders".' Singh mimicked the man's tone with sufficient accuracy to draw a smile from Menhay. He could sense the tension ebb from Chhean but he was not sure that she had good reason for relief. He could keep his suspicions to himself for a short while – hope that another solution presented itself – but in the end he would have to tell the colonel about the judge, whatever the consequences to the war crimes trial. Singh told himself firmly that he was just buying a bit of time, not obstructing justice.

'Ah, here is our guest,' said Menhay in an even tone. He sounded like a man determined not to pre-judge an issue.

Singh swivelled his body with difficulty and was taken aback to see the lean, cadaverous figure of François Gaudin. 'The mad Frenchman? What's he got to do with anything?'

'We're about to find out,' whispered the colonel. He stood up and ushered the man into a chair.

Gaudin was in better shape than when Singh had last seen him. His gait was steady and his eyes less bloodshot than on the day of the murder.

A waitress arrived bearing Singh's chicken curry. There was an awkward silence while Singh supervised the delivery of his food with the concentration of a drug addict administering heroin intravenously.

The inspector sniffed appreciatively. 'This looks good,' he exclaimed and then, remembering his manners, he addressed the Frenchman. 'Would you like something?' He sampled his lunch – 'I can recommend the chicken curry.'

François Gaudin, who appeared bemused by his surroundings or, more likely, his companions, said, 'I would not mind a beer.'

This was duly ordered and arrived with a promptness that caused a broad smile to spread across the Sikh man's face. The service at this place was in marked contrast to the languid efforts at the other dining places Chhean had dragged him to.

'So,' he asked complacently, 'what are we all doing here?'

They turned like puppets to look at the colonel.

Menhay spoke in the heavy portentous tone that seemed to come naturally to all successful policemen. It indicated authority and hinted at secrets. 'We believe that you might know something about the murder of Cheah Huon.' He was staring at the Frenchman full in the face as he said this.

To his obvious disappointment, this opening gambit was met with a look of genuine bewilderment. 'That man who was stabbed at the ECCC?'

Menhay nodded. Singh shovelled some chicken curry and rice into his mouth. The truth was that it was fairly ordinary. But the lunch-time entertainment provided by Menhay and his witness was fascinating.

'I have information that you tried to hire a hit man.'

'That's a lie!'

'My informant briefed me that you offered him a large sum of money to kill a witness at the war crimes tribunal. *He* turned you down but he was certain that you would look elsewhere.'

'I have no idea what you're talking about.'

He was completely unconvincing. Singh had the feeling that he wasn't even trying, almost hoping that the other man would delve deeper and compel him to tell what he knew. But he still had a residual sense of self-preservation – enough to prevent him from volunteering the truth.

The inspector leaned back in his chair and clasped his hands over his belly. He contemplated the Frenchman, his expression thoughtful. He had seen the man in so many guises: sobbing at the testimony of Ta Ieng, demanding to know who had been killed at the tribunal and now sipping his beer nervously at the FCC. He had heard of his collapse at Tuol Sleng prison. Menhay claimed that Gaudin had hired a hit man. But whom had he wanted dead? Surely not Huon? A memory of Gaudin's shock when he learnt the identity of the murder victim came back to him. He suddenly had a fair idea of what had happened.

Singh reached into his pocket for the reproduction of the painting by Vann Nath. He held it up to Gaudin.

'This is why you did it?'

Gaudin appeared to deflate – all the fight went out of him and it left him a limp and tired old man. The inspector had seen it before. When those who were not hardened to a life of crime were found out, they sometimes treated the revelation of their conduct as a relief. The secrecy of criminality was too great a burden for the usually law-abiding.

'You know what that man did to the children. Perhaps they were mine as well. I just felt that if I could destroy him, it would be some retribution for my family. Some rest for me . . .' His voice trailed off into silence.

'The children, your family?' Menhay sounded like a sporadic questioning echo.

'Yes, I have told you they disappeared in the early days of the Khmer Rouge . . .'

'But what have they got to do with Huon?'

'Huon? Nothing! I didn't even hear his testimony. I hired someone to kill *Ta Ieng* . . . and as I understand that he is still alive and well, I assume that the assassin has pocketed my money and done nothing for me.'

'But you did hire a hit man?' Menhay was trying to get the questioning back on track.

The Gallic shrug of the shoulders was wonderfully obscure. Gaudin, it turned out, was disputing the description, rather than the underlying accusation. 'A hit man? I thought so – a seedy character with dirty hands who said he would kill Ta Ieng for me. He insisted on the money in advance – because it would be too dangerous for both of us if he approached me again after the killing.'

'How much did you pay him?' asked Singh, his appetite for food temporarily sated but his appetite for information still keen.

'A thousand US dollars.'

'That would be a very good retirement package in Cambodia for your murderer,' muttered Menhay.

'I guess you think I'm a fool,' said Gaudin bitterly. 'Perhaps you are right. I just wanted to do *something* . . . that's all.'

'Murder is not "something",' admonished Singh, turning his attention to the dessert menu.

'Ta Ieng deserves to die,' protested Gaudin, waving long fingers in the air like a concert pianist.

'But he's not dead,' pointed out Menhay. 'Singh saw him this morning. Only Cheah Huon is dead.'

'Well, I had nothing at all to do with the killing of this . . . Huon, you say? Who is he to me? I hired someone to kill Ta Ieng. You will have to look elsewhere for your murderer.'

There was a brief interval in which the Sikh policeman ordered chocolate cake. Chhean nibbled a biscuit and wondered why the fates had made her an unwilling fourth to the table.

'What now?' asked Menhay in a depressed voice.

Chhean had some sympathy. His wonderful lead in the murder investigation had just petered out. The Frenchman with the long face was innocent of Huon's killing despite having hired a hit man. She shook her head – a thousand US dollars. That was big money in Cambodia. Even she might be prepared to bump someone off for that amount. Especially if it was someone she already disliked. One of the government naysayers for instance, who kept insisting that the trial of Samrin should be postponed indefinitely – Cambodian-speak for abandoned once and for all.

'Wait a minute.' Singh was poised with his fork halfway to his mouth, a chunk of chocolate cake impaled on the end.

Chhean was amused. It was clearly something of great importance if it prevented Singh from effecting an immediate transfer of food to mouth.

'What is it?' asked Menhay, raising his head hopefully like a dog who'd heard the fridge door open.

Singh put his fork down on the plate and stared at François Gaudin. 'You hired a hit man to kill Ta Ieng?'

'That's what I just said,' grumbled the Frenchman with a moody expression.

'All right – what did you say to him exactly?'

'To whom?'

'Your hit man!' Singh was getting impatient and it showed in voice and expression.

'To kill the child killer . . .'

'Did you name him?'

'Of course.'

'Are you sure – this is important.'

Menhay was sitting a little straighter in his chair. Chhean

was already leaning forward. She sensed that the fat man was on to something.

'I met the man at a karaoke joint. The first guy – your informant, I guess – mentioned where I could find him,' said Gaudin carefully.

'I knew I should have arrested that bastard,' growled Menhay. No one paid him any attention. The focus was on the inspector from Singapore.

'You said earlier that you only heard the testimony of Ta Ieng, not Cheah Huon?' he asked.

'Yes – after Ta Ieng testified I was too upset to stay in the courtroom.'

'Here's my question then,' said Singh. 'Did you ask this hit man of yours to kill the *witness* or did you identify Ta Ieng by name?'

'I know what you're trying to suggest – and I refuse to accept it. I had nothing to do with the death of Cheah Huon.'

Gaudin's family was gone, destroyed by the Khmer Rouge. He had sought revenge – if not on the killer of his family, one very like him. He had admitted as much. But he refused to accept the possibility that a mistake had been made. Chhean realised with a burst of perspicuity that he did not fear the consequences to himself. Gaudin was just reluctant to live with the possibility – and the guilt – of having killed the wrong man.

'There's a woman in a Cambodian jail,' said Singh, his voice barely above a whisper. 'She fled Cambodia when she was fifteen. Before that she watched her whole family die of starvation – except for her father. Him, she witnessed beaten to death by a Khmer Rouge cadre. I don't think I need to

246

describe to you the conditions in a Phnom Penh prison or this woman's emotional fragility.'

'Why's she there?' whispered Gaudin.

'She's been arrested for the murder of Huon.'

Gaudin took a deep breath and placed his two hands flat on the surface of the table.

'You can help her by doing the right thing,' urged Singh.

Gaudin nodded once and answered Singh's original question. 'I may have said, "Kill the witness." I think I mentioned Ta Ieng's name as well.'

Chhean closed her eyes for a moment. Singh's reading of Gaudin's character had been unnervingly accurate. He was too decent a man to allow someone to remain in jail for a crime he might have committed.

'Anything else?' asked Singh.

'I suggested that he was a child killer – I can't remember the exact words I used. You have to remember I don't speak Khmer and his English, not to mention his French, wasn't very good. There were moments when I wasn't sure he understood that I wanted a man dead, let alone that it was Ta Ieng.' He looked rueful. 'I'd been drinking as well.'

Singh was blunt. 'So your guy killed the wrong man?'

'It's possible,' admitted Gaudin finally.

Chhean doubted he would be prepared to go any further than that. But the circumstantial evidence was building up.

'I'm not convinced,' complained Menhay. 'Could an assassin really be so hopeless?'

'Not an assassin,' pointed out Singh. 'A cut-price thug with whom François didn't share a common language.'

Menhay sighed.

'Otherwise, we have to accept that there was more than one killer running around. Our so-called hit man and someone *else* who killed Huon,' said Singh.

'In Cambodia, such things are possible,' remarked the colonel.

'It must be the solution,' insisted Singh. 'A simple case of mistaken identity.'

'I suppose you're right,' admitted Menhay at last.

'Time to order the release of Jeremy and Sovann Armstrong,' murmured the fat man.

'I know I was wrong,' François said pleadingly, 'but you can understand why I did it, can't you?'

Chhean looked around the table. Menhay was impassive but Singh nodded his great head, wagging the turban to indicate comprehension of Gaudin's motives. As she had suspected, the fat man had a well-disguised compassionate streak.

'I understand why you tried to kill Ta Ieng too,' she added obstinately.

'I didn't know it was the role of interpreters to condone murder,' grumbled Menhay.

Gaudin on the other hand, gave her a small smile. He reached into his wallet and took out a small black-and-white photograph which he placed on the table. He said simply, 'This is my family – they've been missing for thirty years. It's why I did it.'

Singh reached for the photo and stared at it, his heavy-lidded eyes almost overlapping in concentration. 'Chhean, where's that picture of yours? The one of your family that you always carry around?'

Chhean felt a wave of nausea sweep over her. She had to close her eyes and let it pass. She reached slowly into her pocket and removed the photograph that she had shown Singh earlier. She handed it to the inspector, who gently placed both photos side by side on the table. Two photos of a mother and her children. Both pictures were much handled, much loved and faded with age. The mother in each was smiling at the camera – or the cameraman – and cradling a baby in her arms.

François covered his face with long nicotine-stained fingers. Chhean felt hot tears trickle down her cheeks and slowly drip off her chin.

Sixteen

It was Singh who found the courage to speak first. 'I'm so sorry,' he whispered. 'I was so sure that they were the same.'

Chhean nodded an acknowledgement. François was lost in his own world.

The fat policeman bit his bottom lip so hard he could taste blood. His famous investigative instincts – that had put two and two together and found a lost family for the lost souls at the table – had been completely and utterly wrong.

The photos were similar, but weren't so many happy family pictures? Two women and their children. The only thing they had in common was that their smiles indicated that no premonition of the future had darkened the moment.

Menhay cleared his throat. 'François Gaudin – I am arresting you for the murder of Cheah Huon.'

The Frenchman looked up at this and smiled wanly. When he spoke, it was to Chhean. 'Look, I know how much it would have meant to both of us to find some family. But I'm not the father for you – not now when it seems that I have killed a man by mistake.' He sighed. 'Perhaps not even before . . .'

It was a brave thing to say – and an unselfish gesture. Singh was suddenly glad that the death penalty had been abolished in Cambodia. He wouldn't have wanted to see this tired old man hanged for his errors. It was a timely reminder as well that, in Cambodia, there were no happy endings. Even if François Gaudin had turned out to be Chhean's father, their initial delight would have been subsumed in the knowledge that his destiny was to live out his remaining years behind bars.

Trying to comfort the man she had believed was her father for a few short precious moments, Chhean said quickly, 'We have information that Huon was ex-Khmer Rouge. You didn't kill an innocent man.'

Menhay raised an admonishing finger at her but she had said what she wanted.

'Thank you,' whispered Gaudin.

Far better, it appeared, to be the killer of Khmer Rouge than an innocent person. It seemed, thought Singh, that this elderly Frenchman had something in common with the vigilante who was executing Khmer Rouge cadres.

Menhay cleared his throat and got to his feet. 'It's time to go.'

Gaudin looked as if he wanted to say more to Chhean but words failed him. He followed Menhay out of the room, not stopping to look back.

Chhean sat across from Singh, staring out of the window. She was dry-eyed but the blankness of her gaze hinted at her inner turmoil.

At last, she said, 'For a moment, just a moment, I thought I'd found my father.'

'I'm so sorry,' said Singh again, wondering whether there was enough time left in the world for him to apologise sufficiently for what he'd done. An error made in all good faith, but devastating to his young and vulnerable sidekick.

'It's not your fault.'

He had no adequate response to this piece of kindness.

'I just feel – I don't know if you can understand – that if I had some family, if I could find some trace of them, I wouldn't feel so alone . . .'

Singh thought of the network of relatives that surrounded him. His wife's nagging soundtrack to his life, his sister in Kuala Lumpur echoing the criticisms, his mother, growing old in Penang but still fiercely independent, and innumerable cousins and nephews and nieces and distant uncles and aunts. He spent his whole life avoiding them, doing his best to alienate them, but – probably due to the efforts of Mrs Singh – they remained in his life, talking politics and house prices and nagging him to give up smoking. What would he do without them all? Usually, he assumed that he'd head for the nearest coffee shop to have a cold beer in celebration. Today, he had a small glimpse of the void they would leave behind.

However, the realisation that he needed his family, warts and all, would not be helpful to his young companion.

'I just want to *belong* somewhere,' she continued.

This he could deal with. 'You belong here,' he insisted. 'In Cambodia.'

It drew a small smile.

'I'm quite serious, young lady. People like you – honest, hard working, decent – are the future of this country. You're not alone at all, you're surrounded by people who need you.'

'To do the "odd jobs"?'

He cracked a smile. Chhean was back. 'Exactly. To do the odd jobs – you know, track down a murderer, save a tribunal, find justice for your people . . .'

Singh was in a taxi on his own heading back to the tribunal compound. The inspector had been anxious to get away from the scene of the painful disappointment of Chhean and Gaudin, orchestrated by his own well-meaning, but disastrous intervention. Chhean had insisted she was fine but that she wanted to be alone with her thoughts for a while. He'd called Menhay, who assured Singh that he would release Sovann and Jeremy Armstrong. There was hesitation in the colonel's voice but also relief. He would never admit it but Gaudin was a much more convenient solution than the Armstrong couple, each trying to shoulder the blame for Huon's death and leaving the police none the wiser. Singh hoped he wasn't taking the path of least resistance as well. He shook his head. He knew Sovann was innocent. And it made sense that Armstrong had just confessed to protect his wife. According to Menhay, François Gaudin was willing to admit that he had given the hit man incorrect, or at least inadequate, instructions. His attitude was that of a man with nothing to lose. Just as well, really, that he hadn't found a daughter. He might have fought harder for his freedom if he had.

The taxi trundled towards the tribunal compound, running

the usual gauntlet of aggressive driving by an assortment of unroadworthy vehicles. Tomorrow, the tribunal would recommence hearings. They would do it convinced that the murder of Cheah Huon had been the mistake of a deeply unhappy old man looking for some retribution. It was the best possible solution – one that did not cast a shadow over proceedings or provide ammunition to the doubters.

But there was still the problem of the judge. Singh was on his way to confront Sopheap but he was not looking forward to it. Ta Ieng had said a judge stepped in to prevent Huon saying too much. Singh remembered the moment. He had been at the tribunal when the angry Huon had leaned forward and insisted he had more to say – but been cut off before he could finish. It was that same justice who had asked Menhay whether the colonel had any leads and been relieved that the answer had been in the negative.

Thankfully for the tribunal, this judge was not a killer. That unhappy role had been assigned to Gaudin. But the inspector knew he could not leave this stone unturned although he dreaded what lurked underneath. He could not let the institution of the war crimes tribunal be tainted because one of its judges was crooked. He desperately wanted to get to the bottom of this for the sake of Cambodians like Chhean and Menhay. The other sort, the Samrins and Ta Iengs, could not be allowed to win the day. But he feared that any outing of the judge would throw the tribunal, still reeling from Huon's murder, into disrepute. It was a classic no-win situation. Like trying to argue a point of principle with Mrs Singh.

The inspector remembered Som, another chap who'd been

dealt a rotten hand. An innocent – perhaps the only person with clean hands in this entire mess – who had paid for knowing too much with his life. But what had he known? How was his death related to this migraine-inducing Cambodian conundrum? Singh's bottom lip was in full pout – an indication that he was, like Hercule Poirot, bringing all his little grey cells to the contemplation of a problem.

He ran over the events leading up to Som's death in his head, wishing that he had Chhean with him to jog his memory and provide a sounding board. What had Som the amputee said and then been engulfed in laughter? That Singh and Chhean could be the *judge* of the quality of the evidence he was offering? Chhean had emphasised the word 'judge' when she translated Som's words. The amputee had been amusing himself at their expense – he must have belatedly recognised the man in the Mercedes as Judge Sopheap. It made sense. It would explain Huon's hinting at secrets at the tribunal, hoping to milk the man presiding for more cash. And no wonder he'd become afraid when Sopheap cut short proceedings so abruptly.

The inspector wondered how Som had identified Sopheap. Perhaps the amputee had seen a picture of the judge in a newspaper, no doubt in an article about Cambodia's finest sons. But before he could finger Sopheap as the man who had bought all the books and paid Huon enough for that gold chain around his neck, Som had been gunned down. The first question was whether Sopheap had been working for someone else or protecting himself. The second was how, in the absence of any hard evidence, he was going to persuade the judge to talk.

Singh leaned forward, his stomach compressing into folds like an accordion, and tapped the driver on the shoulder. He needed to make a detour.

They reached the compound and Singh submitted his large form to the x-ray machines and a body search that took longer than the average. He assumed it was his bulk rather than any misplaced suspicions that rendered the search such an event. He collected his wallet and passport from the plastic container and headed for the judges' chambers. The tribunal compound was a hive of activity. Chairs were being rearranged, wiring checked, passages swept. There was a palpable sense of excitement and relief that the hearing of Samrin was to continue.

Singh gritted his teeth. He didn't want to be the proverbial fly in the ointment. He skirted a large Mercedes – *the* Mercedes? – showed his ID to a guard and was allowed up the stairs. He knocked on the door, firmly but not aggressively. There was time enough for that when he had Sopheap where he wanted him.

A curt 'come in' and Singh pushed against the door and walked in. The judge was behind a desk on which documents were stacked neatly and at right angles. An orderly man in a disorderly country. Sopheap looked quizzically at the inspector, and said, 'Inspector Singh – what I can I do for you?'

The fat man was relieved that he spoke in English. It had crossed his mind on the threshold that he had only ever heard the judge speak Khmer and French. Without an interpreter, without Chhean, this could have been a short visit.

Singh leaned against a wall and crossed his arms so that they rested over his fat belly. 'Who are you protecting?'

'What are you talking about?' There was wariness in Sopheap's eyes as he answered question with question.

Singh cut to the chase. 'I've received credible information that you prevented Huon from continuing his testimony – and I was in court on that day. I saw you do it.'

'I was feeling ill and decided to stop proceedings,' insisted Sopheap. Singh felt in his gut that the excuse was rehearsed. Sopheap had feared this moment. But he was a clever man and he had also prepared for it. Singh had seen it often enough – the smart ones didn't rely on blank denial, they provided an alternative explanation that fitted the facts.

'You look well enough.'

The judge was more than a match for this. 'I'm much better now, thank you.'

As if he'd been asking after the bastard's health, thought Singh irritably. 'I've read your CV,' he remarked, keeping his annoyance under wraps. 'You've worked hard to get here – on the bench of the most important tribunal in your country's history. You have a reputation for honest dealing. Why did you throw it all away?'

'What exactly are you accusing me of doing, Inspector Singh?'

It was a good question. Not murder because Colonel Menhay was, probably at that very moment, charging François Gaudin with the killing of Huon. Perhaps the judge was still in the dark about the arrest.

'You were determined to keep Huon quiet. You stopped the hearing. What was the next step? Murder?'

'Of course not! Besides, the police have made an arrest – an unbalanced Frenchman, I hear.'

The fat man scowled. Sopheap was in the loop. Not a huge surprise, he supposed reluctantly. After all, the tribunal was set to recommence hearings the following day. Singh continued to stare at the man across the table, causing him to fidget with the papers on his desk. This fellow was an academic, a judge. He could imagine him fixing a case, perhaps paying a bribe, but not much more than that.

'You didn't kill him. But you paid him enough so that he could buy that rope of gold around his neck. Even my wife would have envied him that piece of jewellery and she's hard to please.'

'I have no idea what you're talking about.'

'One of the other amputees who was with Huon that day recognised you – the rich man in the Mercedes who bought a lot of books.'

Singh debated whether to tell Sopheap that Som was dead. He had a suspicion that the man didn't know. He took a folded piece of newspaper from his pocket and smoothed it out on the desk. It was an article from a Khmer-language newspaper about the war crimes tribunal. A picture of Sopheap had been circled in red ink.

'He recognised you from this . . .'

Singh's detour on the way to the tribunal had been worthwhile. He'd remembered Som's fellow amputee, sitting next to him under the shade of a tree, corroborating his tale about the rich man in the Mercedes and putting a comforting hand on his arm when Som had begged Singh to find Huon's killer. The inspector had backed a sudden hunch that Som would have told his friend what he knew before going to keep his appointment with death. He'd been right.

The judge was picking at a loose thread on the shiny gown hanging over the arm of his chair, refusing after the initial glance to look at the newspaper cutting.

If he was a gambling man, he'd have wagered money that Sopheap didn't know about Som's murder, decided Singh.

'Why did you pay Huon yourself?'

'I just bought some books, that's all. That's all any witness would have seen. You can't prove anything else.'

'You're a judge – used to weighing the evidence. Do you really think anyone is going to believe you? This is Cambodia. Once I tell the police – and the newspapers – about your visit to Huon, the way you stepped in to stop his testimony and show them that,' he nodded at the newspaper, 'do you really think anyone is going to believe you were stocking up on reading material?' He looked at the judge thoughtfully – it was time to test his theory that as far as Sopheap knew, Som was alive and well. 'And the police and press – they'll talk to Som, of course,' he continued.

Sopheap looked as if he was close to tears.

Singh had guessed right. The justice didn't know about the second murder.

'The court of public opinion doesn't need proof beyond reasonable doubt,' pointed out Singh.

Sopheap was staring blankly out of the window. Watching his precious career go up in flames, thought Singh snidely.

'Why didn't you get some runner to pay Huon instead of exposing yourself?' The inspector's voice was quiet but penetrating.

'I didn't know anyone I could trust.'

It was like the first crack in an eggshell – soon the truth would emerge, covered in lies and self-justifications, but the truth nonetheless.

'What did Huon have to say that you feared so much?'

'Not me . . .'

'Someone you worked for?'

'I was approached by a man over the phone. He said he could guarantee my place on the bench.'

Singh nodded his understanding.

Sopheap was still talking, trying to defend his actions. 'He wasn't asking that I manipulate the outcome of Samrin's trial.' He stopped picking at the thread and met Singh's gaze. 'I insisted on that.'

'You're a real hero,' growled the fat man.

'Later, he asked me to pay Huon to keep quiet. I found the money in here.' His eyes darted about the room like a moth looking for an exit. 'He has people everywhere and I don't know who they are – none of them.'

That accounted for the haunted air of the man in front of him. Sopheap was jumping at shadows, terrified of his mysterious paymaster.

'I did as he requested. It seemed a small thing – nothing to do with the trial,' continued Sopheap.

'Bribing witnesses had nothing to do with the trial?' Singh could not keep the sarcasm out of his voice. Som's body, what was left of it, was firmly in his mind's eye.

'I meant nothing to do with Samrin,' muttered the other man. 'That's what this trial is about.'

Singh ignored this legal solipsism. 'Who was it? Who was this man?'

'I don't know.' He looked up at Singh, his expression pleading. 'I swear I don't know.'

Singh debated whether to believe him.

The other man was still talking. 'Huon told me that he knew for a fact that a high-ranking government official had been senior in the Khmer Rouge. This man, when he saw that the Khmer Rouge was doomed, he fled to Vietnam. He returned when it was safe and claimed that he had been hiding out in Vietnam all those years.'

'And you're still trying to tell me you don't know who this is?'

'Huon wanted to tell me but I stopped him. I didn't want to know. I was too afraid.'

See no evil, hear no evil, thought Singh with disgust. But sometimes one did evil by choosing to remain ignorant. His sidekick, Chhean, came to mind. She walked through life with her eyes wide open, unwilling to ignore the corruption in Cambodian society. This man was made of weaker stuff.

'Did he ask you to kill Huon? When the bribes stopped working – when Huon hinted at secrets in court?'

Sopheap shook his head, gesturing with flat palms for the inspector to stop hurling accusations at him. 'He said I had to do *something*. I couldn't think what to do. I was in a panic.'

From his rolling eyes and the way his body was pressed back against his seat, Singh knew he was not exaggerating.

'I could never kill a man, you see.'

He sounded like he meant it but Singh was in no mood to be charitable.

'In fact, when I heard the news of Huon, I thought he had

done it or found someone else to do it. I was shocked. I didn't know what to do.'

'What changed your mind?'

'He thought *I* had killed Huon.' He sounded genuinely aggrieved.

'Did you deny it?'

'Of course, but he wouldn't believe me. He just laughed and insisted that I had done well.'

'What about Som?'

'What do you mean?'

'The amputee who recognised you – he's dead too, I'm afraid.'

'How?' A whisper of sound.

'Murdered.'

After a long pause, it was the judge's turn for a question. 'Do you think this man killed Som?'

Singh nodded without hesitation. He had no doubts on the subject.

A small sigh greeted his response.

'What about Huon?'

'That probably *was* the unbalanced Frenchman.'

There was pregnant silence as each man considered his next step. Sopheap rose and walked to the window. If Singh had been a superstitious man, he would have imagined that Som's spirit was there in the room with them, demanding an accounting.

'What happened to Som? I mean, how did he die?'

'Gunned down in cold blood at Choeng Ek.'

Judge Sopheap returned to his chair and sat down. Once again he was presiding over events – a man whom life had taught the gift of command but who had traded it in for a position that he would probably have received anyway. 'Inspector Singh – what do you plan to do with this information?'

'I guess that's up to you.'

Singh was down the stairs and halfway across the compound when he heard the unmistakeable sound of a single gunshot.

The policeman turned around slowly. People were hurrying in the direction of the noise, towards the judges' chambers. A high-pitched scream pierced the air – someone had found the body, he guessed. He spotted Menhay hurrying out of his office. He considered going back, hesitated on the spot for a long time. But in the end decided against it. He knew what he would find, didn't have to see it.

Cambodia had claimed another life.

Seventeen

Singh waited in Menhay's office, reading the newspapers until the colonel returned.

'What happened? I noticed a bit of a commotion.'

'One of the judges, Sopheap, killed himself – single shot to the head.'

'Will it affect the trial?' asked Singh quickly.

Menhay shook his head. 'There are two reserve judges who sit in on the hearings . . .'

Singh had sensed a streak of integrity in the judge. And he'd been right. The news that his anonymous master had killed a man – gunned down an amputee – had been too much for him. He had done the decent thing and taken the only way out that did not affect the war crimes tribunal.

'I wonder why he did it?' Menhay sounded puzzled and worried.

'The strain of presiding over the tribunal must have been

too much,' suggested Singh. 'Let's hope the reserve judges are made of sterner stuff.'

Menhay nodded.

Singh fervently hoped that neither of the reserve judges was in the pay of this mysterious character who had suborned Sopheap. The tentacles of corruption were hard to disentangle in Cambodia. The inspector debated telling Menhay about Sopheap and decided against it. He might feel obliged to reveal the information – and that would be the end of the trial of Samrin. There was no way it would survive the discovery that one of the judges was corrupt. A mistrial would be declared and Samrin would die of old age before it recommenced. Sopheap's – and Som's – sacrifice deserved a better ending. It would have been different if he could see a way to find the puppet master – this high-ranking government official who was a former Khmer Rouge leader. The man who had paid Huon and Sopheap and killed Som. But Sopheap had only felt the pull and jerk of the strings.

Singh rubbed his eyes with the heel of his palms. They had solved the murder of Huon and he at least understood how Som had come to his death although the face of that killer was still hidden from view. It would have to do. In Cambodia, he feared, there were only small successes, no grand triumphs. At least they had saved the tribunal and with it the possibility that at least some of the big fish would face justice, even if many – so many more – eluded it.

He decided to focus on the small fry for a moment. 'What's the story with the Armstrongs?' he asked. 'Have they been released?'

'Yes.' Menhay was in a taciturn mood.

'Did Armstrong retract his confession?'

'Very quickly. He apologised for wasting police time. They plan to go to Siem Reap to recuperate from their experience. I guess they'll be staying at the Raffles there too.'

Singh ignored this mild envy of a working class man for the habits of the rich. He asked, 'Are you going to charge Armstrong with anything?'

'He was just trying to protect his wife.'

'That's what I said.'

'Do you want a medal?'

Singh slapped the colonel on the back. 'Why are you so grumpy anyway? You've found your murderer. The trial will recommence tomorrow. You should be in a good mood. Colonel Menhay saves the day. *You'll* get a medal.'

The other man essayed a small smile. 'You're right. And I know I should thank you.'

Singh shook his head. 'It was your contact who came through. It shows that only someone with his ear to the ground can solve a murder. I would never have fingered the Frenchman if you hadn't brought him in. It will be a lesson for Adnan Muhammad not to import policemen and expect them to get the job done.'

Neither man looked convinced that the UN man was the sort to derive lessons from experience, only from white papers and PhD theses.

'You were convinced of Sovann Armstrong's innocence in spite of the evidence . . . you fought for time – and we found Gaudin.' Menhay was generous with praise.

'I was just lucky,' remarked the fat man jovially. He was prepared to be self-deprecating now that the case was closed. He was pleased with himself though – he'd backed his instincts on Sovann and they had come up trumps. The Singh's nose for crime was still a finely tuned instrument.

'Where's Chhean?' asked Menhay suddenly.

Singh's face drooped like that of a snowman in the warmth. 'I don't know. She said she needed some time on her own.'

'Poor kid, it was a big disappointment.'

'When I saw the photos . . .' It was not difficult to remember the feeling – it had been like a punch to the gut, almost as shocking as when Som had been murdered in the killing fields. 'I was just so sure they were one and the same.'

'At the end of the day, I think she's better off without such a man for a father.' Menhay looked at Singh hopefully as if seeking corroboration that it was more desirable that Chhean spend the rest of her life trawling through documents in dusty archives than have a murderer for a parent.

'You're probably right,' agreed Singh. The two men sat in melancholy companionship, all their glee over the resolution of the case lost in the memory of Chhean, her face ashen and her eyes like dark wounds, as she realised that she had not, after all, found a family.

A few hours later, as a bright day turned into a golden dusk, Singh walked along the river front dragging his feet and scuffing his heels as he went. He had left Menhay to his own thoughts and regrets and spent the afternoon nursing a beer at the Foreign Correspondents' Club. It had not improved his mood – well, that was not strictly true: it had improved his mood but not sufficiently. He had decided to walk back to the Cambodiana despite all his previous walking adventures having been such disasters. He waved away the usual offers – as it was late evening these now included the services of young women – and the repetitive chorus of 'You remember me?'. He would not remember them. Only Chhean with her brusque manner and glossy short hair would stay in his memory. In a way, he realised to his surprise, his erstwhile assistant was clearer in his mind's eye than Sovann Armstrong. The latter had left him with a fleeting impression of elegance, the scent of expensive perfume, but it was difficult at that moment to form a mental picture of her face. His wife would be pleased, he decided. Perhaps he was less susceptible to a pretty face than she usually suspected.

Thoughts of his wife led him to shove his wallet deeper into his pocket. Her universe was peopled with pickpockets and petty thieves and she would have been horrified to see him sauntering along so carelessly. Mrs Singh moved like a secret agent through the streets of a strange town, always on the lookout for miscreants, her bag clutched to her side like a gold ingot. 'You can't just swing-swing and walk,' she had said to him sharply once, referring to women who foolishly dangled their handbags on their arms as they ambled down sidewalks. Singh sighed. He missed his wife. He wished he was home now, sniffing the rich curry smells coming from the kitchen rather than returning to the shiny impersonality of his hotel.

As he turned into the driveway, carefully manicured bushes on each side, he was surprised to see a police car parked outside the main entrance. An anxious uniform was scanning the horizon. As Singh hove into view, there was a sudden outbreak of wild waving. The policeman jumped into the vehicle and shot towards Singh with such energy that the fat man cautiously climbed onto the pavement. Lights and sirens rendered the man inaudible as he pulled up, hopped out and flung open the back door. The policeman was almost lip reading before he understood the message. It was a summons from Menhay.

Unfortunately, the driver hardly spoke English so Singh was forced to restrain his curiosity and while away the time with mental threats if it turned out not to be important. The colonel had come between him and his dinner and that was a serious transgression in Singh's eyes. To his mild surprise they headed towards the outskirts of town instead of the police headquarters. It seemed that they were on the way to the tribunal compound.

Forty-five minutes later, Singh was in Menhay's office. The colonel was nowhere to be found. He sat on the edge of the desk, swinging his feet like a lonely child. What was the use of dragging him away from his dinner and then leaving him to his own devices?

It was Chhean who came to fetch him. He stared at her in surprise. 'What are you doing here?'

'The colonel sent for me. He said it was important – and it is.'

'Enough games, young lady. What's this about?'

Another smile – what was the matter with her? 'Come with me,' she said and led him out of the office.

She turned in the direction of the block where Huon had been killed a week ago. He could see that she was desperate that he question her further, bubbling with excitement like an overflowing pot. Singh, however, was feeling rebellious so they walked in silence, short legs moving in rhythm but the owners at odds.

Chhean knocked on a door and the harsh voice of the colonel barked permission to come in. Singh entered cautiously. The last time Menhay had waved him into one of these rooms, a dead man had been sprawled across the floor. The scene that met his eyes this time was almost as disturbing.

Menhay sat in a plastic chair. Across from him, about six feet away, another man sat in an almost identical chair. It reminded Singh of a stage play, one of those dull arty ones with a lot of conversation and complex lighting. Here, the only light was coming through a small window behind the colonel, darkening his swarthy complexion into invisibility. It lit up the other man's face and reflected off the handcuffs that encircled his wrists behind the chair. Singh noted that the prisoner's flat unlined face was badly bruised and that his bottom lip was cut; only congealed blood held the fault line together.

'What's going on?' he demanded. Singh was upset and he didn't bother to hide it. He was happy to take liberties with police procedure but he drew a line at beating prisoners and he was genuinely shocked at the scene before him. The victim didn't look up, his spirit well and truly defeated. Chhean and Menhay both faced the inspector. Neither looked guilty or embarrassed. Singh wished he had not grown so fond of these two – the gulf between them was very wide indeed at that moment.

Menhay's developing frown was like the slow movement of tectonic plates. 'What do you think I'm doing? Beating up this rat?'

'Yes, that's what it looks like.' Singh's tone was even but his anger was fizzing beneath the surface.

'I thought you knew me better than that.'

Singh quickly revised his thinking. 'Who is he?'

'An assassin.'

'What? Whom did he kill?' Singh was pale in the half light. Had Samrin cheated justice? Or was this the serial killer?

'No one.'

Singh wished there was a third chair in the room. He felt like sitting down. 'Stop playing the fool, Menhay.'

Chhean butted in, her voice high-pitched with excitement. 'This man tried to kill Ta Ieng! But Ta Ieng managed to hold him off and call for help. Security arrested him.'

'*That's* how he got his injuries,' said the colonel dryly. 'Ta Ieng is not in great shape either but he should live – assuming our Cambodian hospitals don't finish off the job, of course.'

'I'm sorry,' said Singh. 'I should have trusted you.'

Menhay shrugged. 'You are right to be cautious. People are not always what they appear.'

The inspector decided to ignore this piece of homespun wisdom as he had no idea what Menhay meant. 'So, why did he try to kill Ta Ieng?'

'Ask him!'

Singh turned to the man and Chhean translated his hasty question.

The man muttered a response that was almost inaudible.

Chhean's translation however was loud and clear. 'He was hired to do it by a *barang* who paid him US$1,000.'

The hair on Singh's arms stood up. 'You mean . . .'

'Yes, this is the man François Gaudin hired to kill Ta Ieng. Both men have confirmed it.' Menhay spoke matter-of-factly.

Again it was Chhean who embellished the explanation. 'It wasn't a case of mistaken identity. François did *not* name the victim but he did refer to him as a child killer. This man did some investigation and discovered that he meant Ta Ieng.'

Singh glared at the would-be killer. Whoever heard of a paid assassin who did research? So much for his theory on cut-price thugs. This one apparently took pride in his work.

'Do you understand what this means?' It was Chhean again, insistent, demanding their acknowledgement of what she knew to be the truth. 'François Gaudin is innocent.'

'He did hire a hit man – I wouldn't call that innocent,' grumbled Menhay.

'You know what I mean.' She sounded almost as pleased as if Gaudin had been her father. 'He didn't kill Huon!'

Eighteen

Singh and Menhay drank strong coffee at the tribunal canteen. A gloomier pair would have been difficult to find in Cambodia. Sagging jowls and down-turned lips created a similarity of appearance despite the superficial differences. The waitress had placed the coffee before them and hurried away. It was the Cambodian way to smile and smile despite setbacks. These two didn't seem to know that and it was unnerving.

'My other suspect is sitting by the pool at the Raffles in Siem Reap,' grumbled the colonel.

Singh might have added that yet another one had just committed suicide but he did not. Sopheap was dead by his own hand. But he didn't think he'd killed Huon. His story, and unfeigned indignation as he described being accused of murder by his paymaster, had rung true. 'Are you going to re-arrest the Armstrongs?'

'I'll look like a real fool if I do that without further

evidence. And it's not them – it's her. *He's* withdrawn his confession.'

Singh sighed and the lines that ran from nose to mouth deepened. They had come full circle and the woman with the fingerprints on the knife was once again the main, the only, suspect. Sovann Armstrong needed more than a fat Sikh champion to keep her out of trouble this time.

Menhay's telephone rang. He reached into his breast pocket and held the device to his ear. He listened without saying a single word although Singh sensed that his initial lack of interest had been superseded by curiosity.

'What is it?' he demanded as Menhay terminated the call.

'Ta Ieng has regained consciousness. He wants to speak to us. In fact, he wants to speak to *you*.'

Singh rose to his feet, using the table for support. Menhay was able to assume a standing position under the power of his leg muscles alone. The fat man scowled. He really needed to get into shape. He and the colonel were almost the same height and the same heavyset build but there the similarities ended. Menhay's muscular thighs and forearms bulged through his olive green uniform. It was probably because they were still physically chasing down the bad guys in Cambodia while in Singapore his work was mostly cerebral, decided Singh, as he panted after the fast-moving figure of the colonel.

Yet another car journey later, Singh winced with dismay as they walked through the open wards crowded with beds and hot and humid at this late hour. Although the would-be killer of Ta Ieng had been apprehended, Menhay was taking no chances and Ta Ieng had a private room. There were some unexpected advantages to being ex-Khmer Rouge. Singh noted the policeman at the door and nodded approvingly.

Ta Ieng turned to face them the minute they walked in. He was lying under a thin blanket drawn up to his waist. His upper body was bare and Singh could see the blood-stained bandages across his chest from the attack.

'What was the weapon?' he asked Menhay.

'Switch blade. The assassin claims to have thrown it over the fence yesterday and collected it this evening.'

Singh thought of the overweight guards carefully manning the x-ray machines at the entrance. It didn't seem that difficult to circumvent them.

'Lucky he didn't have a gun, eh?' Singh said in a cheerful loud voice to the injured man. Menhay translated with an expression of distaste on his face.

Ta Ieng held out an injured claw-like hand, the drip needle taped to the surface. 'I need your help. I'm afraid I will be killed.'

'The man who attacked you is behind bars,' explained the inspector. 'I think you're safe.'

The man on the bed was not reassured. His eyes were wide pools of fear. Singh felt a sudden overwhelming sense of revulsion. How many of this man's victims had looked at him with just such an expression? How much mercy had he shown?

'Why are you so afraid?' he asked.

'I know too much,' whispered Ta Ieng. 'I know too much.'

Singh shrugged burly shoulders to convey his indifference. 'Why don't you tell us what you know and we'll decide if you need any more protection.'

275

Menhay repeated his words in Khmer and added to the inspector, 'I also told him that I would remove the guard at the door if he didn't speak up.'

The fat man scratched an armpit. He suspected fleas. The hospital was the most unhygienic one he had ever been in. There were streaks of dirt on the floor and the walls were stained with damp. Ta Ieng's blanket didn't look too clean either. He wondered whether they sterilised the needles. Singh fervently hoped he never ended up in a Cambodian hospital. He suspected that the survival rates weren't very high. In fact, it was the sort of place where the death rates probably exceeded the number of patients as friends and relatives also caught deadly diseases.

Ta Ieng turned away from them and stared at the opposite wall. Considering his limited options, suspected Singh.

'Did Huon tell you anything?'

The stick-like man turned back. He shook his head. 'He hinted that he knew that one of the government bigwigs was ex-Khmer Rouge, one of the cadres reporting directly to Pol Pot, but he wouldn't tell me which one. We had a big quarrel.'

The sounds of the argument that Sovann had heard on her way to see Huon. Singh wondered whether Ta Ieng was cautiously feeling his way to a confession of murder. That would be very convenient indeed. He might have immunity from his Khmer Rouge-era crimes but Menhay would enjoy locking him up for a present-day murder.

'I hit Cheah Huon.' Ta Ieng gestured to his own chin to indicate where the blow had landed.

Menhay and Singh exchanged glances. That explained the bruising on his chin that Savuth had identified.

'He fell down – his balance was not so good because of the leg.'

The policemen waited in silence.

Ta Ieng, clearly unnerved by their impassive faces, became voluble. 'He was lying on the ground. One leg was like this.' He indicated how the prosthetic limb lay across the man on the floor.

And then you grabbed a knife and stabbed him, thought Singh. And that also explains why the knife wound was horizontal – it was not an indication of the height of the killer. Huon had been prone on the floor – and unconscious – when he was stabbed.

'You killed him?' asked Singh.

Ta Ieng shook his head rapidly from side to side. His eyes were wild with terror. 'No, I ran from the room. I was afraid that he was already dead. He was so still and white. I didn't have a knife.'

Singh's entire body sagged with disappointment. He had been so certain that Ta Ieng was about to admit to murder.

The thin figure lying on the bed was still speaking, his voice reduced to a whisper so that they had to lean forward to hear him. 'I heard footsteps so I hid in a doorway. I was terrified that I would be caught. I still thought that I might have really hurt him. Someone passed me. The person stopped at the door to Huon's room to look around. Huon must have been still unconscious because there was no sound. I saw a knife in the hand.'

'Did you see who it was?' shouted Menhay, unable to stand the convoluted explanation – and the added burden of a simultaneous translation – any more.

'Yes . . .'

'Well, who was it?'

'I didn't recognise her at the time.'

Singh froze at the use of the female pronoun.

'Later I saw her picture in the newspaper when she was arrested for the murder.'

'Who was it?'

'Will you provide security for me? I must have protection!'

Singh still didn't understand his fear. It seemed out of proportion to the threat. The man who had attacked him was in custody and so was the Frenchman who had paid for the attack. Was he such a coward?

Menhay nodded – just once – but it was enough for the other man.

'I think her name was Sovann Armstrong.'

'Why didn't you tell us?' Menhay was leaning over Ta Ieng as if he was a priest performing the last rites.

'I didn't want to get involved.'

'And now? What's changed your mind?' Singh was convinced there was more and he needed to know what it was.

'When you released the man and wife – I approached them.'

It was like a lightning flash of understanding. Singh knew exactly where Ta Ieng was going with his long-winded, self-serving tale. It was with utmost restraint that he prevented himself from barging in with his version of events.

Ta Ieng pressed his head against the pillow so that his eyes and chin were facing the discoloured ceiling. 'I asked for money ... the husband, he gave me a few hundred dollars and he promised me more – if I kept my mouth shut.'

'And now you think that they might murder you rather than pay you?'

'The police say that a Frenchman sent the killer. I don't believe it. I think it was the American – the husband. I am sure he will try to have me murdered again. He will not rest until I am dead and their secret is safe.'

It was the constant fear of a blackmailer. Singh had seen it so many times before. When did the victim decide to take matters into their own hands? How much money was too much? Ta Ieng's story made sense. He had witnessed something important but kept quiet about it – his instinct for secrecy so much greater than any desire to tell what he had seen. His information must have appeared worthless – until the Armstrongs were released. And then, instead of revealing what he knew, he had decided to milk a cash cow. No wonder he was afraid. No wonder he was sceptical that just because one hit man had been arrested, another wouldn't follow.

'Will you protect me from them?' asked Ta Ieng.

'If you keep your mouth shut about what you've just told us, if you agree to testify in court about what you saw and what you did – then yes, I will keep you alive because you are more valuable to me alive than dead.' Menhay sounded like he meant it but only within those limited parameters.

Ta Ieng did not protest the terms of the bargain – all his cards were on the table. He nodded rapidly and the tears that were nestling in his eyes spilt over.

'I still can't believe it,' grumbled Singh.

Menhay threw him a sideways glance. They were at the airport, waiting for a flight to Siem Reap.

'Fingerprints on the knife, eyewitness sees her go into the room *with* knife, Huon is unconscious so the stab wound is horizontal *and* they paid Ta Ieng to keep quiet . . . sounds like a guilty conscience to me.' The colonel recited the facts in a liturgical voice.

'I know the evidence,' snapped Singh irritably. He was already dreading the flight, knowing that his nerves would be put to the test. And this time they were flying a domestic Cambodian airline which didn't fill him with great confidence either.

'Why do we have to go to Siem Reap anyway? Why couldn't you just have them arrested and shipped back?' asked Singh in a querulous voice.

'Best not to leave something like this in the hands of others. We know the case – and them – best.'

Singh remarked with his usual perspicuity, 'You're worried they'll pay off the cops and slip across the border?'

'Why take the risk?'

It was a fair point. This case had generated enough negative publicity. The newspapers had started to refer to the Cambodian police's 'revolving door policy' when it came to suspects. It was probably best to avoid any further public relations disasters. Sovann and her husband had already shown themselves willing to pay to avoid trouble. It was sensible that the only two policemen in Cambodia that they personally knew to be incorruptible be in at the end.

'Why do I have to come?' The fat man acknowledged to himself that he sounded like a whiny child.

'You're still jointly in charge of this investigation,' pointed out Menhay, leading the way across the tarmac to where the plane was parked. 'We wouldn't want to upset Adnan Muhammad.'

Singh didn't bother to respond. If it wasn't for him, Sovann would have been charged at least a week ago and a lot of trouble since might have been avoided. He was fairly sure that Menhay had been conscious of that irony as he brought up Singh's notional place in the investigative hierarchy. Anyway, if it was only a question of annoying the man from the UN, they would have both opted to leave the inspector behind. Adnan had been furious that, yet again, they had arrested the wrong person – the Frenchman – and then had to exonerate him of Huon's killing.

'Actually, I just want you to be convinced that she did it,' explained the colonel. 'Besides, I don't like my deputies,' he added with a wry smile.

'I wish Chhean was coming along,' said Singh, determined to preserve his melancholy mood by seeking clouds instead of silver linings.

'No budget. And the suspects speak English so you don't need a translator,' replied Menhay, fastening his seat belt loosely. Singh watched with dismay and then fixed his own as tightly as possible, neatly bisecting his belly into two wobbly halves. Menhay watched him quizzically but Singh didn't care. Better safe than sorry.

'And you will have a chance to see Angkor Wat!'

'I prefer Angkor beer,' growled the Singaporean.

The Cambodian, if his lowered brow was evidence, had not taken kindly to this lack of respect for the ruins regularly acknowledged to be one of the wonders of the world. Singh changed the subject to mollify him. 'Are you going to charge Gaudin with attempted murder?'

'Not sure – I thought I would let the excitement die down

and then see if I can let him go. He won't try again. We owe him too – he frightened Ta Ieng into telling us what he knew.'

Singh was grateful for the compassionate streak exhibited by the colonel. He didn't look like he had a softer side with his sunglasses, sideburns and surly expression. But he did. Just a big teddy bear like me, thought Singh, repressing a giggle.

The plane was taxi-ing down the runway and Singh searched desperately for a topic that would take his mind off the impending gravity-defying moment.

'I was sure I was right,' he remarked hastily. 'About the mistaken identity. You know, that Gaudin's hired assassin killed the wrong man.'

'It was a good theory,' agreed the colonel in a soothing tone.

'It happens all the time!' insisted Singh, annoyed at the colonel's mildly patronising tone. 'Just look at your serial killer. That's what gave me the idea in the first place.'

'What are you talking about?'

'Chhean hasn't reported back? She's been preoccupied, I suppose.' The plane was lifting off, the entire fuselage shuddering with the physical effort. Singh was sure he should have taken a taxi – or maybe a boat down the Tonle Sap – to Siem Reap. Who was afraid of bandits and landmines anyway? He continued quickly, 'Apparently the serial killer got one of the identities wrong . . . the tenth victim, I think.'

Menhay was staring at Singh intensely, waiting for him to continue.

'The victim was someone with the same *name* as a notorious Khmer Rouge commander – but the fellow who got killed was just a farmer.' The fat man shook his head. 'It's typical of these vigilante types – always trying to find short cuts to justice. Eventually, they kill the wrong guy and that's when they realise why there are cops and lawyers, judges and juries . . . it's to prevent this sort of mistake. We might look ridiculous for having arrested half of Phnom Penh for the murder of Huon and then releasing them one by one. But at least we didn't put a bullet in the wrong suspect!'

He turned to look at his travelling companion. Menhay was as white as a sheet. Singh felt smug – it appeared he wasn't the only one afraid of flying.

He sought comfort from the newspaper but the lead article was on the widespread contamination of the Cambodian countryside with landmines and unexploded ordnance.

'Is Siem Reap safe?' he demanded, pointing to a map which suggested that the area around the city centre was still dangerous. He might dread an eventual autopsy by Dr Maniam but he didn't want to be in too many pieces to rule out the possibility.

Menhay turned to look at him with reddened eyes. 'Siem Reap? Yes, quite safe – the nearest landmine fields are about fifty kilometres towards the Thai border.'

'Remind me to stay in town then,' said Singh grimly, folding his arms across his chest as if he was trying to hold his blubbery mass together.

Menhay shrugged with the indifference of one of life's soldiers. 'I don't know . . . I've always thought it would be a good way to go.'

'Rather you than me,' muttered Singh.

'Don't worry. I know the area so you should be safe.'

'How come?'

283

My home village is just outside Siem Reap, towards Poipet near the Thai border.'

'Maybe you'll get a chance to visit,' said Singh optimistically. He was feeling better now that they were airborne and the skies were clear.

There was a quick but firm shake of the head from the other man. 'It's been abandoned. Khmer Rouge mined the area during their retreat in '79. The only people who go there now are from bomb disposal units.'

Singh scowled and then clutched at the arm rests as the plane banked. Making small talk in Cambodia really was well nigh impossible.

It was with immense disappointment that they were told that the Armstrongs were out. Singh, gazing around the elegant lobby, found it difficult to believe that anyone would choose to leave the Raffles. Say what you liked about the Armstrongs, they enjoyed nestling in the lap of luxury. Menhay was equally sceptical that they were out because he prowled through the hotel, walking around the pool and gardens, glaring at diners in the expensive restaurants and sitting moodily at the bar watching the denizens come and go. To Singh's agreeable surprise, he eventually consented to have a beer. As they sipped Angkor beer in sullen silence, they had their first breakthrough. A bellhop sidled over and asked if they were looking for the Armstrongs. Singh nodded while Menhay perfected the glare he had been practising all morning.

'I called the driver for them this morning,' he whispered. Singh's heart sank – had they made a dash for Thailand?

Money made borders porous in countries like Cambodia. And he didn't want to chase them through any minefields.

'They went to Angkor Wat for the day,' the bellhop continued to the relief of the two policemen.

Singh nodded his thanks and the young man, dressed in that fashion best known as hotel-exotic, crept away.

The inspector raised his hand to order another beer. It appeared that they would spend the afternoon at the hotel waiting for their prey to return. He could think of worse places to be and worse things to do.

Menhay, however, waved the waiter away. 'We will go looking for them,' he announced, slipping easily into action man mode.

Singh demurred hastily. 'What's the point? We'll probably miss them if these Angkor ruins are as extensive as I've been led to believe. Why can't we just wait here?' He looked hopefully at the barman, who was hovering within earshot, uncertain whether his summons or his dismissal had precedence.

'We will go looking for them,' insisted Menhay. 'I will leave a few policemen here to wait.'

If he meant the dodgy examples of Cambodian policing that had driven them from the airport, Singh was not optimistic. But the colonel's mouth was set in a stubborn line and the fat man was mildly curious to see these great monoliths of Angkor. Especially if the alternative was spending a long afternoon with the bad-tempered Cambodian. His sour face would curdle beer, let alone milk. The inspector had no idea what was bothering his counterpart, but he was certainly anything but cordial company.

The Raffles provided a car, no doubt to expedite the departure of the threatening Colonel Menhay. It meant, at least, the comfort of a limousine with a functioning air conditioner and decent suspension although the roads in Siem Reap, lined with luxury hotels as the Cambodians sought to monetise their past, were in rather better condition than those in Phnom Penh. In a relatively short while, they were dropped off at one of the entrances.

Angkor Wat truly was stupendous. In the clear afternoon light, the grey stupas rose out of the horizon like the remnants of a vast lost civilisation, which indeed they were. The walkway was crowded with tourists and street vendors but for once Singh felt a sense of complete isolation, engulfed by the great buildings in the distance. It really was a shame that two-dimensional images of Angkor were used to advertise every product in Cambodia, thought Singh wistfully. It did a disservice to the reality.

As they got closer, Menhay snapped, 'Stop staring at the buildings and look out for our suspects!'

Singh looked around guiltily. He had been so enamoured of the ruins he had forgotten the mission. He began to scan the faces, saying as he did so, 'They must be inside – and anyway, the pair of them together are unmissable.'

'Unless they see us first,' responded Menhay darkly.

They were soon inside the temple compound. The grey and white buildings were golden where they caught the light. Flashes of colour, the bright orange of monks' robes, created a delightful counterpoint. Singh ran his hand over a cool grey statue, admiring the peaceful, full-lipped stone face. He remembered walking through the museum and being likened to the elephant god sculpture by Chhean. It made such a difference to see the figures in their original setting.

Menhay was striding ahead purposefully and Singh hurried to catch up. He seemed to know his way around the compound so the inspector resigned himself to following meekly in his footsteps, occasionally glancing around for a sign of the large American and his delicate wife. They wandered into a shady grove where nature was battling to reclaim Angkor. Singh stared at the enormous roots emerging through crevices, grasping entire structures with greedy pale limbs while root buttresses dominated adjacent walls. The inspector shivered. In the half light, the trunks looked covetous, as if they hankered after the spaces occupied by the buildings and would not be content until nothing was left of the vast human imprint on the landscape. He was so lost in thought that when Menhay put a hand on his shoulder, he almost yelped out loud. Fortunately for his relationship with the Cambodian, he managed to suppress the sound. The colonel nodded in the direction of a small alcove ringed with carved heads, their expressions fractious and unforgiving. The American couple was sitting within. She had her head on his shoulder. They were talking quietly – probably seeking some shade and rest.

Menhay didn't hesitate. He strode over, the fat man hard on his heels. Singh did not miss the quick action of his right hand – the colonel had unbuttoned the holster of his gun. The inspector gritted his teeth. There had been too much violence already. He didn't want more – didn't want any blood around Sovann. He reminded himself that she had stabbed an unconscious man to death – this was not the time for some dormant

287

masculine protective instinct to kick in. Besides, she had her enormous husband to look after her.

'Mrs Armstrong?'

They turned in surprise but without fear. Neither of them had heard the approach, the soft earth had muffled their footsteps.

'Colonel Menhay?' Sovann spoke and there was no questioning her surprise at seeing them.

'What do you want? Why are you here?' It was her husband who realised the implication of their unexpected presence. He stood forward so that he was shielding his wife with his body.

She stepped up so that she was side by side with her husband.

'There was an eyewitness, Sovann,' said Singh, unable to hide the sadness in his voice. 'He saw you go into the room where he knew Huon was unconscious. He also saw the knife. It's too late for any more denials.' He was facing Sovann, speaking directly to her, ignoring the hulking figure of her husband.

Her thin frame could not withstand such body blows. She sat down on a rock and folded her arms tightly.

'That's a lie,' said Jeremy Armstrong roughly but unconvincingly.

'Ta Ieng was the witness. You paid him to keep quiet,' snapped Menhay.

There was a small smile from Sovann as she came to terms with her fate. 'It doesn't seem to have worked.'

Jeremy Armstrong was still standing, a tall man with a broad chest and a large stomach. Why were Americans so big? wondered Singh. Was it all those hamburgers with cheese?

'I did it,' stammered the American, stepping forward a stride.

The colonel stepped forward as well as if they were playing a childish game of chicken. Despite being a foot shorter than Armstrong, he conveyed menace. It was the khaki uniform and the aggressive expression. Not to mention the gun. 'If you waste any more of my time, you'll spend as much time in prison as your wife.'

Sovann put her hand on her husband's arm. Although it was a light touch, he subsided immediately. 'Enough,' she said quietly. She turned to the policemen and faced them squarely. Singh was struck again by her preternatural calm. 'You're quite right. I killed Huon. I went to see him. I took a knife. For self-defence, I thought. When I got to his room, he was lying on the ground unconscious.' She paused and took a deep breath, her gaze failing to meet theirs for the first time. 'I stabbed him while he was lying there.'

'Honey, no . . .'

She sounded like a maths teacher admonishing a child over the quality of his homework when she spoke. 'Enough, Jeremy. My fingerprints were on the knife.'

Menhay walked over to her. He grasped her by the arm, firmly but not aggressively. The other hand was hanging loosely by his side but Singh sensed that he was coiled as tight as a spring. The colonel expected trouble from Jeremy Armstrong. Singh turned to the couple. They were still staring at each other but he was caught by their expressions – this was no fond farewell. Her eyes were trained on him like a laser beam and he had the hangdog look of a puppy, albeit a large one, who had just been kicked by a much-loved master. Their expressions were a conversation in another language. One for whom he did not have an interpreter.

The sun was now low in the sky and the last rays were bright and painful in his eyes. The light turned the moss-covered stones a vivid green. The statues seemed to have their blank stone eyes trained on him, expressions ranging from disgust to anger. What did they know that he didn't? He turned his attention to Sovann Armstrong. For a cold-blooded, self-confessed killer, she radiated an inner peace. He sensed again that core strength he had first observed when they were unlikely luncheon companions at the war crimes tribunal canteen.

For a moment, under the shade of the encroaching trees at Angkor Wat, time stood still. And then a picture formed in Singh's mind. A picture of what might have actually happened that night.

Nineteen

'Stop!' barked Singh. 'This isn't right.'

Menhay didn't even turn around, although his back stiffened. 'We don't have time for this, Singh.'

'Yes, we do. I know you don't want to make a mistake any more than I do.'

'A mistake? You think *this* is the mistake? There are others far worse.'

Singh ignored this detour into the hierarchy of errors. His whole attention was focused on the couple before him. 'I need five minutes, Menhay . . .'

'I don't want to wait – please let's go. I've *said* I killed him.'

Menhay's face, usually an ugly mask, was just ugly. However, Sovann's interruption seemed to have a contrary effect on him. The colonel was nothing if not bloody-minded. He spat on the ground in disgust but said, 'All right. You want five minutes, you've got five minutes.' He pulled his gun out of the holster and waved it at the Armstrongs. 'But no funny business.'

This would be a good scene for when they made a movie of his life, decided Singh. It was very atmospheric with the gun-toting colonel, the beautiful woman and the ruins of Angkor Wat as a backdrop. On the other hand, it had probably been done before.

He addressed his next question to Jeremy Armstrong. 'You insist that you did it? You killed Cheah Huon?'

'We've been through this already,' grumbled Menhay. 'Don't encourage him to confess *again*.'

The big man ignored the policeman and nodded slowly. Sovann's fingers tightened on his arm. Her knuckles were white. She must have been hurting him with her grip but he gave no sign.

'How?' asked Singh.

'I followed Sovann when she went to see Huon. I didn't know where she was going but she had been acting really weird lately and I was worried. I saw her stop by the kitchen and pick up the knife. I stayed right back because I didn't want to be spotted.'

'Why not?'

'Sovann would have stopped me from going with her. My wife – well, she can be pretty independent sometimes.' He smiled down at her and all the love in the world was contained in the moment. 'She'd told me about Huon being the murderer of her dad.' He raised a helpless hand. 'I guess she thought Huon was more likely to tell her the truth if she was alone.'

There was a silence broken only by the gentle rolling cry of an early nightjar.

Armstrong took up his tale again without prompting. 'I followed her into the room.'

292

'Why didn't Ta Ieng see you?' asked Menhay sharply.

'I don't know – he must have left by then or gone further into the room where he was hiding.'

'What was Sovann doing?' This was Singh. His only interest was the sequence of events in the room, the sequence that had led to the death of a man.

'She was kneeling by Huon, crying her eyes out.'

'He was dead?'

'To be truthful, that's what I thought at first. When I felt for a pulse, I realised that he'd just passed out – I didn't have a clue why.'

'Ta Ieng hit him,' explained Singh helpfully.

'I tried to get Sovann to calm down – she was almost hysterical. And then Huon started to stir. He was coming round.' Armstrong was no longer looking at any of them. He was staring into the distance as if he was watching a film trailer and describing the plot to his companions.

'And then I stabbed him,' said Sovann calmly as if she was remarking on the weather. She slipped her arm through her husband's, a gesture of reassurance that she was strong enough to take the consequences of her confession. It struck the inspector in that moment how much she loved her husband. She was not as obvious in her affections as the big American, but her feelings ran deep for the man who had rescued her from her past. Singh felt a stab of some emotion. Was it jealousy . . . or regret?

'And then *I* stabbed him,' corrected her husband.

Menhay snorted his disbelief.

Singh didn't blame him. The inspector persisted despite the absurdity of the situation, once again addressing his question to Jeremy Armstrong. 'Why?'

'I could see that Sovann would never be able to rest while this man was alive. There was no way he would be tried for what he had done to her father. The policeman – when Sovann made her report – treated her like she was mad. The war crimes tribunal is only interested in the big shots. Huon was literally getting away with murder – just like Ta Ieng.' He was rehearsing old arguments about the tribunal but he sounded like he meant it. 'The knife was lying by Huon – Sovann must have put it down or dropped it. I saw Sovann's tears – I don't know what came over me – I . . . I killed him.'

'What about the fingerprints?' Menhay was shouting now.

Armstrong hung his head. 'I wiped the knife handle clean . . . and then wrapped Huon's fingers around the hilt. I had this wild idea the death might be taken as suicide or an accident. Later, when I calmed down, I realised it was unlikely.'

'What about Sovann's prints?' asked Singh.

'My fingerprints, *my* murder,' said Sovann adamantly.

'I agree with the lady,' muttered the colonel, watching with annoyance as his murder investigation turned into a farce.

'Did you leave her alone in there?' Singh was adept at ignoring the Cambodian policeman when it suited him.

'I went ahead to the door – to check that the coast was clear. Sovann must have handled the knife then.'

'And why would she do that?' asked Menhay in a tone of extreme resignation.

'I don't know.' The big man was almost in tears. 'To take the rap for me?'

The sun was sinking rapidly over the horizon. The stupas of Angkor Wat were glowing angry red in the light. Blood, thought Singh. Angkor Wat, awash in blood just like the whole damn country. He knew what he had to do, had known since a few minutes ago when it became clear to him what had happened. But he didn't like it – didn't want to do it – knew he would get no thanks from those he was trying to help. Should that stand in his way? It was difficult to know. He glanced across at Menhay. A man of certainties. A policeman to the core, doing his job with a single-minded tenacity while all around him people sold their pride, their honour, even their children, for a few extra American dollars. But he had suggested that he would let the Frenchman go – Menhay had the ability to be benevolent – while what Singh was about to do was cruel. Or was it? Perhaps it was also just. He was a policeman, decided the fat man ruefully. He would err on the side of justice. And that meant that no one should be allowed to take the blame for a murder they didn't commit.

'Sovann?'

She was watching him. The fear was on the surface, visible in the rigidity of her body and the paleness of her skin, like an antelope catching sight of a lion in the bushes and too frightened to run.

'Sovann, your husband was a B-52 bomber pilot before he met you. He flew dozens of sorties over Cambodia.'

He had Menhay to thank that he avoided injury. With a loud scream of 'No,' Armstrong launched himself at the fat man. The colonel stepped neatly in the way and tripped him. The big man came crashing down like old wood in a rainforest. He turned over but stayed down. He whispered, 'No, please . . .no,' but it was already too late.

Singh had refocused his attention on the woman the minute it was apparent that he was not going to have his head knocked in. Menhay had his gun trained on the prone figure.

'What did you say?'

He almost had to read her lips, her words were spoken so quietly.

'He was a pilot during the "secret war".'

Sovann would not look at her husband directly but she addressed her next question to him. 'Why didn't you tell me?'

'I was afraid of hurting you.' He paused. 'I was afraid of losing you.'

'What about the people *you* hurt? My people? My family?'

'I've worked my whole life to make amends . . .'

When he had spoken to Singh earlier in the week, Armstrong had made the same argument. He hadn't sounded convinced then and he didn't sounded convinced now that his reparation was sufficient or complete. What a burden of guilt for a man to carry, thought Singh sadly, his own shoulders drooping under the weight of what he had done.

The harsh cry of a night animal reflected the agony of the couple before him. It was time to close this case. He asked quietly, 'Who killed Cheah Huon?'

'He did,' said Sovann, her voice loud and clear. 'My husband murdered Cheah Huon.' Her rejection of her husband was complete and the whimper from the crumpled figure on the ground suggested he knew it.

'Fingerprints?' asked Menhay.

'While he was looking out of the door, I wrapped my hands around the hilt,' explained Sovann.

'Why?' Even Menhay was not immune to the stark

emotion of the protagonists. His voice was husky as he asked the question.

'It was my fault that he killed Huon. He did it for me – knowing how I would suffer if the man who killed my father was alive and free. The police would not rest until they found Huon's killer – the tribunal is just too important for a murder to remain unsolved in its midst. Because of my police report, I knew the trail would eventually lead to me – to us.'

She nodded her head in the direction of her husband, unable even to speak his name. 'I thought I owed him everything, you see . . .'

'But you didn't confess immediately?'

There was a hint of the old Sovann in her answer. 'Inspector Singh seemed determined to protect me – I decided to give him a chance.'

Singh grimaced. An old fool, that's what he was – but he had been right about Sovann's innocence. 'Why didn't you tell her?' He addressed the question to the man who was sitting up against a stone wall now. 'If you were so determined to save her from going to jail for murder, why didn't you tell her about your past? God knows, she's not protecting you now.'

The head drooped like a week-old flower. One open hand gestured at his wife. 'I was weak. I didn't want to lose her . . . didn't want her to live with the knowledge of what I had done. I was hoping . . . that there was another way.'

Sovann Armstong turned to leave.

'Can't you forgive me, honey? After all we've been through together?' Jeremy Armstrong asked the question of his wife but stared at the ground by his feet.

Singh watched the couple carefully. He was praying that

this woman would find some previously untapped capacity for forgiveness.

Her words when she spoke were almost an echo of Menhay's when Chhean had posed the same question hypothetically. 'You weren't on the ground during the bombings. The earth was flattened as if God's fist had descended. The villages were burning. We children would scream when we heard the engine sounds, even before we saw the distant specks in the sky. My brother died – and my grandparents. That's why we were refugees in Phnom Penh in the first place . . . before Pol Pot evacuated the cities and we marched towards death again.'

Her husband watched her walk slowly away from the little group. He made no further attempt to stop her. As she passed Inspector Singh, she paused. 'I would have preferred not to know,' she said sadly. 'I would have preferred to go to jail.'

He knew she meant it, knew it was true. 'I'm so sorry,' said the inspector. 'I did what I believed was right.'

She looked up and her gaze met and held his as powerfully as a magnet. 'You aren't the first person in Cambodia to believe that he knew best.'

Singh awoke the next morning with a profound sense of dislocation. He lay in bed, noting the luxurious four-poster and the filmy white mosquito netting. He was under starched white bedding. His tummy bulged underneath like a snow-covered hill. He turned slowly and glanced over the side of the high bed. His white sneakers lay on the floor but he could feel that he still had his socks on – and his shirt, pants and belt. He thought as hard as he could although it hurt his head and slowly the recollection of a long evening at the Raffles Bar followed by the decision to take a room at the luxurious hotel for the night came back to him in drips and drabs. He lay back, his big head resting against the cool pillow. He remembered being certain he could fob off the cost of the hotel on the Singapore government or Adnan Muhammad. After all, hadn't he solved their precious case? A memory of Sovann's soft brown eyes looking at him with an almost unfathomable sadness came to him. 'I would have preferred not to know,' she had said. 'I would have preferred to go to jail.'

He deserved a real pat on the back for solving this one, thought Singh bitterly. It was no wonder that he had such a towering headache – he must have spent the best part of the night trying to drink away the memory of those eyes and those words.

He rose slowly, splashed cold water on his face, retied his turban which had unfurled enough to be used as a hangman's rope and walked slowly downstairs. It was time to have a big breakfast to assuage the pain in his head, find Menhay, get back to Phnom Penh and then return to Singapore by hook or by crook. He was through with Cambodia. He had seen enough, done enough and destroyed enough. Only the company of his wife was sufficient punishment under the circumstances.

As he sat down to breakfast, ordered a large coffee and sniffed hopefully at the smell of fresh toast, the bellhop from the front door handed him a sealed envelope with his name on the front in the firm stroke he recognised as Menhay's. The colonel had probably deserted him and headed back to Phnom Penh with his prisoner, decided Singh, with anticipatory annoyance. He pursed his lips and felt the tickle of his encroaching moustache. Coffee first, then Menhay's excuses. He sipped the caffeine slowly, wishing there was a way he could imbibe it intravenously. He felt slightly better and tore open the envelope, surprised to find it was quite a long missive. What was this – a love letter from the colonel? He held it a foot away from his blunt nose and began to read.

'Dear Inspector Singh,

I am sorry to write to you like this – I would have preferred to speak to you in person. But I was afraid you would try to stop me, persuade me that there are other, better ways. You would be wrong, of course, but I fear that a part of me would have been tempted.'

Singh reread the first paragraph in some puzzlement. What in the world was Menhay going on about? From this meandering opening, it sounded like the colonel had been hitting the bottle hard as well.

'You don't have to worry about the Huon case. I have arranged for Armstrong to be escorted to Phnom Penh and charged with Huon's murder. As for François Gaudin, I have given instructions for him to be released. If he has any sense he will take the first plane out of the country.'

Had Menhay resigned from the force? Why now in his hour of triumph?

'I am sure you feel guilty about revealing her husband's past as a B-52 bomber to Sovann Armstrong. Don't be. It is the most important element of our job – that only the guilty should suffer for their crimes.'

Was that true? Singh pondered the question for a moment. It was good to know that the colonel was on his side although he still didn't know why he had felt the need to write this Jane Austen-esque letter. What was wrong with using the telephone if he was on his way to Phnom Penh?

'You must be wondering why I am going on like this' – bloody right, thought Singh – *'and I will tell you although my heart is filled with shame. You will remember the eleven men – ex-Khmer Rouge – who were killed? I am afraid I was the one – I am the murderer of those men.'*

Singh blinked rapidly a few times. His hands trembled but he kept reading.

'I believed that I was the hand of justice. Those men were living the lives of the innocent, growing old and looking forward to dying peacefully. And yet the blood of my family, my friends, my comrades and my countrymen was on their hands. I tried to apprehend them – and men like them – legally but government policy was not to charge Khmer Rouge excepting only those at the very top. I could not stand it.

And yet, you must believe me, I tried not to act in anger. I sought my targets carefully and executed them without the guilt of revenge but with a strong sense of the necessity of my actions.

But yesterday you told me that I had made a mistake. All these vigilantes kill the wrong man eventually, you said, and it seems that I was no exception. I called Chhean. She was quite certain that the killer had made an error. A simple case of mistaken identity and an innocent man died. Which makes me no better than the Khmer Rouge.

I am sure you will understand that I must pay for this crime with my life.

I think you will guess where I have gone. Do not try to follow me. It is too late now anyway.'

It has been a pleasure working with you, Inspector Singh. I leave in your good hands the decision of what to do with this letter.'

It was signed and dated by the colonel.

Focus on the salient point. Forget the fact that his fellow policeman and recent companion had just admitted to being a serial killer. Menhay expected him to guess where he had gone. Was this a last cry to be saved – like with so many would-be suicides? Singh glanced at the letter again. Except for the beginning, where Menhay had – understandably – struggled to get to the point, the letter did not have the tone of panic or regret of someone seeking a reprieve. It was not a cry for help, it had been too emotionless for that. Singh winced. This was just practical information for the collection of the body – and a desire to leave his story with someone.

Singh's mobile rang. It was Chhean. He answered hastily.

'Inspector, how are things? I heard that Jeremy Armstrong has been arrested.'

Singh could barely concentrate, his mind full of Menhay's confession.

'Inspector, are you there?'

'How did you know – about Armstrong, I mean?'

'The colonel called me yesterday. He wanted some information on one of the victims of the serial killers. You know, the one where the killer got the wrong man, killed the farmer by mistake.'

Menhay had said as much in his letter.

'Did he say anything else?'

'What do you mean? Is something wrong?'

302

He obviously sounded as panicked as he felt. 'Just think, Chhean – did the colonel say anything else, anything at all?'

Her voice was puzzled but she complied. 'Nothing important, only that he might visit his village. It's somewhere near Siem Reap.'

His village. But Menhay had said that his village had been abandoned after it was mined by the Khmer Rouge.

'I've always thought it would be a good way to go.' The colonel's words came back to Singh. It made sense – the thought of his own suicide must have been on his mind when he made that remark to Singh.

'Chhean,' he said desperately. 'I need you to find out exactly where Menhay's village is and call me right back. Can you do that?'

'Of course,' she said, ever efficient. 'But I don't understand. What's wrong?'

'I can't explain now.' Could he ever explain? 'Just do it.'

The inspector rose to his feet quickly and rushed to the door, shouting for a hotel limousine. He clutched the letter in a moist, urgent grip. There would be time enough to think of what to do with it after he tried to stop Menhay.

He urged the careful Cambodian driver to set off towards the Thai border in the direction of Poipet, praying that Chhean would call him back, noting that his phone battery was down to the last bar. He'd forgotten to charge it the previous evening, too intent on getting drunk, trying to forget the expression on Jeremy Armstrong's face as his wife had walked away. In what seemed like hours but was only fifteen minutes by his watch, Chhean called back with the address. He passed the phone to the driver and listened to the exchange in Khmer, hoping that the battery would last long enough and that her directions were detailed and accurate, having no way of verifying the information himself.

'Do you know where to go?' he asked after his phone had been returned.

'Yes, no problem.'

Time flew and yet stood still as Singh stared out of the window, noted the storm clouds rolling in and tried to get his head around his friend's confession. Menhay was the killer. The most honest man in the Cambodian police force was a mass murderer. He thought of the plain-speaking, hard-working, fundamentally decent colonel who had given him every opportunity, despite his personal reluctance, to prove Sovann innocent. Singh found his mind shying away from the thought that this man was a killer. Then he remembered the bloodshed in Cambodia's past and what it had done to the psyche of the nation as well as to so many, many individuals. In a way, he supposed sadly, it was more of a surprise that many of these traumatised souls found a way to get on with all the little vicissitudes of life instead of lashing out against the injustices inflicted upon them.

They had arrived. Singh looked out over the small collection of dilapidated huts and the surrounding fields, uneven muddy ground with patches of grass and moss, flat as a pancake and decorated with the tall spindly sugar palms. Despite the quietude of the day, the true nature of the place was revealed in the signposts: grinning skulls and crossbones against weather-faded red backgrounds with the words 'Danger!! Mines!!' written in Khmer and English. Singh felt a shiver run down his spine like a drop of cold water. It was the double exclamation marks, with their slightly comic overtones, when juxtaposed against the reality of the round metal objects of death scattered through Cambodia, which brought home the horror to the fat policeman. He remembered Som, the landmine victim, and felt his heart clench like an angry fist. He needed to find Menhay.

There was hardly anyone about – it was still early in the morning. The figures in the distance appeared to be those poor creatures that made a living from selling the metals of unexploded mines and other ordnance. Some of them were on their bellies with metal detectors held out in front of them. The sheer awfulness was overwhelming to the Sikh inspector and he put a hand over his eyes for a moment. When he looked up again, he spotted the squat shape of Colonel Menhay in the distance.

'Hey! Colonel! Wait,' he shouted as he hurried in his direction, jogging and then suddenly, as he sensed time growing short, running as fast as he could towards the distant figure who was silhouetted in black as the rain clouds shut out the sun. He closed the distance and fell silent, suddenly convinced that the colonel would expedite his plans if he realised Singh was almost upon him. The inspector still gripped the letter in a sweaty fist – just as well, it was not something for the eyes of an inquisitive driver.

He didn't make much noise, just the sound of sneakers on the dusty path and his breath coming in puffs like a steam engine, so it must have been some sixth sense that caused the colonel to turn around and look in his direction. As Singh drew closer he realised that Menhay was already fifty metres into the fields, no longer on the relative safety of the well-trodden trail along the perimeter.

'Menhay, stop!' he shouted.

'You shouldn't have come here, Singh.'

'Let's talk about it – work something out.' Singh's hands were on his knees as his heart thumped against the walls of his chest like a battering ram. At this rate, he would die before the colonel, thought Singh in disgust.

'There is nothing further to say or do. I am not unhappy at this ending. It is fitting.' He took a few steps backwards, his wary eyes still fixed on the policeman from Singapore.

The rain began to fall, large individual drops splashing down with intent. Could raindrops set off landmines? Singh wondered, looking nervously about him. Presumably not, otherwise there wouldn't still be so many littered throughout the countryside. The colonel took another few steps into the field and Singh a few tentative steps forward as if he was tied to the other man with an invisible string.

'Maybe Chhean was wrong – maybe you only killed Khmer Rouge.'

Menhay actually laughed. 'Is Chhean ever wrong?'

'Please, Menhay. There has to be another way.'

Menhay shouted to be heard against the encroaching storm. 'Go back, Singh! It's over.' He turned and started walking rapidly into the distance. Singh hovered on the edge indecisively for a few long moments and then took off at a run after the colonel.

He had closed to within twenty metres – felt that he could grab Menhay by the shoulder, look him in the eye, talk to him and then very carefully make his way back to safety – when the colonel was lost in the bright yellow-orange light and dark grey cloud of a violent detonation. Singh saw the ground explode and contract in an instant, saw his friend disintegrate into a red haze, felt the noise impact his eardrums like a blunt instrument and then the shrapnel reached him like flying knives. As he fell to the ground and felt his fingers loosen, his last conscious thought as the blackness descended was that the letter would be lost too, just like the man.

Epilogue

Singh came to in a bright white room and he blinked and his
eyes teared against the light. He looked around and saw faces
that seemed familiar although he did not know them, could
not place them. It reminded him of a family wedding – the
impossibility of remembering the names and O-level results
of all his young relatives to the grave disapproval of his wife.
The thought of his wife caused the head to swivel around
again and this time he saw her.

'Where am I?' he asked, pleased that the words came out
clearly from a mouth that seemed filled with cotton wool.

'Singapore GH,' she replied tersely, referring to the
Singapore General Hospital.

'You were medivac-ed out,' stated a thin voice that contrived
to annoy Singh despite his condition. He didn't have to turn
his head again to recognise the dulcet tones of Superintendent
Chen. 'It was very expensive,' he continued, implying that if it
had been his choice, he would have left Singh in the tender
hands of the Cambodian medical profession.

Singh ignored him and fixed his attention on the other person in the room.

'Chhean,' he whispered.

'The UN sent me with you as an escort since you were so unwell,' she replied.

'Another "odd job"?'

She smiled but did not answer.

'You should thank her,' interjected the superintendent. 'If she hadn't insisted that the police track you to that village, it would have been too late to save you.'

'I realised when I was looking for the colonel's address that the area was mined,' she explained. 'I tried to call you back but your phone was dead.'

The recent past was coming back to him, bright flashes of individual images, as if he was a child looking into a kaleidoscope. He saw Menhay turn away from him. He was shouting as loud as he could although the sound was distant and tinny. And then the explosion.

'The colonel?' he asked.

'Dead,' said the superintendent. 'Blown to smithereens. The Cambodians and the UN want to know why he decided to go for a walk in a minefield. I want to know why you went with him.'

Singh touched his face and realised he was wrapped in bandages. He felt his head. It was swathed in cloth. 'Turban?' he asked suspiciously.

'Bandages,' replied his wife, who was being unusually economical with her words. Perhaps there was a silver lining to his present condition.

'Well?' demanded Superintendent Chen.

Singh thought about what Menhay had done – killed eleven men. And then he remembered Ta Ieng and Huon, who had escaped all forms of formal justice. He would not judge his friend and colleague, would not decide what was right and wrong, as he had done with Sovann Armstrong. Menhay had made a mistake and chosen to pay the ultimate price. Who was he to gainsay that?

His senior officer was glaring at him, demanding answers.

Singh shrugged and winced as the movement pulled on various cuts and bruises he didn't even know he had. 'It was just an accident,' he said firmly. He sighed. 'A real waste of a good man,' he added and he meant it.

Superintendent Chen looked disbelieving but something in Singh's eyes told him that no further information would be forthcoming. He muttered reluctantly, 'You've received a lot of praise for wrapping up the Huon investigation.'

Singh raised his right hand in a gesture of acknowledgement and dismissal and saw the intravenous drip embedded on the surface. He demanded loudly, his voice petulant, 'I'm hungry *and* I'm thirsty. Can't I have some beer or curry put through this thing?' He turned his back on the superintendent and saw that his wife, who had been watching him carefully from the end of the bed, was smiling.

Do you love crime fiction?

Want the chance to hear news about your favourite authors (and the chance to win free books)?

Kate Brady
Frances Brody
Nick Brownlee
Kate Ellis
Shamini Flint
Linda Howard
Julie Kramer
Kathleen McCaul
J. D. Robb
Jeffrey Siger

Then visit the Piatkus website and blog
www.piatkus.co.uk | www.piatkusbooks.net

And follow us on Facebook and Twitter
www.facebook.com/piatkusfiction | www.twitter.com/piatkusbooks

piatkus